I0708624

COPYRIGHT

Marie Cadieux and the Liberty Conspiracy by David Gennard published by Prana.creative.

ISBN: 978-1-7395023-1-7

Cover design by: David Gennard

ARE YOU READY FOR ADVENTURE?

Thank you for purchasing this book. I'd love for you to become a part of my reading crew and keep up to date with all of my latest stories, news and special offers. Feel free to head over to: www.davidgennardauthor.com

Also by David Gennard

Marie Cadieux and the Fever Coast

MARIE CADIEUX
AND THE
LIBERTY
CONSPIRACY

DAVID GENNARD

CHAPTER 1

1886

Everyone and everything in Manhattan moved constantly close to collision. Marie Cadieux's steps were giddy. She walked fast down the sidewalk of the bustling Avenue of the Americas, almost, but not quite, breaking into a run.

A woman thrust a bouquet of carnations towards her. 'Hey Miss, wanna buy some flowers?'

'No, no merci,' Marie said, sidestepping around the woman and nearly colliding with a boy shining shoes. She hitched her skirt, jumped over the outstretched leg, and avoided tripping.

'Watch where you're going, lady!' the man shouted. He instinctively withdrew his shiny boot and stepped back into a puddle.

Marie ignored his cusses. She continued, plotting a route through the many push-cart pedlars on the street.

'Missy, you want a Mickey?' an all-hot man asked. His steaming, mobile baked potato oven sat on a cart.

A row of boys ran past carrying baskets of oysters on top of their heads.

'Hot jumbo peanuts. Turkish Halvah. Indian Nuts. Sugared peanuts!' a vendor shouted, his cigarette dancing up and down between his lips.

On the street, a man ushered along a couple of cows, keeping them in check with a stick. Nobody blinked at the sight. People stood deep in conversation or rushed or strolled to the many stores lining the thriving street: butchers, grocers, hardware suppliers, confectioners, tobacconists and above them, several varying levels of apartments. The smell of warm rye bread, bagels and pumpernickel drifted out of Horowitz's bakery. Marie's stomach grumbled. She wasn't sure if it was nerves or hunger, having skipped breakfast because she was eager to tell her sister Capucine her news.

That morning, Marie received a letter confirming her place to study art at the Académie Julien in Paris. Her grin evaporated when she thought about telling her sister. Marie had left France a couple of years ago after her grandfather's death and arrived in America to live with her sister. She didn't think Capucine would take the news well.

Capucine had picked several quarrels with Marie about her not coming home at night and sleeping in her art studio. Marie retaliated by not returning home in nearly a month. Though the sisters had seen each other, their relationship was strained.

Marie's pace slowed. She sighed at the thought of the unnecessary conflict. Then her defiance returned. Why should she tell her sister her every move? It's not like Capucine had cared when she'd emigrated and left Marie in France with her grandfather. A policeman stopped Marie from striding into the street.

'Keep your eyes off the floor,' he said. 'Look where you're going.'

A huge horse clomped along the cobbles, dragging a cart loaded with barrels. Its hooves struck the street like the steady hammer of a blacksmith. The cartwheels groaned as they ground through the deep mud holes. Steam rose from the horse's shiny black hair. The leather horse collar and reins and brass buckles slapped and creaked. As soon as they'd passed, Marie strode on. She weaved around the missing cobbles, puddles, mud and manure and arrived at the sidewalk outside Robert R Brown's millinery shop.

Marie gazed up at her sister's apartment above. She took a deep breath. 'Cueille le jour,' she said to herself.

Marie went up the entrance steps beside the milliners and into the narrow corridor, past the mailboxes and bounded up the stairs two steps at a time to the landing on the second floor, sidestepping the squeaky floorboard and across to her sister's apartment. She knocked on the door. Light barely filtered through the frosted glass skylight above. There was no answer. Marie checked her watch. It was mid-morning on a Wednesday, and her sister should've been home. She knocked again. A door opened across the hallway, and Mrs Kepler stuck her head through the gap. 'You after your sister?'

'Yes,' Marie said. 'Though she doesn't appear to be home.'

'She's not. She hasn't been home for over a week.'

Marie turned to face the woman. 'Not been home?'

'That's what I said.'

'Did she say where she was going?'

'No,' Mrs Kepler said. 'She went out last Tuesday and hasn't been back since.'

Marie reached into her satchel and removed the key. She didn't say anything else to the woman, who craned her neck to watch as she unlocked the door and went in.

'Cap,' Marie called out as she stood in the hallway. Silence. She closed the front door behind her. The apartment smelled unoccupied. Marie shivered.

'Cap, it's Marie. Are you home?'

There was no reply.

The side table by the front door, where they'd usually leave each other notes about their comings and goings, was empty.

She went down the corridor, clutching her satchel's strap. Nothing appeared out of place. She stopped at the thought of finding her sister's body in one of the rooms. Kepler saw her leave and not return, Marie reminded herself. The old woman never missed a coming or going. Even if she hadn't seen her return the day she left, she would've seen or heard her since. Their neighbour was that sort of woman. The suspense became too much for Marie. She swung open her bedroom door, disturbing the thin layer of dust on the furniture. It was all how she'd left it.

She strode across the corridor to the kitchen; neat and tidy with everything where it should be.

She dreaded opening the door to her sister's bedroom. Her hand hesitated on the doorknob. She sighed. Closing her eyes, she twisted it and pushed the door. It swung open and knocked against the wall. She opened her eyes. The duvet lay smooth on the bed tightly tucked in at the corners, and the curtains hung drawn back for the day. Marie shook her head, realising it would've smelled grim if her sister was dead. It didn't. It just smelled unoccupied.

She rushed from the dining room to the parlour. Capucine wasn't home. Everything was neatly in its place. It's strange to be in someone's home without them. The emptiness reminded her of being at the farm after her grandfather had died. It was the same feeling she got when seeing the empty shell of a turtle in the museum.

She wondered if her sister had taken a break and gone to Coney Island or somewhere. That would've only been a couple of days at most, she reasoned. She returned to the side table by the front door, hoping to find a note from Capucine that she'd overlooked. The table was empty and the floor clear. A notepad and pencil lay inside the drawer, but at the back, she found a scrunched-up piece of paper. She took it out, uncrumpled it, and whispered the words written on it. 'I knew you'd come back.'

The guilt hit Marie like a hammer on an anvil. Marie held the scrunched-up piece of paper. She winced, realising Capucine must've balled up the note while feeling hurt. Capucine never lost her temper, Marie thought. She slipped the note into her pocket and reasoned Capucine must've taken off without saying anything to teach her a lesson. But that wasn't like her either. Capucine would never do something like that.

Marie looked over the rooms one last time and even checked inside her sister's wardrobe. Her clothes hung neatly, and the suitcase remained at the bottom. However, Capucine's necklace and rings were missing from her dressing table. She only kept the jewellery there at night, so she must be wearing them.

Marie left the apartment and locked the door behind her.

Mrs Kepler opened her door again. 'Was she there?' Her voice actually sounded concerned.

'No.'

'And she didn't tell you where she was going?'

'I'm sure she's fine,' Marie said.

'Probably gone on one of those suffragette rallies somewhere out of town,' Mrs Kepler said.

Marie felt a sense of relief. 'Yes. Probably. You know what Cap's like.'

'Well, this happens when a woman gets too much agency. They go missing. I'd vote for us not to get the vote.'

'I don't think you'd be allowed to,' Marie said. The irony was lost on Mrs Kepler. Marie walked away, stepping on the creaky floorboard and headed down the stairs. She checked the mailbox in the hallway, took the letters out and went outside into the light.

There were four envelopes. Two were handwritten, and two were typed. Marie slid her nail into the corner of one of the written ones. She frowned. This is ridiculous, Marie thought. She stuffed the letters into her satchel and stomped down the steps onto the sidewalk. She looked back at the building. Something wasn't right. She just knew it.

CHAPTER 2

Marie arrived at the Astor Library on Lafayette Street. It looked like a Roman palace with graceful arched windows. She went up the steps off the street, through the tall doors, and into the reception hall. A woman stood behind the main desk. Like Marie, she looked to be in her early twenties. She wore an enamel sunflower pin on the lapel of her jacket. Marie recognised the symbol of the suffragettes. Her sister wore one, too.

'Can I help you?' she asked.

'Yes, I hope so. My sister is Capucine Cadieux. I was—'

'Oh,' the woman said.

'Oh?'

'Just wait here a moment, would you?'

The receptionist scuttled out from behind the desk and ran off through an arch, up a broad staircase, and past a sign that read to the South Hall.

Marie shook her head in disbelief and then followed after the woman.

Marie marvelled at the sight as she walked up the stairs into the South Hall; a cathedral-like room with skylights in the roof and tall windows. Lining the hall, bays filled with bookcases stood twenty feet tall. Above them another set of bays and cases full of books filled the gallery. People stood on ladders to reach the tallest shelves, and sat reading at tables.

The receptionist led a man wearing spectacles and a tweed suit. When she spotted Marie, she brought him over to her.

'You are Capucine's sister? Where is she?' he asked,

spreading his arms wide as if seeking answers.

Marie's heart sank. 'I hoped you could tell me.'

The man shooed the receptionist away, and then led Marie to one of the alcoves with an empty table.

'I am Richard Everett, the head librarian here,' he said, sitting.

'Marie Cadieux.'

'It's nice to meet you. She has told us all about her young sister, the artist.'

Marie felt guilty again. She couldn't remember telling anyone about her sister or what she did. 'Capucine has not been to work, then?' she asked.

'No. It's been over a week now.'

Marie frowned. 'And you haven't thought to tell anyone?'

'I went to her address personally and left a letter,' he said.

Marie opened her satchel and removed the letters. She placed them on the table. He reached out and slid one of the handwritten envelopes to the side.

'This is mine,' he said, frowning. 'It's unopened.'

Marie stared at the books behind him, lost in thought.

'Had she not taken leave from work then for a holiday?' Marie eventually asked.

'No. Is she on holiday?'

'She's not. When did you last see her?'

'I said over a week ago. If Capucine's on holiday—'

'So, she's been missing a week,' Marie said absently.

'Missing? Let me clarify,' he said. 'You've not seen her either?'

'It's been a couple of weeks since I last saw Cap.'

'I thought you lived with her?'

'No, I live at my art studio now.' She rubbed her forehead as she tried to make sense of Capucine's disappearance.

There must be a million questions, but she couldn't think of any helpful ones.

'I take it you've not reported this to the police?' he asked.

'The police?' she asked, looking up at him.

'You should really report a missing person.'

Marie shook her head. 'Capucine's not missing. Not like that. She's just...'

He reached out across the table and put his hands on hers. Marie flinched. He moved his hands away.

'Has she ever missed work before?' she asked, knowing the answer.

He solemnly shook his head. 'If you'd like me to accompany you to the station?'

'What? No. She's not missing.' As Marie stood, she remembered what Mrs Kepler had said. 'It's probably just that damn suffragette cause. She'll have gone on a rally. Out of town.' Marie grabbed the letters and stashed them in her satchel, leaving the head librarian looking as confused as she felt.

As Marie rushed down the staircase from the South Hall and entered the reception hall, she diverted from her exit and returned to the desk. 'Excuse me. You're a suffragette?' Marie asked, pointing at the enamel sunflower pin on the woman's lapel.

She nodded. 'Yes. I am.'

'Then you know my sister is too.'

'Oh yes. Capucine is very inspiring.'

'Is she?' Marie asked, surprised her sister apparently inspired people in this manner.

'Of course. Capucine is a brilliant speaker and a great advocate of the cause.'

'Yes! Indeed. So that must be it, no?'

'What must be it?'

'She must be giving a speech somewhere.'

'Not that I'm aware of.'

'Come on. You must know what's happening. Is there not a rally taking place? Something. Anything happening out of town?'

The receptionist looked flustered. 'No. I'm not sure. I don't think so. She would've said. She always talked to me about the movement. She's the reason I joined.'

Marie sighed. 'Then perhaps you might know somebody that does.'

Marie waited until the evening when the New York City Woman Suffrage Association met in a hall on Fifth Avenue. The Astor Library's young receptionist, Amelia, greeted Marie on the steps outside, and they went in together. They arrived early, hoping to find out if anyone had seen Capucine.

The rows of benches in the hall were filled with people, though nobody had taken to the stage. Marie hoped Capucine would be mingling with the other women. She didn't know whether to hit her or hug her when she eventually saw her.

'Over there, look,' Amelia said.

Marie spun around as Amelia pointed towards a group of women standing near the stage.

'Capucine? Where? I can't see her.'

'No, sorry. That lady over there. She's introduced Capucine to talk before.'

'Capucine spoke? On stage?'

'Of course. Capucine is an amazing speaker.'

'Really?' Marie asked, shaking her head in disbelief. It dawned on her how separate their lives were despite having lived together. Capucine had tried to integrate Marie into her life, but Marie was too independent. Since arriving from France, Marie sought to build her own life, pursuing her art. She'd preferred to mix in art circles and not waste time with suffragism. She did not care whether she could vote for one politician or another. They were all idiots. She remembered how her sister would call her immature and selfish for such views.

'Who is she?' Marie asked.

'She's Matilda Joslyn Gage. She's a senior member of the association.' The woman had a stern, forthright look about her. She reminded Marie of a schoolmarm. She wore a black silk dress with a high ruffled collar. The only colour she wore was a gold, white and purple ribbon pinned to her chest. Her long, white hair sat pinned high on her head, except for a couple of shoulder length braids.

'Do you know her? Can you introduce me?'

Amelia seemed to shrink. She shook her head. 'I wish. No, I don't know her personally, I'm afraid.'

Marie considered Amelia for a moment, then decided not to say anything.

'I'll save you a seat,' Amelia said, pointing to some spaces on the end of the bench next to the aisle.

Marie nodded. She made her way down the aisle to the stage and squeezed between people deep in conversation who were oblivious to her presence. Marie sighed and stood with her hand on her hip when she got to Gage. The leader was also conversing and didn't realise Marie waited to speak to her.

'Excusez-moi,' Marie said, slipping into her native French, which she tended to do when annoyed. Both women turned to Marie at the interruption.

'Can I help you, miss,' Gage asked.

Marie held out her hand. 'Mrs Gage—'

'You may call me Matilda,' she said, shaking Marie's hand.

'My name is Marie Cadieux. My sister is Capucine.'

The woman's stern face melted into a warm smile. 'Ah, finally, she has persuaded you to join us.'

Marie winced. 'Not quite. Have you seen Capucine recently?'

'No. In fact, we were expecting her tonight. Is your sister here? Is she not well?'

Marie closed her eyes and took a deep breath. Her head lowered.

'Marie. Is everything okay?' Gage asked again.

'I don't know,' Marie said. 'Nobody has seen her for at least a week. Have you?'

Matilda's smile faded. She looked concerned. 'Your sister doesn't miss these meetings.'

'Nor does she miss work,' Marie said. 'Or take leave without telling me. Even when we have quarrelled.'

Matilda considered Marie. 'Do you know Voltairine Kingma?'

Marie shook her head. 'Would you mean Vee? Capucine has spoken of a friend called Vee.'

'It's likely to be her.'

Matilda led Marie over to a tall, confident looking woman. 'Voltairine,' Matilda called out. The woman turned to them both, and though her curious eyes darted up and down Marie, she did so with a smile. She looked to be a similar age to Capucine, in her late twenties or early thirties.

'This is Capucine's sister, Marie.'

A brief hint of confusion crossed her face. Then, she broke into a broad smile. She took her hand and shook it.

'At last!' she announced. The woman's accent sounded Dutch. Capucine finally got you here. Is she here?' she asked, looking around the hall.

'It seems not,' Matilda said. 'Capucine hasn't been seen for what. How long was it?'

'She's been missing a week,' Marie confirmed.

'A week?'

'I think,' Marie said.

Voltairine's smile faded like everyone else's when Marie revealed the news.

'Am I okay to leave you in the company of Miss Kingma?' Matilda asked, placing her hand warmly on Marie's back. Marie nodded and felt the older woman gently push her towards Voltairine.

Voltairine instantly slid her arm through the crook of Marie's arm and guided her towards one of the benches.

Marie tried to indicate she had a seat with Amelia, but Voltairine swept her down to the bench. Marie sat in silence for a short while, and sitting so close to Voltairine, she could smell her neroli-scented perfume.

Voltairine released her arm from Marie's. She twisted in her seat to face her. She frowned. Marie studied her and felt a surge of admiration. Voltairine was confident, fashionable and beautiful.

'You know my sister well?' Marie asked.

'Yes. Of course. Capucine is one of my closest friends.'

Marie frowned. 'But, I have never seen you before. You've never visited our home,' Marie said.

She smiled and shrugged. 'She's never invited me.'

Marie sighed. Capucine didn't like visitors to their home. She'd fallen out with Marie about bringing her art friends and models there. It was one of the reasons she'd moved out.

'She's ashamed of where we live. That's why.'

Voltairine tilted her head in acknowledgement but didn't say anything.

'It's stupid really. I recently brought some artist friends back, and she was furious.'

'Is that why you left home?'

'One of the reasons. She told you then?'

Voltairine nodded. 'Yes, Capucine missed you. She said it was too quiet, too empty without an easel to trip up on in the hallway.'

Marie choked back her tears and coughed her throat clear. 'I'm worried about her. It's not like her to go missing like this. And now. Now, I don't even know where to look. Everywhere I've been, I thought she'd be there. I thought I'd either hug her or hit her.' She smiled, but it swiftly faded into a frown.

'Have you contacted the police?' Voltairine asked.

'No.'

'Why not? You should do.'

'What will they do?'

'She might be in hospital.'

'Hurt?'

Her mouth twisted as if she were having difficulty saying: 'Maybe. She could even be in jail.'

Marie laughed.

'No. I'm serious. The police have not been known to be kind to us. Capucine might be in trouble if she has argued with them or done something.'

Recognition dawned on Marie's face. 'I didn't think.'

'Look, the talk is about to start,' Voltairine said, indicating to Matilda Joslyn-Gage, who took to the stage. Marie stood. 'What are you doing?' Voltairine asked.

Marie pushed past Voltairine, who caught her hand, causing her to stop and answer. 'I can't sit and wait,' Marie said. 'I have to go look for her. If you don't know where she is, you can't help me.'

'I'm due to talk shortly,' Voltairine said, gesturing to the stage.

'It's okay. I don't need you to come with me.'

'If you wait until I've delivered my speech, I can come with you.'

Marie's forehead creased as she pulled her hand free. 'I can't just sit here doing nothing,' she said.

'Well, at least do you have a pen?'

'Why?'

'Take my address.' Marie took out her sketchbook and a pencil. She handed them to Voltairine, who scribbled her address in the book. 'Let me know if you find her, and I'll help. If you don't find out anything tonight, come back here. We'll be here until late.'

CHAPTER 3

Despite fervently supporting the suffrage cause, Capucine Cadieux was not the type of woman to get herself arrested. At least, Marie didn't think so. Marie decided to go to the police station first to discover if her sister was detained. It was the quickest outcome to be eliminated, though she would prefer to find her in a cell than injured in a hospital bed or worse.

The police station looked like an Italian castle looming on the corner of the street with an imposing tower and tall arched windows. As Marie stood looking up at it, two policemen on horseback sloped past her and towards the stables at the back of the building. A dog walking with them veered towards Marie and sniffed at her leg. One of the policemen whistled, and the dog caught up with them. Marie took a deep breath and strode into the lamplight and up the steps.

The waiting room smelled sterile. The white glazed bricks looked grimy in the dank light. A rotund man in uniform stood behind the desk and eyed her as she came in. Marie grimaced and walked right up to the desk. The Desk Officer spread his hands on the surface and leaned towards her.

'Can I help you, ma'am?' he said with a deep voice.

'My sister has gone missing.'

He reached for a notepad without taking his eyes off her and laid his hands on it first time. He slid the pencil out of its holder and ran the tip across his tongue. He didn't say anything. They just stared at each other. She raised an eyebrow.

'You tell me your name. You tell me who's gone missing.

You tell me when.'

Marie's nostrils flared. 'Marie Cadieux.' She took a deep breath and waited for him to write that down. He spelt it wrong. 'My sister is Capucine Cadieux.' He spelt that wrong, too. She spelt out her sister's name. By the time he'd rewritten that, she sighed. 'Is there not anyone I can speak to? A detective, maybe?'

'They require details first.'

She forced a smile. 'I last saw her two weeks ago. The last time anyone saw her was a week ago. She hasn't turned up for work at the Astor Library on Lafayette Street, which is unlike her. She is a...' Marie hesitated from saying it, then decided it better he had all the details down, no matter how long it took to write them. 'She is a suffragette. A passionate one. By all accounts, she's an inspirational one. She hasn't attended their meetings or been in touch with her friends there for a week.'

The Desk Officer still wrote down the name of the library. Marie sighed. 'I should've hired a damn Pinkerton instead.' She placed her hand on the notebook when he licked the pencil again. He looked up at her and raised an eyebrow.

'Is anyone here locked up who goes by that description?' Marie asked.

'Ma'am, you haven't yet given me a description.'

'It's okay, Knowles. I've heard enough. I'll take it from here,' an American-Italian voice said from the room behind. Marie peered around the large Desk Officer to see who spoke. A short man in his mid-twenties came over. He finished buttoning the shiny brass buttons on his blue coat. He took his hat off and placed it on the desk. The Desk Officer slid the notebook over to him.

'So your sister's gone missing, that right?'

'Yes,' Marie said.

'Is she known to us. She a troublemaker? I don't know you.'

'No, she's not. Not at all.'

'Thought you said she was a suffragette?'

'Does that make her a troublemaker?'

'No, not in my eyes, it doesn't.'

A commotion entered the station. A couple of policemen led a drunk man into the waiting room.

'We need to book him in for the night,' one of the policemen said.

'You again?' the Desk Officer said. 'Shoulda taken him straight to The Tombs.'

The drunkard grinned. Then he turned to Marie and tilted his head at her. His grin grew broader still when he looked at her face. 'And sure, what are you in for? Booked for breaking hearts, missy?'

One of the policemen escorting him shoved him in the back. 'Eyes front.'

The Desk Officer lifted the hatch in the desk and turned sideways to fit himself through. The drunkard laughed and was greeted with a punch to the stomach. He doubled over. The Desk Officer grabbed his collar and dragged him to the cells.

'I sure hope you haven't treated my sister like that.'

'You believe her to be in our custody then?'

'I don't know.'

The Italian-American waved her towards him. 'Come on through. Let's have a chat.'

The young Officer's name was Joe Petrosino. He was about to go home, but he took Marie over to a desk instead, and she recounted everything she knew.

'I'll send a memo to the other precincts,' he said. 'And we'll see if anything comes back. If she tends to stay local like you suggest, I'd try checking the hospital in case she's been in an accident of some sort.'

After the interview, Joe Petrosino walked Marie back to her sister's apartment, several blocks away. A nearby clock bell chimed eleven times. Marie regretted not wearing a warmer coat than her jacket. She shivered. Joe glanced at her. 'You cold?'

'Yes.'

'It's probably just nerves. Try not to worry too much. There's a good chance she'll turn up,' he said, vigilantly watching the shadows as he strode. She felt safe in his company, which was just as well.

A drunk man flew out of the doors of a concert saloon and clattered into the gutter. He got up and picked up a sign leaning against a gas lamp that read Punches and Julep. An arrow on the sign pointed towards the establishment he'd unceremoniously been escorted from. Two men with broken noses and cauliflower ears stood in the doorway. Music, smoke and light came out of the room behind them. Joe withdrew his truncheon from his belt and weighed it in his hand. The drunk man saw Joe in his police uniform. He held the sign above his head. He swayed and hiccuped. Deciding a night in a seven-cent lodging house was better than the cells, he put the sign down and staggered off down the street.

'This whole city's getting more and more ridiculous,' Joe said.

They continued walking. A dead horse lay decaying on

the filth-covered cobbles in the gutter. They could see the silhouettes of the rats scurrying and hear them gnawing and picking at the flesh, emboldened by the darkness.

The sound of a train or a boat blowing off steam drifted between the buildings. Carriage wheels and horse hooves pounded the cobbles. Somebody walked out of a building and threw the contents of a bedpan into the street.

They got to the steps of the door to Capucine's apartment building. A collection of heads wearing hats peered out from behind the milliner's dark window.

'I'll leave a note for you in the mailbox to contact me if I hear anything. Try to have hope. It doesn't always end badly.'

Marie thanked him, and he strode off into the night. She stood looking up at the building as she used the boot scrape. She hoped there'd be light coming from her sister's windows. There wasn't.

She'd never called it home despite Capucine insisting she should. Home was her grandfather's farm in France. She missed the open skies and fields. Thankfully, as she arrived at the apartment's second-floor door, it was too late for even Mrs Kepler to be lingering in the hall, seeking gossip. But that only added to the eerie, quiet sense pervading her sister's apartment. She checked each room one last time, hoping Capucine had returned and would be asleep on a chair or quietly reading, but she wasn't. Marie fell asleep on her sister's bed without changing her clothes.

A door slammed shut. Marie startled awake. It took her a moment to recognise the room. She got up too quickly, stumbled towards the bedroom door, and looked into the hallway. 'Capucine?'

There was no reply. Marie leaned against the doorframe and realised she had probably heard the sounds of the city coming through the ajar window. She looked at her watch. It was nine-thirty a.m. She rubbed the tiredness from her face and headed for the kitchen.

While making coffee on the stove, she thought of the things Joe had suggested she do: Visit the hospital, create a missing person's poster, contact the newspaper for an article, and visit all of the places Capucine frequented.

Marie sat by the apartment's door, crossed her legs and laced her calf-length boots. Her sister always teased her for how she dressed. You can take the girl out of the Midi-Pyrénées, but you can't make her dress civilised.

Marie resisted the fashion of high necks, tight corsets and bodices with lots of silk and lace, and she dressed more like a pioneer of the plains than a woman living in Manhattan.

She wore a simple calico skirt, hemmed three inches shorter than the city streets were used to. She slipped on her waistcoat over her white blouse and fastened a belt around it.

Slipping her satchel over her shoulder and checking what was inside, Marie realised she hadn't read the letters. She went over to the sash window, pushed it open and sat on the sill. She opened the typed letters first. One was from the New York City Woman Suffrage Association, and the other was about rent, which she didn't care to read.

She knew one of the letters was from the head librarian, who had enquired about where she was, and a quick glance confirmed that. This left one remaining handwritten letter. C.Cadieux, appt 5. was written on the envelope. Marie turned it over and thumbed it open.

The letter was from a recipient on the Upper East Side,

dated Wednesday, 8 September, two days ago. It read:

Capucine,

Have you seen Phillip? It's been almost a week since I saw you both together. I haven't been able to contact him since. As you know, he has a production at our theatre in a couple of days. Now is not the time to be running off. He has a job to do. I hope you have not imposed your views on him. I'd be most obliged if you let me know your whereabouts at your earliest convenience.

Jonathan.

Marie's hand dropped to her lap. She leaned back against the window frame and stared outside. The sun shone, and the trees still clung to their verdancy. People walked on the sidewalks, and a trolley car trundled by. 'Phillip,' she whispered to herself. 'Who is Phillip?' She reread the letter, and her eyes lingered on the sender's signature, Jonathan.

She went over to the side table in the hall and took out her sister's address book. She flicked through it, searching for Jonathan or Phillip's name. There wasn't an entry for either of them.

Marie left the apartment, ran past Mrs Kepler on the landing, ignoring her questions, and went down the staircase. She found the mailbox empty and headed out of the front doors, nearly running straight into Joe Petrosino.

'You okay, miss?' he said, grabbing her shoulders so she wouldn't fall over. 'I might have a lead.'

'Really? Me too.'

'Where you headed?' he asked.

'The Upper East Side.'
'You're kidding me.'
'No, why?'
'Because that's where I'm headed too.'

CHAPTER 4

Marie and Joe walked down the sidewalk and headed for the elevated railway station on Christopher Street.

'We had a note from the 19th Precinct to go check out your sister here this morning,' Joe said, thumbing back towards Capucine's apartment building. 'Turns out a guy over on nineteenth has gone missing too, and your sister was one of the last to have seen him.'

'Phillip?'

'Yeah, that's his name. D'you know him?'

'No. I have never heard of him until today.'

She thumbed inside her satchel, plucked out the letter and handed it to Joe for him to read.

'Well, well,' he said. 'It looks like this Jonathan's the person we need to pay a visit to.'

They caught the Ninth Avenue Line of the elevated railway up to the corner of Central Park, and from there, they took a route through the park. Marie had instantly warmed to Joe, and seemingly, she thought he had to her. As they walked, they reminisced about their home countries. Joe had grown up in the Campania region of Italy but didn't share Marie's yearning to be back in the countryside on the other side of the world.

'I lived with my grandfather, too, when I was younger,' he said. My cousin Pup and I came over and lived with him until he had an accident with a streetcar.'

'Your cousin or your grandfather?'

'My grandfather.'

'So you lived with your cousin?'

'Kinda. We were too young to fend for ourselves, but rather than send us to the orphanage, the judge took us into his care, believe it or not, until our family in Italy discovered our plight. The judge looked after us and put us into school until our family emigrated here.'

'I wonder what it would've been like with more family here,' Marie said.

'So it's just you two?'

'Yes.'

'You get on with your sister?'

'She acts like she's my mother. Even though she left France years before I arrived here. We're both very passionate about our pursuits.'

'So, is this Phillip like her suitor then?'

Marie shook her head. 'No. Well, I don't know. This is the first I heard of it,' Marie said, waving the letter.

'Strange. Don't you two talk about things like that?'

'Yes. No. I don't know. You know how it is. I never thought she kept secrets, though.'

'Everyone keeps secrets, Marie.'

'Is that your professional opinion?'

'Indeed it is.'

It was gone lunchtime by the time they'd made their way over to the Upper East Side and the address on East 78th Street where Jonathan Moses resided.

A tall, thin man in his early forties wearing spectacles and a suit opened the door.

'Mr Moses?' Joe asked.

'Yes?

'I am Officer Petrosino. And this is Miss Cadieux.'

His brow raised when he heard her name, and he looked her up and down. 'I guess you're here about my brother?'

He led them into his parlour, and his maid bought them each a drink of lemon water.

'It appears your brother and Miss Cadieux's sister have gone missing. Presumably together?' Joe asked.

Jonathan looked furtively at Marie, then took his glasses off and cleaned them with his handkerchief.

'Can you tell us more about their connection?' Marie asked. 'I had no knowledge of their relationship.'

'It is a...delicate matter.'

'Delicate matter or not, they're missing. And so they can't inform or object, but you can,' Joe said.

'Yes. Yes, it would appear so. I told Phillip no good would come of it, that it would court controversy.'

'Monsieur Moses. Mr Moses. Please. What is their connection?' Marie asked.

'They are lovers.'

Marie's face scrunched up. 'Lovers? Capucine? Mon dieu.' His jaw clenched.

'Why is their relationship such a secret? Is he married?' Joe asked.

Both Marie and Jonathan remonstrated with Joe for his comment.

He held up his hands in surrender. 'I'm only trying to ascertain the facts. I'm hearing a lot of secrecy and have two missing people. So I suggest you start being more forthcoming with your answers if you want to help me find them.'

'Capucine has never even hinted she has a suitor.'

'No, well, I dare say she would.'

'And why is that?' Joe asked.

Jonathan squirmed in his seat. 'I feel like I am betraying their trust, but if this is the position they have put me in with their sneaking around, then...'

Marie and Joe's stare suggested they would expect an answer the next time he opened his mouth.

He sighed. 'Your sister is some kind of prominent suffragette, is she not?'

'So I'm beginning to believe.'

'Well, Phillip is not. He's quite the opposite.'

'What do you mean?' Marie asked.

'He is a playwright. And like your sister, he is somewhat of a rising star.'

'And that surrounds this affair in secrecy because?' Joe asked.

'You've not heard of Philip Moses?'

'We are quite in the dark as to who your brother is,' Marie said.

'Philip is an anti-suffragette. And he writes satirical plays mocking the suffrage cause.'

'Yet they are lovers?' Joe asked.

'Why would Capucine fall for a man like this? I do not believe it.'

'I have funded Phillip. I have supported him for many years while he pursued this aim of becoming a writer, but alas, he found no success until he started writing plays of this kind. And now he has become one of the most celebrated playwrights in New York.'

'So celebrated I have never heard his name,' Marie said.

'Nor I,' Joe said.

'Are you not informed on the suffrage debate, Officer Petrosino?' Jonathan asked.

'My sister would not have a relationship with a man like that, Joe.'

'Your sister is madly in love with my brother.'

'Yet she keeps it a secret even from me.'

'Yes, well. I've heard about you, Marie.'

'And what is that supposed to mean?'

'You are like my brother and care only for your artistic pursuits.'

'Is that what she told you?'

'It's what I deducted. Her benevolence allows you to pursue your art. I at least have that in common with your sister.'

'We're not here to discuss Marie's artistic capabilities, sir,' Joe said. 'What effect would exposing their relationship have on their respective pursuits?'

'Well, they'd be ruined, wouldn't they? Their credibility would be shot. Philip is not really an anti-suffragette. I can't say he particularly cares for either side of the cause. But, he saw an opportunity to make his writing known and to get some measure of fame and success. Then the damn fool only goes and falls in love with your sister, but he is now too committed to this ruse despite his affections. And it's the same for your sister. If she steps out with my brother on her arm. Her career, or whatever you'd wish to call it, as an ardent suffragette...well, it wouldn't go down well with the Suffrage Association.'

'I dare say it would,' Marie said.

They sat in silence and sipped their drinks. The grandfather clock's pendulum swung back and forth.

'Could they have simply had enough of the stress of this situation and took a break somewhere together?' Joe eventually asked.

'Capucine would have sought leave from her work.'

'And my brother always attends his performances. The opening night of one of his plays is tonight. It's a sellout.'

Joe leaned forward. 'Excuse me. You say that like it's still going ahead?'

'Of course it is.'

'Well, I suppose, but—'

'The show must go on, Officer. The show must go on.'

That night, Marie and Joe went to the theatre. The name of the production, The Rights of Man, was emblazoned across the sign. Light bulbs burned brightly around it, and crowds filled the sidewalk.

'I still think it's strange, don't you?' Marie asked.

'A little. But if it can continue without Phillip, then I suppose it makes good business sense,' Joe said.

'Well, it is big business around here.'

'True. If Jonathan Moses invested money in this venture, he would never have turned away a box office like this. What did you think of him?' Joe asked.

'He is a mercenary like all businessmen. I don't know what my sister would see in a man like his brother.'

'Assuming he's like his brother.'

'He couldn't be like him. Nothing seems right about this, Joe.'

'I'd have to agree with you.'

'Do you think we're going to learn something tonight?'

'We're no closer to finding your sister. So anything's better than sitting at home, right?'

'I don't know. I could be creating a missing poster or something.'

'Just let's keep an eye on Jonathan.'

'You suspect him?'

'Don't you?' Joe asked as they arrived at the box office. 'Say, Mr Moses has put aside a couple of tickets for us.'

'Your name?' the box office assistant asked.

'Petrosino.'

The box office assistant opened a drawer and thumbed through a wad of envelopes. 'I'm sorry, but there isn't one put aside for that name.'

Joe twisted his lips. 'Check again,' he said.

The woman thumbed through the envelopes again. 'Nothing,' she said.

'Is there anything under the name Cadieux?' Marie asked.

The woman thumbed through the envelopes and found one with Marie's surname written on it. She slid the tickets through the hatch and glared at Marie.

'Is there a problem?' Marie asked.

'Yeah. You're holding up the line. Next, please,' she shouted, ushering through the people behind Marie and Joe.

'What was that about, Joe?'

Joe shook his head. 'How well known is your sister?'

'Cap? You think that was because of my name?'

'Her tone couldn't have changed more when you said your surname.'

'Jonathan Moses is more au fait with the situation than either of us. Why use my name and not yours if that was the case?'

'Who knows. Let's find our seats.'

Marie didn't say anything as Joe led them through the theatre to their seats, which gave her time to theorise about the situation. Her thoughts kept leading to dark places. They sat at the end of the row next to the aisle, and she stared at the safety curtain. Joe watched as she pondered and frowned. 'What is it?' he eventually asked.

'How do you think this will turn out?'

'It's no use speculating.'

'I thought that was your job,' she said.

'Then leave that to me.'

'You think it's bad, don't you?'

'Do you believe their relationship, under the circumstances, might incur enemies?'

'Enemies?' Marie asked.

'There have been a few cases across the city regarding suffragettes and anti-suffragettes, an escalation of sorts. It appeared like a tit-for-tat: One side does something, and the others do something in return.'

'Retaliation?' Marie asked.

'I can't be sure. I've just noticed a pattern. Hopefully, they're unrelated events, and it's just a coincidence.'

'What would retaliation incur?'

'I wouldn't like to speculate. I just wondered if either your sister or Philip had enemies.'

'You could try that woman at the box office for a start. But I'm guessing there's a whole theatre full of them in here,' she said and looked around at the patrons. 'Have any of these incidents you speak of involved abduction?' She turned and eyeballed him.

He stared straight back. 'No. Not yet. Why?'

She shook her head. 'I just can't imagine Capucine being in love with a man like him.'

'You've not even met him, Marie. Siblings can be very different. You're different from your sister.'

'What if they've abducted Capucine?'

'To what end?' Joe asked.

'Surely, this Phillip wouldn't have gone missing, not when all this is happening. And besides, if they had, there'd be some posturing. They wouldn't keep it a secret.' Marie rubbed her forehead. 'Maybe I'm just tired.'

The orchestra in the pit started tuning and warming up their instruments. The fire curtain lifted, revealing lush red curtains.

Marie reached out and patted Joe's leg just as the light dimmed. She could see him blush. He tilted his head and frowned at her.

'Thank you, Joe.'

'What for?'

'This. Helping me.'

'Just doing my job, ma'am.'

'I know, but you didn't have to. So thank you.'

The orchestra went silent. The conductor tapped on the lectern. He lifted his hand. Expectations filled the theatre. He swung the baton. The curtains drew back dramatically, revealing a chorus line of dancing girls.

Marie didn't want to be sitting in the stalls doing nothing. She twisted in her chair and looked around the theatre. She glanced up at the dress circle and the boxes. On the stage, the chorus line was shaped into a v, and a man ran to the front and started singing. Marie wasn't paying attention to the lyrics, but whatever he sang made the audience laugh. She slipped a penny into the holder on the back of the chair, releasing the opera glasses. The scene was magnified through the cloudy eyepiece. She glassed from the man on the stage to one of the boxes. She could make out Jonathan Moses sat wearing a top hat. A woman sat next to him, presumably his wife. She hoped to see her sister lingering in the back of the box with the man she apparently loved. Capucine wasn't there. Marie scanned the other box but didn't recognise them.

A couple of journalists sat in the front row, enjoying seeing the chorus girls up close.

She nudged Joe. 'He's up there,' she whispered, offering him the binoculars. He declined.

'I see him.'

'Do you think it strange he didn't invite us into his box?'

'Why would he invite the sister of his missing brother's lover?' he said ironically.

'Don't call her that.'

The chorus line finished their musical number and scattered off the stage, leaving the actor to deliver a speech. Marie rolled her eyes as the audience laughed. She dropped the binoculars in Joe's lap and stood.

'Where are you going?'

'You said to keep an eye on him up there. So, that's what I'm going to do,' she said. Then she decided she needed the binoculars. She grabbed them from his hands and took them with her.

Marie slipped out of the stalls and into a side corridor. An usherette leaned against a wall, smoking, while a man whispered into her ear. They paid Marie no attention. She took a back set of stairs to the dress circle and got behind the audience. She had a better view of Jonathan Moses in his box but stayed low so he didn't spot her. Engrossed, he beat his hand on the handrail and laughed heartily. Marie wanted to throw the binoculars across the theatre and smack him off his head. How could he act like this with his brother missing?

She took a deep breath and scanned the other occupants in the box. The woman beside him seemed to enjoy her privileged position more than the show. Another couple sat with them and howled at the play. Marie hadn't gotten involved in the suffrage cause with her sister. Not because she didn't believe in it but because she didn't want distractions from pursuing her art. She knew people like those in the audience would anger her too much, and then she'd get too involved. It was better to stay out of it. But not tonight. She dropped the binoculars from her eyes and pondered doing something. She shook the thought from her head. She was there to try and find her sister. She lifted the binoculars to the box.

Again, Marie had hoped to see her sister and his brother further back in the shadows, but they weren't there. At the back of the box, Marie saw a man with a stern face, half hidden by a low, wide-brimmed hat, sitting by the door. He stared blankly at the stage. The man looked out of place compared to the others sitting there. He was dressed casually, unlike the others. It was as if he wasn't with them. Security, maybe, she thought. Why would Jonathan Moses need security?

She lowered the opera glasses and went back out into the corridor. With Jonathan and his guests occupied, she went to find out if he or his brother had an office. The front of the house contained the box office and a bar on the floor above it. Marie made her way backstage, where it was a flurry of activity. The chorus line had changed clothes and were waiting in the wings to head back on stage. Through the curtains, Marie saw an actress arguing with the actor who'd been on from the start. The actress seemed to be hamming up her role as a suffragette, and the actor's pithy put-downs created more raucous laughter from the audience.

At the back of the stage was a corridor with a row of dressing rooms. Marie walked down it, looking for a sign that indicated their office.

The actress who had been on stage just before clomped down the corridor towards Marie. She reached for her hair and suddenly whipped it off. It was a man.

'Jesus Christ,' the man in the dress said. He saw Marie standing there staring open-mouthed. 'Nothing here is as it seems, honey.' Then he went into one of the dressing rooms.

Marie followed after him and opened his door without knocking. He sat at a dressing table and turned to see who'd walked in. 'Sorry, autographs can be given at the stage door.'

The room was stuffy and smelled sweaty. A single, dim Edison bulb lit the room.

'What do you want?' he asked.

'Do you know Phillip?'

He frowned and thought for a moment. 'Philip, the writer?'

'Yes.'

He raised an eyebrow and then stood and started taking off his dress. 'If you're gonna stand there, you could at least hand me that dress—the green one.'

He nodded to a rail of clothes by the door.

She took the hanger with the green dress off the rail and held it to him. When he went to take it, she pulled it away.

'Who are you?' he asked as he stood in his long johns, hands on his hips.

'When was the last time you saw Phillip?' She tossed him the dress to keep him sweet.

'Thanks. I was beginning to get cold,' he said dryly.

'I know. I could see.'

He laughed. 'I like you.'

He started climbing into the dress. 'What are you? His girlfriend or something?'

'I just want to know if he's okay.'

'You don't look like his type.'

'And what would his type be?'

'Tall, dark. Dramatic.'

Her sister was two of those things, so she went with the one she wasn't. 'So he likes dramatic women?'

The man puffed out his cheeks. 'You'd better believe it. Say, you couldn't help me with these buttons?' he said, trying to reach around to his back and turning around on the spot. 'Come on, I don't bite.'

She walked over from the door, and he turned his back to her. She started fastening the buttons on the dress. 'If I were you, honey, I'd stay clear of him.'

'Why?'

'Well, any man who writes a play like this doesn't have much respect for his mother.'

'You're a suffragette?'

He laughed. 'I couldn't care less. Besides, it's a job, and the money's real.' He turned around. 'How do I look?'

'Like you're missing a wig.'

He suddenly remembered and touched his head. 'Oh yeah!'

He took it from the mannequin's head on the dressing table and put it on.

'Don't you think it strange he'd miss the opening night of his play?'

The man sighed and put his hand on Marie's shoulder. 'No. Phillip likes the ladies too much. I've known him for a while now, and he does stupid things for women. They'll be the ruin of him, that's for sure.'

There was a knock on the door, and someone shouted. 'Benny, what's taking you? You're on stage in less than a minute.'

'Shit!' he said, pushing past Marie. His wig was lopsided. As he opened the door, she asked, 'Where's his room, his office? I've got a note I want to leave him.'

He looked flustered. 'Just over the way behind that curtain,' he said before returning to the stage.

Marie looked around the dressing room. There were no more answers here, she thought.

She pulled the large curtain to the side in the corridor and found the door behind it. She tried the handle, expecting it to be locked. But it clicked open, and she went in. The smell hit her. She wanted to vomit. She raised her sleeve to cover her nose and fumbled for the light switch, flicking it on. A mouse spotted her and ran away. A mouldy chicken carcass sat on the table.

She grimaced.

The room was messy, but nothing seemed out of place. A typewriter sat on the desk. Pages of scripts were piled up next to it. Scrunched-up balls of pages spilt out of the wastepaper basket. How could Capucine love a man like this? Her sister would get annoyed if Marie tried to paint or draw in the house, telling her that was what her studio was for. I guess this is his studio, though, she countered to herself.

She went around the desk and tried the drawers. They, too, were full of bits of scripts and correspondence. Nothing stood out to her. She looked around the room. It was a shabby, dark mess of failed work. Nobody could be inspired in a place like this. Yet from the theatre, she could hear eruptions of laughter. Marie decided there was nothing to be found in Phillip's office. The chicken carcass looked like it corroborated he hadn't been there for some time.

As she walked down the corridor from his office, the man who had lurked at the back of Jonathan Moses' box came towards her.

I haven't done anything wrong, she told herself. They kept walking towards each other. What could he do? He seemed to stare straight at her. Was he coming to stop her from snooping around? His fingers flexed at his sides as he approached. What did Jonathan Moses have to hide so much he'd send someone like this to stop her looking around? He went straight past her. She sighed, glanced over her shoulder, and watched as he ascended a narrow, iron, spiral staircase to the fly tower above the stage.

She shook her head. You're being ridiculous, she thought. Just because he had a mean-looking face, you thought he was a thug when he's probably a chief curtain puller or something. She allowed herself a smile. Perhaps leaving home had given her sister a chance to live her own life and do something reckless for once.

If he was going to drop a curtain, it would be time for the interval. Marie headed around the back of the cyclorama and waited in the backstage left wing for the interval.

Marie watched Benny belting out a musical number in his dress as he walked forward from centre stage. He was singing about wanting to be a man and was making splendid use of his deep and surprisingly good baritone voice. But as he reached the front of the stage and the music built to a crescendo, there was a sudden unfurling noise from above. Marie staggered back as she saw the objects falling from the rafters. Bodies. Two of them. They jerked as they reached the end of the rope, and there was a sickening crack as their necks broke from the height of the fall. A man and a woman swung there. The crowd sat in stunned silence. The orchestra abruptly stopped playing their instruments. And Benny, oblivious to what happened behind him, extended his arms to the roof and the deep baritone note at the end of his song. For him, it was a triumph. For everyone else in the theatre, it was an unfolding drama nobody had wished to see. People realised the hanging bodies were not part of the show. Murmurs turned to shrieks. Panic began to spread.

Marie stood motionless in shock. She stared at the two hanging bodies. At first, she couldn't understand what was happening. The man hanging there wore the woman's clothes, and the woman wore the man's clothes. Marie recognised the dress but not the man wearing it, who now spun idly around. She couldn't bring herself to look up at the woman's face. She knew who it would be.

By now, the theatre had erupted into chaos. Benny stood shrieking on the stage. The audience was screaming and scrambling to exit. The journalists who had come to review the show stood in the front row, gazing up at the scoop of their careers. A hand grabbed her shoulders.

'Marie? Marie?'

She blinked away the shock. It was Joe. She grabbed him and hugged him. He just let her. She turned her buried face from his shoulder to look up at the bodies again. Capucine twisted on the rope. Her head was tilted to the side. Her pale face stared blankly out.

'It's your sister, isn't it?'

Marie began to sob.

'Don't look,' he said, turning her away. Joe witnessed the chaos unfolding. It turned into a stampede as people pushed and shoved their way out. Some still sat or stood transfixed by the horror. But if they were in the way of the majority, they got knocked over.

Joe turned his attention to the box. In his elevated position, Jonathan Moses had his hands on his head. He seemed to be looking aghast at the hanging bodies and the reputation of his theatre flying out of the door with the audience.

Marie suddenly pushed herself out of Joe's embrace. She looked up to the rafters.

'Marie, don't look. Don't do this to yourself,' he said, trying to lead her away from the scene. She shook away his hand. And continued squinting at the roof.

Joe followed her gaze. 'What is it?'

'Up there,' she said. She looked around the stage and saw a spotlight attached to the wall at the side of the stage. She rushed over to it and tried to move it but burnt her hand on the hot metal. Joe realised what she was trying to do. He took off his jacket and threw it over to her. Marie caught it and wrapped it around the light so she could angle the beam up to the rafters. The beam swung up and landed on a man climbing through a skylight. He stopped as the beam hit him. He shielded his eyes with his arm to prevent being dazzled.

'Do you see him, Joe?'

'I see him.'

Marie ran down the corridor and over to the narrow, iron staircase spiralling up to the fly tower above. Joe followed after her as she ran up the stairs. Marie was out of breath when she reached the narrow walkways and beams in the rigging. The spotlight was still pointed at the hatch in the roof. The man had long since exited, but Marie hurried along the narrow walkway, daring not to look at the drop to the stage below or what was swinging beneath it.

When they got to the hatch, Joe stopped her from climbing through.

'Let me go first, in case he's waiting for us.' Marie was about to protest, but he took a gun from his jacket pocket. Joe climbed through the hatch and found himself on the roof. Marie joined him and crouched beside him.

The roof was flat except for various chimneys, leaving no hiding place. There were buildings nearby, but the gap between them was too far to jump. This only left the fire escape, which they went over to. The escape was empty, and so was the alley it led down to. A crowd, made up of the audience, and nosey by-passers lingered outside of the theatre.

Marie slammed her fist against the wall.

'He could be anywhere by now,' Joe said, pocketing the gun.

Marie stared out into the city. Joe put his hand on her shoulder. There was nothing more he could say.

CHAPTER 6

Marie woke up in the bed tucked behind a room divider in her art studio. Sunlight poured through the muslin curtains. Joe had escorted Marie back late in the night. She didn't know how long she'd been asleep. Her head throbbed from a hangover. She'd drunk half a bottle of whiskey before she'd apparently passed out. Joe had also stayed at her studio. A blanket was folded up neatly on the chair he'd slept on. There was a note on top, but Marie couldn't bring herself to sit up, let alone go over and read it.

Marie stared at the sky through the slit in the transparent curtains. It's funny how life can suddenly change, she thought. A few days ago, she prepared to tell her sister she was returning to Paris to study art. Who knows if Marie would've seen her sister again? Now, Marie would never see Capucine again and would likely still go to Paris. Had anything really changed? Of course, everything had changed. Her sister's murderer had robbed them of their choices. Marie would never be able to write to her sister or receive a letter in return. She'd never be able to smile at the thought of Capucine rising to become a leader of the suffragettes. She'd never know if Capucine would've been proud of her or annoyed with her for wanting to go back to France. Capucine would never know if women would receive the vote.

She dreaded reading the headlines in the paper this morning. After they'd climbed down from the fly tower, Joe kicked the journalists out of the theatre. Not long after, more Police rushed to the scene, and eventually, the precinct chief arrived and took over from Joe.

Marie thought about the man who'd fled to the roof and disappeared into the alley via the fire escape. She was convinced he was the killer.

Marie got out of bed. She immediately wanted to get back into it, fall asleep, and forget everything that had happened—not that her dreams would allow it. She stumbled over to the chair, her head swirling, picked up the note Joe had left her, and unfolded it. She sat on the blanket on the chair and let her head recover before she read it.

Marie

We have a lead on the man who escaped onto the roof. I'm heading to The Tombs, but I'll return later with answers.

Joe

Marie scrunched the note into a ball and, despite feeling ill, went to pull on her boots.

The prison known as the Tombs looked like an Egyptian mausoleum. Marie Cadieux leant against the railings. She looked from beneath the shawl she wore over her head, watching, waiting outside the prison on Centre Street in the Five Points. There were many more dressed like her lingering in the street. A boy ran alongside a prison van, jumped onto a railing, and banged on the wall before jumping off when a policeman took a swing at him with a truncheon. Drunk men staggered, and drugged women wandered aimlessly, as lost in their heads as they were in the street. If they had any sense, they would have strayed far away from the immense prison in the heart of The Five Points, but they didn't. She'd arrived at the prison not knowing what she was there to do. Marie knew she couldn't sit in her studio doing nothing.

The man she believed was her sister's killer stalked out of the doors and surveyed his apparent freedom. Marie's heart rate galloped. Adrenaline flooded her. He lit a pipe, then jogged down the stairs onto the street and went past Marie without a glance. It was the closest she'd been to him since he walked past her backstage yesterday, and her whole body shook.

She followed him from a distance, and it was easy. A horse-drawn tram rattled along the middle of Centre Street. Marie walked behind a rag picker carrying a baby and a bundle of salvage before the man she followed turned off the main street. He didn't look back. She hurried towards the turning and peered around the wall. He carried on strolling down into The Bend.

Marie swore under her breath. Mulberry Street was the last place she hoped he'd go, but she knew it was inevitable. Where else would a killer dwell?

She followed him.

Rags of clothes and sheets hung, dripping across narrow alleys between tall, dirty buildings. Piles of ash sat on the greasy paved floor. Women wrapped in shawls leaned out of windows and frowned at her. There was a strong smell of soot, excrement, and dampness.

Marie Cadieux's clothes were too clean, and her boots were too shiny for someone who lived in The Bend. Men glared at her, daring her not to venture too close or inviting her to do the opposite. Every alley she went past had a collection of people like this, all somehow alert to her, as if the gait of her approaching footsteps betrayed she was not from the slums.

The man she was following turned into a side passage. She waited and peered around the wall. Marie let the distance build before following him again. The passage led into a square with looming rundown buildings. An immigrant woman picked through a pile of trash and recovered a chair leg. She shouted in German to her child, who took it. The man headed toward a broken water pump and trough and over to the tenement house opposite. The building had signs up saying it was due for demolition. Every window in the building was smashed. Gutters and pipes dangled from a roof, missing many tiles, which had dropped six storeys and broken into the mud and filth the man crunched and squelched through before disappearing through the doorway.

Marie followed him. She was terrified but compelled; she needed answers. But Marie didn't even know what her aim was. Would she confront him? Would she question him and expect to walk away? She suddenly found clarity as she lingered in the doorway.

'What the hell am I doing?' She turned to walk away.

'Who are you?'

Fear gripped her.

Marie hesitated, realising she should've had an alias ready. Her mind went blank.

'People with a gun to their head usually speak,' he said.

'Maybe it's because of the gun I can't,' she replied, turning and glaring at him.

He narrowed his eyes. 'Alright, let's try another question. Why are you following me?'

'Because you murdered my sister, you bâtard,' she said but then realised what she'd revealed.

'You're the sister?' He lowered the gun.

'Why did you do it?'

He shook his head. 'I didn't.'

'Don't lie. I saw you above the stage.'

He holstered his gun and pulled his coat over it.

'Answer me, damn you!' she said, pushing him.

'You were in the theatre last night,' he said, recognising her. 'I walked past you backstage.'

'Yes. So what were you doing?' Marie asked.

'I was trying to apprehend the one who pushed their bodies off the fly tower.'

'Don't lie to me. I saw only you.'

'If I really was a killer, you'd be dead already. Listen, kid, this ain't the place to talk.'

'Then why lead me here?'

'Because you were acting suspicious. I clocked you outside The Tombs. I thought you were one of them.'

'One of who?'

'Whoever's behind all of this mess.'

Marie frowned. 'Who the hell are you then? I saw you with Jonathan Moses in his box.'

'Look, I'll explain everything. But I really think we should get out of this wretched hole.'

Marie considered him for a moment. 'Yes, I think you might be right.'

The train clattered along the overhead railway and passed the tall, narrow building occupied by Brown's Coffee House and Saloon on Pearl Street. The street was full of carts, drays, and wheelbarrows piled high with bales of cotton, puncheons, tuns, hogsheads and barrels of beer, spirits and sugar.

Marie sat and silently stared at the tall, rangy man. He placed his wide-brimmed hat on the table. It still had dust on from the tenement, but she imagined it was dust from the plains. For that's where he looked like he belonged, on a horse on the frontier far from the cobbles and the fashion of Manhattan. His maroon shirt was open down to his chest, and a bandana hung low around his neck, reaching down to his belt buckle. The gun he'd pointed at her sat menacingly in its holster. He slid the badge and the identity card across the table. She took it and looked it over. He was a Pinkerton Detective called Charlie Blaine.

He leaned back on the chair, rested his foot on his other knee, and scratched at the well-worn leather of his boots.

'I'm sorry for your loss, Miss Cadieux.'

'Please, call me Marie.'

'Were you close to your sister?'

Marie nodded. 'She was the only family member I had left.'

Coffee was brought to their table. Charlie dropped a couple of coins into the waiter's hand. 'When did you leave France?' Charlie asked.

'A few years ago. When my grandfather died, I came to find Capucine, who lived here. Tell me, Charlie. Why are you investigating my sister's murder? You believe there's something more to it. Is there?'

'I was brought on board to investigate exactly that. Not your sister's murder.'

'Are you working for Moses?'

'That idiot?'

'Well, at least we agree on something. So what happened?' Marie asked.

'I got onto Jonathan Moses yesterday like you had. I believe the last tickets went to you and Joe. So he invited me to his box. Midway through the first act, I saw someone acting suspiciously up on the crossbeams amongst all the ropes.'

'Something suspicious like what?'

'Like a man dragging a body, kind of suspicious. By the time I got up there, the bodies were falling. I tried cutting them down. But whether they were alive or not before they fell, I've seen enough hangings to know a neck doesn't survive shorter falls.'

Marie closed her eyes and held her forehead.

'I'm sorry, kid,' Charlie said, recognising how matter of fact he'd said everything.

Marie shook her head. 'It's the reality of it. And the suspect?'

'Went through that hatch. I got onto the roof and followed him down into the alley, but by the time I got down, he was gone.' While he spoke, he watched Marie and admired how her emotion had given way to a steely determination. She leaned across the table and held eye contact with him. 'I need your help, Marie. There is more at play than just your sister's murder.'

Marie's eyes narrowed on him as she fought the sting of

tears. She clenched her jaw and said nothing in reply.

'Marie, I believe there's a conspiracy regarding suffrage in this city. To what end, I don't know. There have been three murders, one averted bombing and lots of vandalism.'

'I didn't realise. Joe mentioned other cases; he thought they might also be connected.'

Charlie nodded. 'I spoke with him. After last night, I thought it wise to clarify my position with the authorities. I also wanted to pose a few questions to someone locked up in The Tombs.'

Marie drank some coffee. 'I just want to find out who killed my sister.'

'Find who's behind the conspiracy, and you'll find who killed your sister.'

'What do you expect me to do, spy for you?'

Charlie nodded.

Marie laughed. 'Mr Blaine, I'm an art student, not a spy.'

'Yet I found you tailing me like one.'

'Then you should know not to hire me. I wasn't very successful.'

Charlie laughed. 'That's true. But I can teach you. You can learn. You wouldn't have to put yourself in danger. What were you even hoping to achieve?'

'Answers, I guess. I just wanted to know if you'd killed Capucine and why.'

'Well. Grief can make us do things we wouldn't normally do.' He shifted position in his chair and leant forward. 'It's highly likely the person who killed your sister knew her. They would also know the suffrage cause well.'

'Which side?'

Charlie spread his hands wide. 'I wouldn't hazard a guess. Marie. Are you involved in the cause like your sister was?'

'It's... it's not my fight,' Marie said. 'Capucine was the French revolutionary,' she smiled, thinking of her sister's strong belief in fighting for the oppressed. 'Suffrage was her interest, her passion. You have the wrong sister, I'm afraid. Capucine would've spied for you.'

'And you have no interest in women's rights?'

'Of course. But I'm not capable of changing the world. You need passion. You need a desire for the fight. I told you. I'm an artist. That's my passion.'

Charlie nodded. 'So you study art?'

'Yes. At the Art Student's League.'

Charlie drank the whole cup of coffee in one gulp. 'Well, if you ever need a model Marie...'

He winked at her and stood. He took his hat off the table.

'What. Is that it? You're leaving?'

'I've got to go and meet Officer Petrosino.'

'You have a lead?' Marie asked.

'He wants me to check something out. And sitting here isn't going to uncover any kind of conspiracy,' he said, placing the hat on his head. He leaned in close to Marie. 'Ma'am, can I count on your discretion regarding this matter?'

'Of course,' Marie said.

'I'm sure Officer Petrosino will be in touch soon. Once more, I'm sorry for your loss, Marie.' He touched her shoulder and then left.

After finishing her coffee, Marie Cadieux took the Sixth Avenue El from Battery Place. She gazed out the carriage window, taking in the buildings as the steam train puffed on the track above the street. Marie was already late for class. She hadn't even thought about attending, but she couldn't just sit and wait for them to carry out the investigation. She had to keep occupied, and she couldn't even begin funeral arrangements until her sister's body was released. At least continuing with her art would occupy her mind.

She got off the station at Fourteenth Street and went to the Art Students League on Thirty-Eight West. Eyes lingered on her as they looked up from their easels as she entered the class and found a space at the back of the warm and stuffy room. At the front of the class, on a plinth, was the head of Venus made out of plaster of Paris. Without concentrating, she began sketching studies of the head onto a piece of paper she had attached to the board on the easel. Every now and again, Marie realised she was just staring at the paper and had been lost in her thoughts. None of her classmates offered condolences. Yet, from their furtive looks, they clearly knew. These were some of the people she'd fallen out with Capuince about.

Marie didn't know what to do next. She wondered whether she should've accepted Charlie's offer. She knew the answer. There was no way she was going to stop searching for her sister's killer.

Charlie smoked his pipe as he waited for Joe Petrosino on Henry Street in the Lower East Side. It was a typical slum district. The once grand row houses built and lived in by wealthy professionals were now overcrowded with migrant workers and their extended families, who had multiplied in the area. Steam from a nearby factory drifted low over the roofs, and the smell of glue stuck in the air.

He spotted Joe hurrying down the road, looking flustered.

'Sorry, I had something to take care of at the precinct,' Joe said.

'And I thought I was the late one.'

'This way,' Joe said, pointing in the direction they needed to head down the street. 'Why were you running late?'

'I had a run-in with the Cadieux girl.'

'With Marie? A run-in? What happened?'

'After I left you at The Tombs this morning, she followed me into The Bends. Presumed I was the killer.'

'Oh,' Joe winced. 'I left her a note to say I was meeting you. That's before I knew you were a Pinkerton, not the killer.'

'You often give away case information?'

'Huh, what? No, Marie's different. What was she thinking, though?'

'She's brave. And with a bit of training...'

Joe looked at him. 'Training? What are you thinking?'

'That's what you meant by she's different? She could be an asset.'

'No!' Joe said.

'You don't think she's capable?'

'Well, she's more than willing, and that's the trouble. She's gonna wind up getting hurt.'

'She doesn't need to get in trouble,' Charlie said. 'She just needs to move in the circles I wouldn't be able to and pass on information. We can take care of the dangerous stuff.'

'We?'

'You're here, aren't you?'

'Sure, but...'

'And your gun's loaded?'

'Always.'

'Well then, my Italian friend.'

'Hey Charlie, remember, this is my investigation,' Joe said, putting his thumb to his chest.

Charlie grinned. 'Granted, it's your lead, Joe. It's an open case, though.'

'Yeah, it's my lead. So just follow my lead.'

Charlie couldn't help but wind up the younger man. He had that confident, youthful swagger, but Charlie needed to know if he could back it up.

Joe led them into the courtyard of a watchmaker factory.

'He works here?'

'Yeah. That's him,' Joe said, pointing at a man.

It was too late for Charlie to bat Joe's hand down. The man had seen Joe picking him out. He threw his cigarette to the floor and bolted, running into a nearby side door into the factory.

'You take the door he went through. I'll see if I can cut him off.'

Joe nodded and headed in the direction the man had gone.

Charlie removed his gun from his holster and ran to the other door. People in the courtyard stood in fear at his sight or edged away in the opposite direction.

He went into the factory's reception hall. A round man with a moustache approached him. 'Excuse me, sir. Is there something I can help you with?' His eyes were fixed on Charlie's revolver the whole time he spoke.

'I'm a detective. Has a man run through here?'

'No.'

Charlie didn't wait to continue the conversation. He stalked off towards the wing of the building where the man had entered. He heard the round-moustached man ordering someone to find police off the street. Charlie hurried down a corridor with several rooms coming off it and headed to the double doors at the end.

A gunshot echoed. Charlie hesitated. Then, another gunshot rang out. Charlie raised his gun and pushed through the doors toward the noise.

People ran out of the shop floor. They raised their hands in the air on seeing Charlie holding a gun but ran away when he ignored them. After navigating several stacked crates and pieces of machinery, he found Joe knelt beside the man sprawled on the floor.

'You found him, then?'

'He found me,' Joe said and stepped aside to show the dead man and a gun next to him. Charlie sighed. Any hope of getting answers was gone. 'Men who aren't guilty don't run.'

'So, do you think he was the killer?' Joe asked.

'It's pretty hard to draw such a confession from him now.'

'Cazzo,' Joe said. He rubbed his forehead. 'What was I to do? He had the draw on me. Shot at me. Barely missed.'

'You're lucky you're alive then. It's the best outcome.'

Joe's hand shook.

Charlie hadn't expected him to react like this. The earlier confidence was clearly bravado. 'Don't sweat it, kid. A man doesn't just shoot at you if he's got nothing to hide.'

'Does it look like him? You said you saw the killer above the stage.'

Charlie didn't recognise him. 'It's hard to say. I saw a silhouette. Have you frisked the body?'

Joe shook his head.

'Come out of the way,' Charlie said. Joe stood, and Charlie knelt beside the man and checked his back pockets. He found a pouch of chewing tobacco and placed it on the floor, and then he turned the body over. The man's face was rendered shocked. A bloody bullet wound lay dead centre in the man's chest. Charlie glanced over his shoulder at Joe. 'That's some shot. Dead centre.'

Joe raised his eyebrows. He still seemed shocked by what had happened.

Charlie patted down the man and opened his jacket. He found a wallet and a pair of reading glasses. 'Look through this.' Charlie handed the wallet to Joe and continued searching the man's pockets. Then he found a matchbook. The words 'The Mills-Parker Building' were printed on it. Charlie slipped it up his sleeve. The only other thing he found was a flick knife.

'Anything in the wallet?' Charlie asked.

'A few dollars.'

'Nothing linking him to anyone?'

'No. But I don't suppose he'd carry anything declaring he was part of a conspiracy,' Joe said.

Two policemen, accompanied by the round-moustached man, entered the room and shouted at them as they approached. Joe sighed.

'I'll go and explain who we are.' He threw the wallet onto the floor, raised his hands and headed towards the two men.

Charlie frowned. He picked up the wallet and thumbed through it. There was just money inside, as Joe had said. It would have been helpful to have asked the man some questions. Not that he thought he would've got many answers. For Charlie Blaine, eliminating the people behind this growing conspiracy was as important as understanding why they were doing this and what it meant for the country. Still, it would've been nice to have received an explanation for why Capucine and Phillip were hung.

Marie looked at her sketch on the easel. The proportions were all off. She hadn't done the basics—she'd just tried to draw. She wanted to pierce the sheet with her pencil and then drag it down. The pencil snapped in her fingers. She closed her eyes and took a deep breath. When she opened them again, she gazed out of the window. She spotted Charlie Blaine standing across the street. She watched as he leaned against the wall and pushed tobacco into a pipe.

'What the hell,' she whispered to herself.

A student sat in front glanced over her shoulder at Marie.

Marie got up from her easel, leaving her bag and pencils on the side table. As she headed for the door, she stopped and diverted to get a palette knife from a pot at the front of the class.

'Are you okay, Marie?' the teacher asked.

'Sorry, yes. I've just remembered I need to do something.'

Marie exited the building via a side door into an alley as she didn't want Charlie to see her. A couple of children threw stones as close to the wall as possible and argued over a dime. When she reached the alley's entrance, she peered around the corner to check he couldn't see her. She waited until a wagon and stagecoach passed each other, obscuring Charlie's potential view of her, and then she slipped across the street. The only way to approach Charlie from behind was to walk around the building. It took her a few minutes to navigate the block, but she found him still leaning against the wall.

There were enough people about that Marie didn't have to disguise her approach. She slipped the palette knife up her sleeve and headed towards him. At the last moment, she stopped directly behind him. The palette knife dropped from her sleeve. She held the wooden handle and pressed the dull blade into Charlie's lower back.

'No wonder you need someone to spy for you,' Marie said, speaking in her native French. 'You can't even watch your own back.'

'I have my back covered well enough, Mademoiselle Cadieux,' Charlie replied in French, but he made no effort to hide his American drawl or even turn to face her.

'If you were more competent, I might have been open to pooling our resources,' she said. 'But I don't wish to be conned into hiring some detective agency with less chance than I do.'

'Frenchie, once you've stopped being emotional,' Charlie said as he switched to English. 'Take a look down.'

She frowned and looked but kept the palette knife pressed to his back.

'If I didn't know you were approaching, why would I have my gun held pointed at you?'

Still leaning against the wall, his arms were crossed, but his gun was held beneath his elbow. He cocked it, and the clicking noise emphasised his point.

'How did you know? You haven't moved. You couldn't have seen me leave.'

'Just slowly remove the paintbrush, pencil, or whatever it is from my back. I wouldn't want you to tickle me and make my finger twitch.'

'It's a palette knife,' she said, moving it away from his back.

As he turned to face her, he reset the hammer on the revolver and holstered the gun. 'You don't need to hire me, Marie. By the time we finish, I'll show you how to use a palette knife or even a paintbrush to kill a man.'

'I'm not going to train to be a killer, Charlie Blaine. I merely wish to find one.'

'Then maybe we can help each other out after all.'

She didn't know what to do with the palette knife, so she held it behind her.

'How did you know what I was going to do?'

'First lesson. Always have intelligence and use your imagination to determine the outcome. Look behind you.'

'What are you going to do? Vanish by the time I've turned back to you?' She turned around. A boy who looked vaguely familiar stood behind her. Charlie threw a dime, and the kid caught it.

'That's bully mister, thanks,' the boy said and ran off.

'The child from the alley?'

'Yeah, he told me you'd left and then tailed you.'

'I saw him playing in the alley but didn't think anything of it. But how did you know I wasn't just leaving for the day? How did you know I would sneak up on you?'

'Okay, I lied. I have a little bit of experience with people, but imagination is key, especially for anyone new to the business. You are headstrong. You want answers enough to follow someone into a deserted, crumbling tenement. I didn't try to hide from you, and I knew our conversation wasn't done. I knew you'd come looking for me.'

Marie narrowed her eyes on him. 'Perhaps Mr Blaine. Maybe we can work together.'

'Good. I'd like that very much, Frenchie.'

A couple of days after what the papers described as an unforgettable performance, Charlie walked around Marie's art studio. He flicked through her canvases leaning against the wall and was surprised at how good she was, not that he knew anything about art.

The studio was one large room. There wasn't a bathroom or a kitchen, but somehow, Marie was making do with living there.

'Are you not planning on moving back to your sister's apartment?'

'I don't think so. No. It never felt like my home.'

'It would be more comfortable than this.'

'Who needs comfort if you can't afford to eat?'

'Things that bad?'

'My job in the art store and my few commissions should sustain me. Besides, I'll only be staying in New York for a few months.'

'Why's that?'

'I'm moving to Paris in the new year.'

Charlie's brow raised. 'Paris? Quite the move.'

'I've got a place to study art and a scholarship at the Académie Julien.'

Charlie nodded. 'If you can make a living off it, then go for it, Frenchie.'

'We've got to find my sister's killer first, though, and I've been thinking.'

'Sounds dangerous,' he said, smiling.

'I think you should come to my sister's funeral.'

'I'm not sure that's a good idea. For all we know, the killer could be in attendance.'

'Then why make our job harder?' Marie asked.

'How'd you mean?'

'If I'm suspected of spying and they see me secretly meeting you, it will blow our cover. If they could be there in the open at my sister's funeral, then so could you. Where did you grow up, Charlie?'

'Colorado.'

'You are my cousin. Great cousin. You are my grandfather's sister's son. You are here because of the funeral.'

'I don't like it.'

'Don't you think it's good to have a cover story? It would give me an alibi to meet with you...'

Charlie wobbled his head as if he wanted to argue but couldn't find a reason because he was actually warming to the idea.

'You think it is a good plan, no?' Marie asked.

'It makes sense, but I don't like it. And you, you'll need to still shake off any surveillance.'

Marie put her hands on her hips. 'Then why don't you show me how.'

Marie and Charlie walked out onto the sidewalk. It was a busy Thursday morning.

'The first thing you must learn to recognise is if someone's following you.'

'New York is one of the busiest cities in the world, Charlie. Am I supposed to look over my shoulder all the time from now on?'

'No. You just need to...open your senses. And once they're

open, you can kind of forget.'

'Ooo sounds mystical.'

'I don't mean like that, Frenchie. Once you know how to act and what to look out for, it'll become second nature.'

Marie nodded.

'Now just hang back, walk behind and follow me.'

Marie did as was instructed. She waited as he walked on and left some space between them. They walked several blocks before Charlie abruptly went to a tobacconist and looked in the window, which, in the sunlight, acted like a mirror. Before she could realise it, Marie saw herself in the reflection. Charlie was looking straight at her. Then he went inside the shop. Marie waited outside. He'd been gone several minutes when there was suddenly a tap on her shoulder. She spun around. Charlie stood behind her.

She frowned. 'What? You were...I mean. You didn't come out of the front doors.'

'Use reflections to see if someone's following you. And if they are, slip inside a shop, museum, or whatever it is and use a different exit.'

He reached into his pocket, took a coin and flicked it over to her. 'Go and get me some tobacco while I wait here. Oh, and tell me what you see.'

Marie entered the tobacconist and went to the counter. She put the coin on the surface but didn't know what to ask for. Boxes, tins, and pouches lined the shelf.

'What can I get for this, please?'

'Bidis, chew, cigarettes, pipe, snuff—'

Marie held up her hands. 'For a pipe.'

While the man fulfilled her request, she saw the branded mirror with a Native American painted on it above the shelves. She could see Charlie standing on the sidewalk in the reflection, and then she understood.

After weighing the tobacco, the man poured it into a paper pouch and handed it to her.

'Anything else?' he asked.

'No, thank you.'

'Good day, miss,' he said as she left the shop. She walked over to Charlie and threw the pouch over to him, which he caught with one hand.

'Did you see?' Charlie asked.

'Yeah, I saw you in the mirror.'

'Good. Try and keep up, okay.'

Charlie walked off again, and she followed him from a distance. As he lazily walked, he filled his pipe with tobacco. Then he stopped to light it and turned towards her, away from the breeze, cupping the match so it didn't blow out.

Marie abruptly came to a stop.

He looked over the pipe at her. Then he waved the flame out and threw the spent matchstick in the gutter. He carried on, his pace faster. He checked his watch as he walked, and then he suddenly veered off the sidewalk, crossing the street, managing his way between the horses and the carts. Then he carried on walking until he stopped by the pharmacy and beckoned her towards him when she'd finally managed to cross.

'The best way to see if someone is following you is to suddenly cross the street. Don't make it seem out of the ordinary. Try and mask it somehow,' Charlie said.

'Like I'm late? Or I suddenly realised I wanted something from a pharmacy?'

'Yeah. And if you're quick enough, you'll be able to see them follow you in the window's reflection. Or if they're really good, in which case you should worry, they'll wait over the street and maybe watch you in a reflection.'

'Do you really think people will follow me? I thought I was supposed to be doing the spying?'

Charlie started walking again, and she fell into step alongside him. 'There might come a time when they become suspicious of you, where you're going, who you're meeting, that kind of thing. It's just prudent to know if that's the case.'

'And what if I need to lose them?'

'Well, I already showed you one method: Use the back door. But they might try to anticipate that. So maybe don't use the first shop you go to. Make it look like you're shopping. Buy something from the first or second shop and then escape from the third one. Understand?'

'Yes.'

He stopped and studied her. With a flick of his finger, Charlie lifted Marie's chin. A sudden feeling of excitement ran through her. She blushed. Charlie obviously saw because he frowned. 'You don't wear makeup,' he said.

'No, I—'

'You should.'

'Is that your professional preference or personal?' she asked, feeling offended.

'Professional. Personally, I don't think you need it, kid.'

Butterflies hit her stomach.

She took a deep breath and continued alongside him. 'Why?' Was all she could ask.

'So you can check your rouge or whatever you choose in one of those little mirrors I've seen ladies carry. Means you don't have to keep using shops.'

'Oh. Oh, I see.'

Charlie glanced at her and frowned again.

Her mind had gone blank. She didn't know what to say

or ask, so they walked silently for what seemed like an uncomfortably long time.

'And that's another lesson,' he eventually said. 'And one I imagine you'll be better at than me. With practice.'

'What?' she asked with a confused look on her face.

'I flicked your chin. Stared into your eyes. Felt intimate, didn't it?'

'You did that on purpose?'

'Even the smallest bit of intimacy can affect people.'

'Like when you placed your hand on my shoulder? When you left the cafe.'

'Warmed to me, didn't you?'

'No,' Marie said, crossing her arms.

'Shame. I genuinely meant that,' Charlie said and continued walking. Marie shook her head, took a deep breath and caught up with him.

'Okay, then, what should I do if I am being followed and can't shake them?'

'Don't meet me or Joe if you've planned to meet us.'

'And if I'm in danger?'

'Definitely don't lead them to me,' he said. 'I don't want to get shot.'

A look of horror crossed Marie's face.

'I'm sorry. That was insensitive.'

'It's okay.'

'But it's true. Don't put anybody at risk. Don't put yourself at risk either unless you're willing to take care of the problem. And that goes for trying to save someone's life.'

'Even if it's you?'

'If I can't stop them. I don't suppose you'll be able to.'

Marie looked down at the floor. She swallowed and tried to subtly brush a tear away.

Charlie sighed. Maybe she wasn't controlling her emotions as well as he'd thought. 'Look, Frenchie, by the time it gets to this, we'll have a plan. We'll know what to do.'

'I'm guessing guilt can have the same effect as intimacy?' She grinned, knowing she'd got the better of him.

He twisted his lips. 'Yeah, it can have the same effect. Now, let's just practice what you've learned.'

Marie and Charlie spent the next hour following each other, spotting each other, and trying to lose each other. They walked from Greenwich Village to the Hudson River and back.

When they got a block from her studio, Charlie said, 'I won't walk you to your door.'

Marie felt sad their time together was up. It had been a welcome distraction from thinking about her sister's death and obsessing over who was responsible. It felt like her time had been spent constructively for the first time in days.

'I'll come back later when it's dark, and we'll discuss what we should do next.'

'Okay,' she said. 'Charlie, won't the alibi of you being a relation help us?'

'Somewhat, yeah. It was a good call to come up with that, kid.'

Marie stood prouder and checked herself when she realised she was doing so.

'Though it'll only work for so long if they think we're sneaking around them,' he said. 'But if we're raising suspicions, it won't matter if they think we're related. They will come after us.'

'Second cousins. You're my grandfather's sister's daughter's son.'

He winked at her. 'See you later, kid. Stay safe.'

The remainder of the day had dragged, and Marie could only think she was wasting time by not doing anything to further the investigation and having to work at the art store instead. The manager had questioned whether she was in the right frame of mind to work after what had happened. He had insisted Marie should observe a period of mourning. But she had argued she needed the money. Now, even more so without her sister to help support her. He'd kindly offered to pay her wage for a few days, but she'd decided to work instead, hoping to use that favour if needed.

When she returned to her studio, she found an envelope pushed under the door. She opened it and found maps inside. A note read, plot various routes to the places you go. Know your way around.

Marie sat at the table and unfolded the Edison power grid map of New York. There was also an Edsalls city guide map detailing the streets, passenger boat routes, piers, and train lines.

She sat staring at the maps, but she couldn't concentrate. Her mind kept going to the Moses brothers and their involvement. Was Jonathan responsible somehow? She took one of the maps and turned it over. Marie wrote her sister Capucine's name in the middle and a line coming off it. She drew two offshoots at the end of that line and wrote Jonathan and Phillip Moses' names. She did the same for the suffragettes she knew. She couldn't remember their names fully. She went to her satchel and took out the address book she'd taken from Capucine's drawer when she still thought she was missing. She also took the sketchpad out where Capucine's friend had written her address. Voltairine. She wrote that name next to the line leading to suffragettes. And then she wrote Matilda Joslyn-Gage and Amelia.

A little while later, Charlie arrived, and she let him in. He carried with him a file and placed it on the table as he looked over the map of names on the back of the map of New York. 'Looks like you've been busy. Say, what's my name doing here?'

'Oh, didn't I cross it out?'

'No,' he said, picking up a pencil. He drew another line and wrote a name next to it. She went over and looked. It was her name.

'Me?'

'Everyone is a suspect,' he said, drawing a line through his and hers. 'But let's assume we can rule ours out.'

'There's over fifty names on there, Charlie. Where do we even know where to begin?'

'Pick five suspects from that list.'

'Any?'

'Top five.'

Marie looked at the map of names. 'Okay, I think I have them. What now?'

'Add another, Michael Byrne.'

'Who?'

Charlie reached across the table and opened the file he'd brought. Inside were lots of newspaper cuttings telling the stories of various incidents that had taken place, including the hanging of Capucine and Phillip. 'Every one of those stories was written by a man called Michael Byrne.'

'Maybe he's a crime writer?'

'Maybe. But he's also sensationalising them. The average

person reads those and will think society is collapsing.'

'They'll twist anything to sell more papers.'

'Oh, definitely,' Charlie said.

'You should go and interview him.'

'Oh, I intend to. Tomorrow. I'm going to pay him a visit.'

At the same time, across town, the Black Veil met on the top floor of the Mills-Parker Building. It was a dark set of rooms with exposed rafters. The wind rattled the glass in their frames. Most of the rooms were full of bales of old newspapers. The busy newsrooms and offices of several newspapers and advertising agencies were on the floors beneath.

The nine members of the Black Veil gathered in the largest room. They sat wherever they could on windowsills, stacks of newspapers and a few mismatching chairs. There wasn't even a table. They didn't need one because they kept no plans or records of their deeds. Every potential act was spoken, and every decision was voted on.

Voltairine looked at the members in the lamplight. They were a motley collection of people, comprising generations-old Americans and immigrants from Europe. She wondered if they could achieve the group's aims. Each member was dedicated and capable of the acts needed to further their cause, but she wondered just how focused they were.

'Be careful you don't bring too much attention upon yourself, James,' Voltairine said.

'The attention I get is as a journalist,' James McGarrity said, letting his Irish accent stretch every word. 'Or should I say the more attention Michael Byrne gets, the less I'll be suspected for anything else.'

Voltairine clenched her jaw and didn't say anything else. McGarrity was a misogynist, and it wouldn't matter what she said anyhow.

'If we're not going to reveal the Black Veil is behind these acts, we must still maximise the amount of fear and panic our organisation creates,' Clément Duval said, pacing around the room. He was a twitchy, little, proud man prone to feeling offended. He was French and a committed anarchist who was never afraid of getting his hands dirty for the cause.

Voltairine thought his hands were too dirty. She glared at him, and he glared back at her.

'If everyone agrees,' Benedict said. 'We will proceed with James's plan for the soirée.'

Voltairine kept her arms crossed as everyone raised a hand.

'Voltairine?' Benedict asked.

She raised her hand.

'Good,' Benedict said. 'Another act, another step closer. Unless anyone else has other business?' He looked at everyone in turn, and with nobody raising anything else, the meeting was concluded.

Everyone staggered their exit, leaving individually or in pairs to avoid arousing suspicion until only Voltairine and Benedict remained. Voltairine stood at the window, gazing out at the people below. Benedict approached her, and she saw his reflection in the glass. She didn't know much about him. His whole manner was diligent in how he spoke, moved and thought. He was in his early sixties, wore spectacles and had a long white moustache.

'Care to tell me what's wrong?' he asked.

Voltairine's shoulders slumped. She turned to look at the man who had initially set up this enterprise, selecting and recruiting the members individually.

'There are too many egos,' she said.

'You doubt the minds I have assembled?'

'I don't doubt their intentions. I doubt their methods. I doubt their impulses. You must share my concerns?'

'The group has the skills and means we need to achieve our aims.'

'That is all very good, but their desires are beginning to surface. Clément is impatient like McGarrity. They both covet fame. They compete to be the most sensational.'

'But we all agree on the approaches we take and the methods used.'

'Not every method is voted on,' Voltairine said.

Benedict lowered his head and nodded.

'And what about Lorenzo? Are you sure he wouldn't put the Camorra above our cause?'

'They could all say similar things about you, Voltairine. Your motivation for joining our endeavour and the means you take—'

'You doubt me?'

'Not at all.'

'Do the others?'

'No. All of the members highly regard your ideas and methods. But you do not have the means to achieve them alone.'

'You're telling me Clément hasn't even questioned me?'

'No. He's not questioned your commitment.'

'He's a Klereneind,' she said, cursing him in Dutch. 'We risk a lot,' Voltairine said. 'One weak link might cause unrepairable damage.'

'After what happened, everybody knows their life is at stake should they be caught.'

'No. It's not just our lives at stake. The cause is.'

'We should all value the cause beyond our own lives,' Benedict said.

'We are all agreed, but let's not get to such an outcome. Not again.'

Voltairine said and went to leave the room.

'Capucine Cadieux's sister. Marie. Is she proving to be a problem?' Benedict asked.

Voltairine stopped at the door and glanced over her shoulder. 'No, not at all.'

She went into the hall and called the service elevator. When it arrived, she opened the grate and operated the mechanism, which caused it to descend. Capucine Cadieux's murder played on her mind. She took a deep breath and then pushed the thought away as she exhaled. Many more would die before America was reborn. She had to remember that.

CHAPTER 10

The grave diggers began shovelling the mud back into Capucine Cadieux's occupied grave. Marie shuddered as each thud of wet earth hit the coffin. It was nearly a week since the theatre incident. The coroner had estimated Capucine and Phillip had been killed at least two days before the hanging. Both had been shot.

The crowd gradually began to leave the burial and either shyly or duly offered their condolences to Marie.

She did not sob, but tears fell steadily. She did not think of the guilt she held for a sisterly spat that had ultimately dragged on too long. Nor did she dare think of the friends she had tried to impress at the expense of the relationship with her sister. They hadn't even bothered to attend the funeral and support Marie.

It was by no means a large funeral, but it surprised Marie how many people in attendance she didn't know. The New York City Woman Suffrage Association had paid for the funeral and many of their members attended.

Joe Petrosino had attended and was dressed in a pristine police uniform. He carried his hat under his arm and had stood near Marie throughout. 'You've done her proud. I'll wait for you at the gate if you need me,' he said, and she watched him as he followed the path down the hill.

Charlie Blaine had attended but kept his distance and didn't associate with Joe. He remained true to what Marie had thought about him. He was quick to offer his condolences and, under the cover story of a distant relative, kissed her on the cheek, put his hat back on, and then went briskly off.

Marie recognised the white-haired woman approaching her, surrounded by several other women. Matilda Joslyn Gage held Marie's hand while she looked empathetically into her eyes. Marie wanted to pull her hand away, but she didn't and smiled politely.

'Marie, we are all so very sorry for your loss. Capucine was a great advocate of our cause. Her presence is felt dearly by all of our members.'

'Thank you. The cause meant a lot to her. I know she found her life's purpose within it.' Marie tried to pull her hand away, but Matilda held on and tapped it.

'Yet until last week, you'd never attended one of our meetings.'

'I don't share the same confidence as my sister speaking in public.'

'Nonsense,' Matilda said. 'And besides. It's the numbers we need. To sit and listen to a speech or volunteer in some capacity. You could really make a difference. We are always in need of art or signage for our cause.'

'I would very much like to honour my sister by doing something.'

'We have a meeting this week. I shall introduce you to everyone you should know. The sister of Capucine Cadieux will be quite welcomed.'

Marie smiled, but inside, she reeled. The grave her sister had been laid to rest in had not even been filled, yet here was this woman trying to recruit her to a political cause that had led to her sister's death. Marie wanted to scream. But she couldn't. It was the perfect way to infiltrate the organisation. She now had to play games and be damn good at them. She had to smile when she didn't want to. Agree when she'd rather oppose. But she promised herself that as soon as she could, she would go to the sea and scream out towards the ocean as loud as she could.

Marie took one last look at the grave. Her sister's coffin was out of sight, covered with mud.

'Goodbye, my sweet sister,' Marie said in her native French. 'You were my hero as a girl. You annoyed me as only a sister could and loved me better than any. You shall always be in my memory. I promise I'll bring to justice the person who killed you.'

As she walked down the slope to catch the ferry from the terminal, Voltairine stood at a nearby grave waiting for her. As Marie came alongside her on the path, Voltairine linked arms with her.

'You're coping just swell, Marie.'

'It doesn't feel like it. How are you?'

'About the same as you, then, I'd imagine.'

'All this is stifling, Vee. All of these people. It's, it's just too much.'

'The day is for them. It shouldn't be, but it is what it is.'

'I didn't realise she knew so many people.'

'They're mostly from the movement just paying their respects. Though there are some who I don't recognise.' Voltairine pointed at a man in a dark suit and top hat who had lingered by some nearby graves during the burial. 'Who is he? I saw him during the interment. Why didn't he stand with everyone else?'

'Because he's an anti,' Marie said. 'That's Jonathan... Phillip's brother.'

'Ah, I see,' Voltairine said.

'Did you ever meet him?' Marie asked.

Voltairine shook her head. 'No, she kept that side of her life private from me.'

'How did they even end up together?'

'I guess opposites attract,' Voltairine said with a smile. As they went through the cemetery gate, the peaceful quiet of the dead gave way to the bustling noise of the living as the cemetery entrance led onto the dock road. The stench of the sewage and industrial wastewater flowing into the creek opposite hung in the air. The mourners were congregated at the ferryboat terminus, waiting for the current passengers to disembark.

'The only other person I don't recognise is him,' Voltairine said, pointing at Charlie Blaine.

'He's a relation,' Marie lied.

'Oh, I didn't think you had any. That's what Capucine once said.'

'He's my grandfather's step-sister's son. At least, I think that's what it is. They live out in Colorado somewhere. He thinks I should go and live with them.'

'You're considering it?'

'Absolutely not. I should imagine the only art they have is cave drawings.'

Voltairine laughed. 'Your sister thought your art was outstanding.'

'She always worried I put it before anything else. Pursuits less noble than hers.'

'She always told me you were busy creating art for adverts, working at the art store, painting and studying. She said nothing would get between you and art. She once joked if men banned women from the arts, then suffrage would have its most vehement supporter.'

Marie smiled. She could imagine her sister talking that way. 'Do you attend all of the meetings?'

'Suffrage?'

'Yes.'

'A lot but not all. Not as many as your sister did.'

'Madame Joslin Gage invited me to a meeting or something next week.'

'She did? You should come, Marie. I'd very much like to get to know you more.'

At the ferry, Marie climbed the ladders onto the upper deck. Jonathan Moses stood smoking at the bow, leaning on the rail. Marie was about to head to the ferry's stern when he turned and spotted her. He went to say something but hesitated and watched the houses and factories. His shoulders rose, then fell, and he faced her again and discarded his cigarette into the murky water.

'My condolences, Miss Cadieux,' he said.

Marie walked over to him. 'My condolences to you too.'

She looked towards the mouth of the creek and the East River it fed into and beyond Manhattan, lined with high-rise buildings, piers, and docks.

'I didn't expect to see you here.'

'It seemed like the right thing to do,' he said.

'Well, thank you. I appreciate it.'

'There was also something I wanted to ask you.'

'Of course, what?' Marie asked.

Jonathan twisted his lips and looked out at the river. Eventually, he looked over his shoulder and leaned in closer to her. 'I haven't told anyone this. Not that Pinkerton detective, nor the police. I wanted to speak to you first.'

Concern crossed Marie's expression. 'Tell me.'

'Before Phillip went missing, he said he was going to meet some pretty serious people.'

'Serious about what?'

He looked over his shoulder once more. 'Anarchism,' he whispered.

Marie was almost amused by his nervousness. 'You say it as if one of them is going to jump up on us and throw us over the side.'

His eyes widened. He looked around again. 'They could be anywhere.'

'You really are worried.'

'Of course. Aren't you? You saw what happened to Philip and your sister?'

'That's not going to happen to us,' Marie said. 'Not here. At least not on the boat.'

'They could blow the boat up.'

Marie cringed at the suggestion. 'To what end? You're being paranoid, Jonathan. If anything, we need to learn why they were killed.'

Jonathan raised his hands in surrender to her. 'I just shouldn't have said anything. Forget I said anything.'

He moved to walk away, but she grabbed his sleeve.

'There's more to this than you're letting on,' she said. 'What else did he tell you? Was it about Capucine?'

He looked around again, then sighed as he leaned in closer once more. 'He was besotted with her. She said she inspired his writing like no one else did. I found a notebook of his. It outlined a story.'

'I imagine he had many outlines. What was it about?'

'Political. As it always was with him. About a female anarchist who set out to kill the president.'

'And you think that was my sister?'

'No. No. I met her. I wouldn't be telling you now if I thought she was one of them. Philip was a fantasist. But his ideas were always rooted in reality. If he'd gotten mixed up with anarchists while researching them. If he'd upset them...'

'You should've told the police.'

'No.' He shook his head. 'The authorities are even more militant than anarchists. I don't need this level of trouble in my life.'

'You should tell Officer Petrosino.'

'You're far too trusting, Miss Cadieux. Maybe I shouldn't have told you.' He took a deep breath, straightened his jacket, and smoothed his sleeves. 'I just wanted to ascertain if more trouble was likely. But it seems you're as unaware of your sibling's dealings as I am. Or at least I know more.'

Marie ignored the jibe. 'Where is it? This outline. Do you have it?'

'I destroyed it. I burnt it.'

Marie raised her eyebrows and looked away as she considered what he'd told her. Jonathan had no doubt grown paranoid after what had happened to his brother and her sister, especially with what Phillip had told him. But she didn't believe Capucine was involved with anarchists. Capucine was more politically motivated with the suffragettes than even Marie had realised, but she'd never shown any hint of extremism. Marie knew she would have to tell Joe and Charlie what Jonathan suspected. But she would need to decide how much she'd reveal.

CHAPTER 11

The New York World newspaper sensationalised many of the incidents Charlie's investigation comprised, and it just so happened the newspaper was located in the Mills-Parker Building. Because the building's name was printed on the matchbook Charlie had found in the pocket of the man suspected of hanging Capucine and Phillip, it seemed only fitting he should pay a visit to the place and the journalist Michael Byrne.

The night of the funeral, Marie had told him Jonathan Moses believed his brother had gotten mixed up with some anarchists before going missing. The newspaper was making so much of a killing out of reporting the incidents Charlie wondered if it wasn't the publisher orchestrating events to increase his circulation and bank balance. As much as Charlie liked to keep an open mind in his investigations, he thought that theory might be too far-fetched.

Charlie found the entrance on Nassau Street and went into the reception. It was all marble floors and mahogany panelling on the walls. There was a reception desk, a harsh-looking receptionist patrolling it, and a sleepy-looking security guard sitting on a chair against the wall. A few people stood around chatting. A brass plaque on the wall listed the businesses occupying the building. None of them stood out except the newspaper.

Charlie rode the elevator up several floors to the newspaper's offices. As he approached, an officious woman at the reception desk looked him up and down, then her eyes lingered on his holstered gun. 'Can I help you, sir?'

'Maybe,' he said. 'I'm looking to talk to a Mr Byrne, one of your reporters.'

'Can I ask what it's about?'

'A story of his, about the theatre murders.'

'I'll go see if he's available.'

Charlie waited until she'd gone through the door behind the counter. 'I'll be back in a moment,' he said to the other receptionist, giving her a wink. She barely glanced up from her typewriter. Charlie hurried across the reception and slipped out of the door into the corridor. He waited behind the door and peered through the gap.

After a little while, the woman returned with the journalist in tow. They stood behind the counter, wondering where Charlie had disappeared, not knowing he was behind the door opposite them. The journalist seemed content to wait. He perched at the edge of the desk and proceeded to sweet talk the receptionist who'd gone to fetch him.

Charlie's mouth dropped open. He recognised the journalist. He wore a beard now, but the piercing blue eyes were unmistakable. Charlie knew him, not as the journalist Michael Byrne, but by his real name, James McGarrity, the Fenian bombmaker. But why was he here? The man should be imprisoned in the British Penal Colony in Western Australia. Charlie shook the shock from his head and immediately turned and left the building. There was no way Charlie could let him see him, or there would be bloodshed. Though Charlie would love nothing more than to put a bullet in him, he needed answers more than revenge.

Charlie slid the newspaper across the table in Marie's studio to her. He tapped on the byline under the headline. 'Michael

Byrne is the alias of one James McGarrity.'

The way he looked at her suggested she should know who he was. She didn't. 'And? You know this man?'

'We had a little run-in across the Atlantic. A couple of years ago, I was hired by Scotland Yard's Special Irish Branch to investigate members of the Clan na Gael operating out of New York. The case took me to England. McGarrity was one of the Fenians I came up against.'

'And now he's a journalist?'

Charlie nodded. 'I couldn't believe it when I saw him. He wears a beard now, but it was him for sure.'

'You think he's connected to the anarchists Jonathan Moses mentioned?'

'That's what I need you to find out.'

'Me? How on earth am I going to do that?'

'James was a devout Irish Republican.'

'Then surely he favours some form of government if he's trying to oust one and replace it with another.'

'I don't think it takes much of a leap from the Irish Republican movement to anarchism. A long time ago, Ireland had a system not a million miles from what the anarchist would like in place today.'

'There's a lot of politically active people, Charlie. We're not focusing on them. So why him?'

'James McGarrity was also a bomb maker. A very good one. Now, here he is sensationalising events in that newspaper—many of the events that have interested us. I went to that building because the person we think hung your sister had a matchbook with the building's name on it. Who's working there under an alias? A bombmaker.'

'So, what do you expect me to do?'

'Can you write?'

'Of course.'

'In English?'

'As well as any American could. Why?'

'The New York World newspaper our Irish friend works for has a job opening.'

'Since you're asking if I can write, I presume it's not as an illustrator.'

'They need a lady who can report on the arts and social scene within the city. You know it?'

'The arts scene, yes. I'm no socialite, though.'

Charlie twisted his lips. 'Yeah. I guess you're right.'

'Lucky for you, I take no offence. And you want me to apply for this job?'

'I want you to get the job.'

'And then what?'

'Then you have an in with James McGarrity.'

'You're forgetting one thing, Charlie.'

'What's that?'

'They reported on my sister's death.'

'I checked. It wasn't Byrne.'

'They'll know I'm her sister. If I go trying to befriend this McGarrity and it turns out whoever he's a part of did kill her, well...'

'That's why it's not going to be Marie Cadieux who applies for the job.'

'Even if I use an alias like this bomb-making reporter, it doesn't matter. They will recognise me. It will be even more suspicious.'

'You won't use your name; we'll also change your appearance. Kid, we're going to give you a disguise.'

Marie stood in front of the mirror. She was dressed like always in her frontier skirt and blouse. She glanced above the room divider and saw Charlie sitting on the windowsill with his legs on the fire escape, sunning himself as he smoked his pipe in the early morning warmth.

First, she unlaced her boots and kicked them off. She unbuckled her belt and dropped it onto the bed. She pulled her blouse from her skirt and unbuttoned it before slipping it off. She dropped the skirt and stood in her underskirt and camisole, looking at how many clothes she needed to put on instead. She rolled her eyes. She first put on a pair of stockings and a different pair of boots. 'God damn it,' she said as she struggled with the button hook to get them fastened. The next thing she put on was the corset. She fastened the hooks at the front and reached around the back to pull the strings tight.

'Goddamn it,' she said again as she kept failing to tie a tight enough knot. She sighed and looked over at Charlie. 'You're going to have to give me a hand with this.'

Charlie pretended not to hear.

'Hey, Charlie Blaine. Help me out here. Please.'

Charlie muttered under his breath. With his thumb, he tamped the tobacco in the pipe and climbed back into the studio.

He walked over to the room divider but avoided looking over. 'What do you want?'

'Help, getting this darn thing done up.'

Charlie glanced over at her. 'Haven't you done one of those before?'

'Not unless I can help it.'

'Ah, geez. What do I do?'

'I thought you'd be the type of man who has taken many of

these things off.'

'Taking them off is one thing, Frenchie.'

'Well, just reverse engineer it,' she said.

Charlie came around the divider, and Marie turned her back to him. He stood behind her, took the strings, and pulled them tight, taking her breath away.

'What was that?' he asked.

'I didn't say anything,' she said with a thin breath.

He slacked off the strings and tied a bow in them.

'What, do I just let these things dangle?' he said, batting at the string like a cat.

'Yes, I'm sure that'll be fine.' She waited a moment, but he didn't move. She turned and caught him looking at her neck. 'I think I can handle the rest,' she said, buttoning up the ruffle corset cover.

'Okay, well, just holler if you need me,' he said, going over to her table and the easel beside it.

She grabbed the bustle and tied that around her waist. She twisted it around so the padded wire frame sat at the back. 'It would be a lot easier to just hem the damn skirts shorter.'

'In the short time I've known you, I don't think I've ever heard you cuss as much as you're doing right now.'

She mouthed another obscenity, this time in French, in his direction as she dropped the petticoat over her head and positioned and fastened it at her waist. Then she added one more and then another. Already, she felt like she had doubled her weight from all the clothes she had on.

'What are you working on at the moment?' he asked.

'Commissioned work mostly,' she said, slipping on the maroon shirtwaist. 'And all of it is Liberty-related. As much as I love her, I tire of painting copper tones. Every advert wants the statue in it.'

Charlie opened a folder and looked at the drawings. On top was a drawing of the statue standing on a reel of blue cotton and holding a thread of red cotton instead of her torch. He carefully placed it to one side and looked at the one beneath advertising tonic.

'Geez, they'll use her to sell anything, won't they?'

'It pays the rent, barely,' she said, adjusting the blonde wig.

'This Annie Oakley?' he asked.

'Yes,' she said without looking up.

'Now that's a girl who can shoot.' When he placed the drawing of Annie Oakley holding a rifle on the table, it looked like she was aiming it at the statue. Charlie frowned.

'So, then. How do I look?' Marie asked, stepping out from behind the screen. Charlie looked over at her. He frowned. Then he looked back at her drawings on the table. Marie placed her hand on her hip. She coughed for a response.

He looked back at her and looked her up and down. His lips parted. 'You look...different.'

'I go to all that trouble, and that's all you can say?'

'Yes. No. I mean,' Charlie said, rubbing the back of his neck. 'You look good.' He looked back down at the drawings on the table.

'I was hoping you'd say you didn't recognise me.'

'Come and take a look at this, would you?'

Marie sighed and went over to the table. She saw the picture of Annie Oakley pointing her gun at the image of the Statue of Liberty. 'Juxtaposition is everything in art.'

'I can't believe I haven't thought of it until now,' he whispered.

'Thought about what?'

'That,' he said, waving at the images. 'That's what they're

building to.'

'You think the anarchists are going to hire Annie to shoot the statue?'

Charlie frowned at her. 'No, I think they intend to sabotage it, though. When's the ceremony?'

'About a month from now.'

'Goddamn it,' Charlie said, pacing away from Marie and the table. 'Each incident has gotten worse.' He started laughing, and Marie shook her head at him.

'You think they're going to target the statue or the unveiling?' she asked.

He turned sharply towards Marie. 'No. Maybe not the statue. Everything they've done so far is symbolic, right?'

'Attacking the statue would be symbolic. If not that, then what?' Marie asked.

'Not what. Who. The President. They're gonna try and kill the president. Where better than to slay the head of authority and try to incite a new age of Libertarian anarchism?'

Marie had now added makeup to her disguise—something she didn't normally wear. She wore light, loose face powder with a soft pink rouge applied to her cheeks, a pink, red lip stain, and darkened lashes. 'Are you really sure this is going to work?' Marie asked.

'You look nothing like you, Frenchie.'

'I wish you'd said that to begin with. I would've felt a hell of a lot better about it.'

'If you're not up to it...'

'I can do this, Charlie,' she said, sounding convincing but unsure if she could actually do it. 'You know, I painted the picture on this perfume box. I hate the perfume. And I hate the box. I feel like I'm something off that box.'

Charlie leaned in and smelled her neck. 'The whole point of wearing it is so it doesn't smell like you.'

They held each other's gaze as he stepped back.

'What about these?' she said, slipping a gold chain with a lorgnette attached over her head. She held the handled spectacles up to her eyes.

'Perfect,' Charlie said. 'And great for covering your face should you need to.'

She turned and took a sidelong look at him.

'That's it,' he said. 'Don't act like Marie Cadieux. Act like...'

'Camille Vallette from Paris,' she said in a deeper voice full of disdain.

Charlie's eyebrows raised. 'I don't know whether to be turned on or afraid.'

'I was hoping for both,' she said again in the same deeper voice.

They both smiled.

CHAPTER 12

Marie strode over to the reception desk in the foyer of the Mills-Parker Building. The receptionist came down the long desk over to her.

'I'm here for the job interview at the newspaper.'

'Which one?' the woman asked.

Marie glanced at the brass panels on the wall on either side of a mirror. Several newspaper names were inscribed upon them. 'Why, the New York World, of course.'

'Your name?' she asked, unimpressed.

'Camille Vallette,' Marie said.

Marie watched the woman go back along the desk, and she was shocked to see Voltairine arrive there. Marie looked away, but it was too late to leave the desk. She watched Voltairine's reflection in the mirror on the wall.

Voltairine said something to the receptionist. She unlocked a drawer, took out an envelope and slid it across the countertop to Voltairine.

Voltairine did not pick it up. She also stared directly at Marie in the mirror. Marie could turn and walk away, but she thought doing that would be the same as going over and revealing who she was. Marie picked up the lorgnette hanging from the chain around her neck. She placed the glasses to her eyes and glanced down the desk at Voltairine. She could hear Charlie's instruction not to make eye contact. Marie sighed as if the woman wasn't worth the effort of carrying on looking at. Then she lowered the glasses back to the dangling position around her neck.

Voltairine took the envelope off the counter and walked

away without giving Marie a second look. Marie watched her exit the building and let out the breath she'd been holding.

The receptionist brought a book over and ran her finger down a list of names.

'Camille Vallette, was it?'

'Oui.'

She crossed Marie's alias off the list. 'Third floor,' she said, nodding to the elevator.

'Your references are excellent, so they are,' the journalist Michael Byrne said. He tapped on the forged letters Marie and Charlie had created, which sat on his desk.

Marie's alias, Camille Vallette, was four years older than Marie. She had studied art at the Academie Julien as Marie intended to and, during her study, had reported on the arts scene for several Parisian newspapers. The letters attested to her abilities and knowledge.

He leant back in his chair and steepled his fingers. He was clearly a confident man. He was traditionally good-looking. He was full of charm, a beguiling smile and a friendly Irish accent. It was hard to imagine the man opposite was capable of creating bombs. It was hard to imagine that he may have been involved with people who had killed her sister.

'I would love nothing more than to give you the job right now, Miss Vallette.'

'And I would love nothing more than to accept your offer.'

He smiled. 'The thing is, while your art credentials are good. You don't have much experience regarding social events.'

Marie leaned forward. 'In Paris, the art scene is the social scene. The two are symbiotic.'

'I must admit the prospect of interviewing for the rest of the afternoon doesn't appeal to me.'

'Then trial me.'

He raised an eyebrow in reply.

'Give me a couple of assignments and see how I get on. Let us get to know each other more professionally,' Marie said, holding his gaze.

'I do have a couple of stories that need following up. An artist named Moran is creating a painting of the Liberty statue. Do you know him?'

'I'm aware of the marine artist Thomas Moran,' Marie said, showing off her knowledge. Luckily, Thomas Moran had guest lectured at the art school she attended. Though his work is traditional—compared to Monet, Degas, and Pissarro, that is. Though I'm guessing you'd prefer a profile to a critique?'

'Maybe not. A more sensational approach might draw more readers. In fact, Miss Vallette, you could create a character for yourself.'

'A character?' Did he know who she really was? 'I'm not sure I follow.'

'A persona. A more outspoken version people might admire the honesty of.'

'Or they might be annoyed by the outspoken words of a woman.'

'Either way, it'll sell more papers. People will buy them to be entertained by you or to be outraged by you.'

'That's how it works here, is it?'

'It's why we have one of the largest circulations in the country.'

'I just wish to give my honest opinion on things.'

'Well, why don't you give me an honest appraisal of his

work, and we'll take it from there?'

The boat ferried Marie out from Manhattan over to Bedloe Island. The water during the crossing was choppy, and Marie was glad to step off the boat and onto the landing stage.

As she composed herself, a man approached and waved. 'You got your sea legs?' he said in a broad, northern English accent.

He was dressed in a paint-covered artist's smock and wore a navy beret. He had a bushy moustache and a long, pointed goatee.

'Mr. Moran. It is a pleasure to meet you.'

'The pleasure is all mine, Miss Vallette, and call me Ed,' he said. His eyes were piercing and intense, but having met him briefly once before at the Artist's League, where he'd given a guest lecture, she knew he was a kind gentleman.

'Liberty enlightening the world,' he said, gesturing towards the statue. Even before its opening, the statue had become such a fixture on the skyline it seemed hard to believe it hadn't always been there. She often caught glimpses of it between the buildings; a defiant, proud figure stood out in the bay. But standing beneath the statue was a different experience entirely. It was colossal.

'She is going to put this city on the map,' he said.

'I'm so pleased to see her up close,' Marie said. 'It feels like I have been reading about her all my life.'

'And how do the French perceive her?'

'Speaking for myself, I can only say I'm proud but possibly a little annoyed.'

'Annoyed? Why on earth?'

'Because it is not standing in the English Channel holding

the beacon of liberty up to England.'

Edward studied her for a moment and saw she was teasing him. 'Miss Vallette, you tease the wrong Englishman. I abandoned my king many years ago in search of liberty,' he said, laughing with her.

'Well, I think you found her.'

They continued on, walking around the base of the statue. Workmen finished various jobs on the structure, and gardeners tended to the grounds around the base.

'Her face is magnificent, I really wish you could see it,' Edward said.

'I just wish I could see its unveiling.'

Edward looked at the floor. 'Yes, unfortunate and silly. Though I plan to be on a boat out there myself, I wish to capture the whole scene, flotilla and all. You should join us.'

'It's likely I'll have to work covering all of the society events. The city is going to be quite the soirée.'

Edward stroked his beard as he thought. 'I have an idea. Would you like to see inside?'

'Inside the base?'

'Inside the statue.'

Edward led her to the doors at the rear of the base and into the pedestal lobby.

'Are we allowed to just walk in? Isn't there anybody guarding the statue?' she asked.

Edward looked bemused at her. 'Why would anyone need to guard her? It's not like anyone can just walk in off the street.'

A few carpenters worked on some cabinets and fittings, sawing and hammering.

The pair continued and trudged up the staircase to the top of the pedestal. Both had to stop and catch their breaths from the climb.

A group of workmen were working at the base of the iron support structure. They stopped and stared at the pair. Then they laughed, and one of them said something in Italian, and they laughed some more. Marie looked over to them and feigned being even more fatigued than she was.

She took a deep breath and looked up at the latticework of iron beams, struts, and stairs running through the statue's centre.

She sighed so they could see.

'A long way up, eh,' one of the men said, grinning.

A tall man, likely his boss, hit him on the shoulder, and the grinning man returned to work. The tall man glared at Marie and Edward. He pointed up at the stairs. 'Are you going?'

'Yes,' Edward said.

The tall man shouted in Italian to a man called Gio, who was somewhere up the spiral staircase. Then he turned his back on them. As they ascended the stairs, Marie tried to look at what the Italian men were doing, but they seemed to block her view as she passed. The tall Italian glared over his shoulder at her.

The spiral staircase was relentless. As they walked up, Edward said, 'Did you know a penny is thicker than the copper covering the whole statue? Incredible, isn't it?'

They were halfway up the statue when they encountered a man called Gio working on a platform at Liberty's neck. He seemed to be waiting for them as he rubbed his hands clean on a rag. A tarp covered some objects on the floor. He stepped in front of them.

'A long way to come to work,' Marie said.

'Been on worse,' he replied. And then he stood there with his arms crossed.

'That goes up to the torch, but we're going this way,' Edward said. Marie and Edward continued up the stairs to the crown. 'Friendly, these workmen aren't they?'

'Indeed. Say, the few times I've been out here, they usually offer more banter.'

'You've seen those before?'

'No, the Irish workers, I mean.'

'Interesting...'

'You lead the way, though,' he said. 'I am shattered. I'll be there in a minute.'

Marie's thighs and calves burned and ached with pain when she reached Liberty's crown ahead of Edward. She smiled as she entered and saw the ripples in Liberty's hair. She reached out and touched them. A tear formed in the corner of her eye. She shook her head and wiped the tear away as Edward arrived, panting out of breath behind her.

At this height, the wind whistled, and the sailcloth buffeted against Liberty's face outside.

'Ah, of course. I was hoping to show you the view, but that damn sail is still covering her face. They intend to swap it for your tricolor I do believe.'

'It's fine, Edward. In fact, it is more than fine. It is incredible to be back here again.'

'You've been in here before?' he asked, looking confused.

'Yes, indeed. Though not on American soil. When my grandpa and I escorted my sister to Paris before she came to New York, he took us to visit, well, this! When the head was displayed at the Paris Exposition, we stood right here... just in another country.'

'Another continent, no less. That's incredible, Camille.'

She ran her hand along the copper plating and thought she would not let them destroy this statue or what it stood for.

Marie, Charlie and Joe sat in a cafe on the Upper East Side. 'There's a whole group of Italians working on the statue,' Marie said and looked at Joe. Charlie looked at him, too.

'What, just because I'm Italian too, you gonna call me Camorra?'

'The thought had crossed my mind,' Charlie said.

'Why do I know you're not joking? You do realise New York is Italy's second city. There are more Italians here than in any city outside of Rome.'

'I know, Marie said. 'Edward commented that the Irish usually worked on it, though. It just seemed like a coincidence.'

Joe shook his head. 'Policing relies on facts...On evidence. Too much of this investigation is relying on coincidence and speculation. We risk conceiving a conspiracy theory to draw connections between these events.

Charlie smiled and raised his eyebrows at Joe's estimation of his investigation. He leaned back in his chair and didn't say anything.

'Well, whatever, they were acting very strange,' Marie said. 'They were doing work on the internal structure. One in particular, he was alone up in the arm. He was very suspicious.'

'Gut feeling kid?' Charlie asked.

'I could just sense something.'

'I think we should discount it until it's the only option left,' Joe said.

Charlie stared at his cup of coffee on the table. Eventually, he looked up. 'You've policed this city for a while now?'

'Several years, yes.'

'Would you say there's more strange crimes happening now than you've ever known?'

'Nothing surprises me in this city. But yeah. I'm not disputing that events are happening, but the links in the chain joining them all together are fragile. It's sporadic. Suffragettes, antis, the army getting robbed. The Camorra. And now Irish Republicanism. It's chaotic.'

'Too chaotic to be joined up?'

'Seemingly.'

'And how does it make you feel?'

'The truth? Unnerved.'

'What are you theorising?' Marie asked. 'What point are you trying to make, Charlie?'

He hesitated from talking, but they both raised their eyebrows at him.

'You've never asked why I was assigned this case.'

'You came on good authority,' Joe said.

'Well, that authority was concerned about something in particular.' Charlie looked over his shoulder. He leaned across the table towards them. Marie and Joe glanced at each other and then reluctantly leaned in. 'Anarchism,' Charlie said as if some monster would leap from the table behind and swallow them whole.

'Is that it?' Marie leant back in her chair. 'Anarchism?'

Charlie frowned at her.

'So, the authorities are worried about anarchism.'

'The President is. Yeah, I thought that would get your attention. Anarchism is on the rise across Europe. Predominantly your lot, Frenchie.'

'And you think it's here?' Joe asked.

'America's had its revolution, Charlie,' Marie said.

'So did France. Didn't stop you having a couple more.'

Joe nodded. 'Based on that theory, it doesn't take much of a leap to link some of these events together.'

'You think my sister's death is related to anarchism?'

Charlie twisted his lips and nodded.

'A suffragette and an anti-suffragette. Murdered lovers from opposing sides. They were chosen for how symbolic it would be and how it would make a mockery of both sides.'

CHAPTER 13

Tobacco smoke filled the bustling newsroom. Typewriters chimed, and the keys clattered as they were punched down by hunched-over reporters. Marie stood in the doorway.

Across the newsroom, Michael Byrne hollered out to her and beckoned Marie over to him. 'Good to see you again, Miss Camille.'

She leaned on the edge of his desk, and he didn't try to hide, staring at the shape of her body through her dress. It felt strange to be looked at like this. Men never usually paid her attention. She was beginning to realise how clothes, makeup, essentially a costume, could have affect the people around her and maybe even to her benefit.

'And how is my favourite Irish journalist?'

'Aye, just grand. How did your interview with the artist go.'

'Well,' Marie said. She handed him the file with her typed interview.'

He slid it out and started reading it. 'You're going to read it now?'

'Gotta decide whether to give you your next assignment,' he said without looking up.

Marie let him read it. She had kept the interview factual, keeping out as much of her opinion as possible, apart from the ending. She felt guilty for giving a critique because she liked Edward Moran. But she reasoned she had written the article in Camille Vallette's voice and needed to keep Michael Byrne happy. Her mind drifted as he read the interview, and she wondered what she would be capable of doing in the name of her alias.

'This is it,' he said.

She was brought from her thoughts.

'This is what we need more of.' He was pointing at the ending. 'It's a grand piece of work, but we need to see more of your personality. Like what you've done at the end.'

'It was my honest opinion.'

'As it should be.' He grinned. 'And I have just the next job for you, so I do.'

Marie touched her cheek as if to dampen her blushes. He grinned. 'The publisher himself would like you to attend a little soirée in honour of the archbishop.'

Marie sighed. 'Here's me thinking you had something exciting for me to attend.'

'Don't be like that,' he said, looking offended.

'Are you going?'

'Aye, so I will.'

'Then why do you need me to attend?'

'You need to prove you can write for the society side of the job. Besides, I need a date.'

'You could've just asked. I'm not working on it. It's a society event.'

'I thought I got to choose what events to report on in the city.'

'Everything so far has been art-related. It's not gone unnoticed. The editor wants more society in your columns. And besides, like I said, the publisher wants this particular event covered, so we all have to jump.'

Though Marie rolled her eyes, this was precisely the opening she sought. 'It is hardly Paris. New York society is...' She twisted her lips and frowned. 'It is full of capitalists.'

His eyebrows raised. 'I didn't see you as political.'

She shook her head from side to side. 'What I mean is, they are dull. Industrialists, businessmen, financiers, lawyers. Ugh.'

'They'll all be there.'

'A writer needs characters to write about, no?'

He nodded.

'Society is made up of more than just the rich. All I will hear about is how some new screw or bolt has made some boring man rich.'

'Concentrate on how rich they are. People want to imagine being rich. They don't want to know the rich bastard's life can be as mundane as theirs. Report the event—the fashion, the champagne, the grand setting the readers will never visit.'

'And I thought you weren't the type of man to be in awe of such people.'

He leaned in conspiratorially. 'Oh, what kind of man did you think I was then?'

'Maybe we'll discuss it later.'

'You see we do, Miss Camille.'

He slid his fingers across the desk towards her leg, and she nearly jumped off the table as he touched her.

He picked up the envelope she sat on and held it out to her. She looked sideways at him, took it from him and found an invite inside.

'I'll be seeing you tonight then.'

The banquet in honour of the archbishop was held at the Metropolitan Hotel. The pre-dinner soirée played out exactly how Marie predicted. She spoke about incredibly dull things, with extremely dull people who were all incredibly rich. Marie despaired. She couldn't see how attending this event was helping her get closer to finding her sister's killer or uncovering a cabal of secret anarchists. Michael Byrne had been nothing but charming to her and everyone else. She watched him effortlessly work the room. His confidence returned smiles and opened conversations. She couldn't imagine him being a man who would detest such power and authority when he moved so easily amongst it. Despite wishing she was at her studio drawing or painting, Marie knew she needed results from the night. If only to keep up pretences. So she copied what he did and worked the room.

After an hour of conversation, they all sat for dinner.

Fifteen tables filled the room, with six people sitting around each.

Marie picked up her spoon. As she was about to take some soup from her bowl, Michael's hand stroked her thigh. Her knee jerked and hit the table. The bowl jumped up and fell over, spilling its contents. Everyone around the table looked at her. Her cheeks flushed.

'Are you okay, miss?' the railway owner opposite asked.

'Sorry. Yes. It is a condition. I have.' Marie wanted to melt into the tablecloth along with the soup. She slowly turned to look at Michael. He leaned in towards her.

'You really should get that looked at, so you should,' he whispered.

'I'm afraid that should the cause be discovered, it might require amputation.'

'That would be a crying shame.' He clicked his fingers, ushering over a waiter who took away the bowl. He stirred his soup with his spoon but didn't eat any.

'Are you not hungry?' she asked.

'I was just thinking, wondering,' he said. He seemed to be

vacant. He looked around the table, watching people eating the soup.

'Wondering what?'

'About your love of art,' he looked directly at her.

She managed to hide her reaction. Stay in character, she thought. 'What about it?'

The railway owner sat opposite began coughing, distracting them from their conversation. The woman next to her started squirming in her seat.

'What inspired your love for it?'

'My father, he was an artist. Was your father a journalist?' Marie asked. She'd rather the conversation was on him instead of her.

Michael laughed. 'The man could barely write, but you've never heard anyone better with words.'

People started to groan and complain. Some coughed. Some retched. People rubbed their stomachs or got up from their tables.

'What's going on?' Marie asked.

'I haven't a clue,' Michael said. But the way he watched everyone suggested he did. His eyes smiled, if not his mouth.

More people started coughing, Some grasped the tablecloth or their cutlery as the pain began to take hold. A man, Marie had heard, was a doctor grabbed a jug of water and emptied salt into it. He grimaced as he drank the whole glassful and vomited immediately onto the table. Nobody seemed to care as they dealt with their own pain. More people got up and left the room. Some hadn't even made it that far as they leaned against the wall and lost their bowels.

'We've been poisoned!' the doctor shouted. His voice was hoarse from retching. He wiped vomit from his mouth with the back of his hands.

Marie was gripped by fear. She had never seen, smelled, or heard anything like what she was witnessing.

'Do you feel ill?'

'No, I feel just grand. Do you?' Michael said.

'No. I don't know. No.'

The waiters stood dumbfounded by the sight. The doctor ordered them to collect as much salt and jugs of water as possible. They then began grabbing drinking glasses and filling them with the improvised emetic.

Marie and Michael stood and edged back to the wall.

'We should help them,' Marie said.

'And do what? What the hell can we do?'

The doctor drank another one and was sick again. People were handed the concoction. Some downed it. Some were repulsed by the thought of drinking it. All were ultimately compelled to take it.

'This is incredible,' Michael said. 'Have you ever seen anything like it?'

Marie remembered to stay in character. 'It is atrocious.'

A woman fell to her knees before Marie. She clasped her stomach and fell to her side.

Marie ran over to one of the waiters and grabbed one of the glasses of saltwater. She took it back to the woman.

'Take this. Drink it,' Marie said.

The woman groaned and tried to push it away. Marie put it to the woman's lips and poured some in. She spluttered and coughed and spat it out.

'You've got to take it. You'll die if you don't.'

The doctor went around everyone, urging them to be sick and to expel the poison from their bodies.

'Michael, stop standing there and help me,' Marie shouted.

Michael strolled over. 'I'm not touching her. I might catch

what she's got. God knows what it is.'

Marie pushed the woman onto her back and grabbed her nose. With the woman gasping for air, Marie poured the saltwater into her mouth.

Marie stood back as the woman vomited a mixture of the emetic and the soup she'd eaten.

Marie knew the soup had been poisoned. It was the only explanation. She went to tell Michael but stopped herself from saying so.

'I've never seen so many people be so sick,' he said, talking into the crook of his elbow.

Marie covered her nose with her hand.

People crawled on their hands and knees. People clung to their chairs. The sound of wailing, shouting and vomiting filled the room. It was like a massacre. No, it was a massacre. The whole scene looked like a dramatic Renaissance painting.

'Keep drinking,' the doctor urged. He was now also orchestrating the handing out spoons scooped full of mustard.

'What do you think's causing it?' Marie asked. 'Why aren't we ill?'

'We're not the only ones,' he said, pointing at the waiters. 'They're all well. I'd say it was a poisoning.'

'Poisoning?'

'Did you eat anything?'

'No. I didn't get a chance to, remember.'

'You mean I saved your life.'

'You think they'll die?' she asked, feigning ignorance.

'That's what poisoning usually leads to.'

'There must be over a hundred people here.'

'Indeed. It's a big story, so it is.'

'Story?'

'Aye. What a scoop,' Michael said, laughing.

Marie said nothing. She dare not say anything lest it reveal her disgust and suspicion of him. So she continued to show her revulsion of the situation instead, which wasn't hard to do. Her intuition told her Michael was involved. He clearly hadn't laced the soup with poison, for she had seen him work the room all night. But she was confident Michael knew it would happen. He had been there for the story. She was presumably accompanied him as part of his alibi. But had he been tipped off by the anarchists? Or was he one of the anarchists himself. Was he the mastermind behind this brutal attack? As she watched him, she wondered if he was annoyed by the doctor who had managed to save, albeit maybe temporarily, the lives of all of these people.

'Tell me, Michael. I'm intrigued. What would've made the better story? All of these people dying, or the good doctor saving the lives of all of them?'

'Neither,' he said. 'I don't think we could've wished for either outcome.'

He seemed too giddy to realise what he'd let slip, so she quickly said, 'I don't think the public will believe it.'

'Oh, they will. We'll paint a picture so damn shocking they'll have no choice but to.'

'But do you think the publisher will let us print it?'

'What's he got to...Oh, I see. It'll be fine. The print sales alone and the sensation it causes will increase his sales and bank balance enough to make him not worry about his morals.'

'Who do you think did it though? Why would they do something like this?'

'Oh, I dare say there are enough people in this room who would've wronged someone on their way to the top.'

'You think it's revenge for something?'

'Aye, why, what do you think?'

'A serial killer?'

He scoffed at her suggestion.

She frowned. 'Why not? There's been some odd deaths recently in this city, do you not think? That couple in the theatre.'

He waved the suggestion away.

'Politically motivated then?' she said.

'Maybe. We'll have to wait and see if anybody claims responsibility for it.'

'You think somebody would just admit to this?'

'If there's a cause.'

'Propaganda of the deed? I don't think so,' she said. 'Surely, if you're hoping to inspire people with actions, then you would do something more inspiring than attempted murder.'

'Oh? You think so, do you?'

'What would you do?'

'Me? Well, I don't know.'

'There you go.' He sounded offended.

'Well, it would depend on what my cause was.'

'Anarchism.'

'What, that's what my cause would be?'

He nodded. His stare was now quite intense. 'Well, I guess I'd do something chaotic. Unpredictable. Maybe this.'

'There, see.'

'What would you do?'

'Exactly this. Exactly this.' His attention had been stolen. A few policemen arrived since the catering staff passed word onto the street about what was happening.

'Maybe we shouldn't be caught here with those policemen

snooping around.'

'Why not?' Marie said. 'We're innocent, aren't we?'

'Well, of course we are, but they might start questioning why we're not ill like everybody else.'

'Just bend the truth a little.'

He raised an eyebrow.

'The truth is we're working. They don't need to know we didn't have the soup.' His eyes narrowed on her. 'I'd rather not draw attention to ourselves. Besides, we've got a front page to write.'

CHAPTER 14

After writing the story, Marie got to do what she had planned with Charlie. She went to celebrate with Michael in a local tavern and made sure he got drunk.

'You're not what I thought you were, Madame Vallette,' he said, slurring his words.

'And what did you think I was?' she asked, staring into his eyes.

'A snob!' he slapped his hand on the table, nearly knocking it over.

Marie shrugged. 'We all have appearances to keep.'

'Why did you leave Paris?'

Marie stared at him. It was the lead-in she'd been hoping for. She smiled. 'Society in Paris.' She shook her head and kept smiling as if recalling a memory.

'You're hiding something, Camille,' he said.

'Are you searching for a story?' Marie asked.

He leaned back and nearly fell off his chair. Marie grabbed his hand and pulled him back down. They both laughed. He held her hand, and she refrained from pulling it away. He stroked her fingers.

'I'm not trying to find a story. I have my own stories,' Michael said.

She returned his strokes, and he turned up his palm. She traced her finger around it, surprising herself with how she could do that. 'A tall, dark, Irish man. Of course, you have stories,' she said.

He sat up straighter in his chair and swayed from side to side.

'Oh, I fight the good fight, Miss.'

'Journalism is a noble endeavour, Michael.'

'There's only one noble endeavour,' he said, leaning conspiratorially across the table.

'And that is?'

'The only fight. Against the English.'

Marie laughed and playfully rolled her eyes. 'All Irish men talk of revolution, yet you've never achieved it.'

Something changed in his eyes. It was as if a dark shadow passed over his soul. He seemed to sober up. 'Oh. Missy. I take it very seriously.'

Marie raised an eyebrow.

'You don't believe me?'

'My father fought in the Commune de Paris. I believe in action, not poetry.'

He clapped slowly.' So your dhaidí fought a battle. Doesn't give you the right to—'

'So did my ma,' she said, mocking his Irish accent before switching back to the broader Parisian accent she used as part of her cover. 'Both my parents were Communards. Revolution is in my blood. And I am proud to continue their fight.' What she said was true. Her parents had fought in the Paris Commune. It was in May of that year, 1871, her father had died during the Bloody Week when the Third Republic Versailles troops had overrun Paris, and the slaughter had begun. Despite being young at the time, Marie remembered the smell of burnt buildings and corpses littering the street. Her mother had barely got Capucine and Marie out of the city alive.

Marie knew she probably shouldn't have used her history as part of her story, but who would've known that?

'You talk as if you left Paris because you did something.'

Marie smiled. 'I believe you're more of a journalist than a revolutionary.'

'How much would you like to bet?'

Marie leaned towards him and gazed into his eyes. She ran her hand along his forearm. 'I don't bet. I'd rather find out how you intend to persuade me.'

A short while later, Michael Byrne led Marie out of the tavern. Charlie sat on a wall nearby and immediately spotted them. She gave a pre-agreed signal, tapping three times on her hip, telling Charlie not to intervene. Charlie followed them as they covered a few blocks and arrived at the Mills-Parker Building.

'Are you trying to prove me right that you're a journalist?'

Though Michael seemed more sober, he still swayed, and Marie felt it safe to check and see if Charlie was still following them. He was. He shook his head as if telling her not to go through with whatever she intended to do.

'You see,' Michael said. 'We're not going to the news desk.' He led her past the entrance on Nassau Street and across the road to another building. He unlocked the door and went in. Marie hesitated on the street.

'Come on,' he said. 'I've got something secret to show you.'

'If I had a franc for every man that's said that.'

'No. I'm being serious,' Michael slurred. He stood inside the doorway, lighting a storm lantern, nearly using a book of matches. Charlie had snuck down the side of the building and stood almost beside Marie, just out of sight. Marie saw him shake his head at her from the corner of her eye. She knew it was stupid but thought it an excellent opportunity.

'Lead the way.'

Charlie dropped his head against the wall as he looked to the heavens.

'I need to lock the door,' Michael said. But he couldn't hold the lantern and find the keyhole with the key in his drunken state.

'Here, let me,' Marie said. Michael gave her the keys, and she pretended to lock the door and gave him them back. The door had led onto some kind of landing, and he started off down the stairs, and she followed. A cellar was at the bottom of the stairs, and running off the basement was a bricked-walled tunnel. She figured it ran under the street towards the Mills-Parker Building.

They stumbled along in the tunnel in the glow of the storm lantern. Marie glanced over her shoulder. If Charlie followed, he did it well, as she couldn't see him in the shadows.

'Where does this lead to?' she asked.

'Consider it a rebirth into revolution.'

They soon arrived at the end of the tunnel, where there was a birdcage elevator.

They went in, and Marie closed the gate behind her. Then Michael pushed some buttons and pulled on a lever, and the elevator juddered to life and began to rise.

If Charlie was following, she had no idea how he'd follow her now.

As they went up, she noticed through the grill it seemed to be one long shaft. There weren't any exit doors on the floors of the building. Michael turned to her in the tight elevator birdcage as if he'd remembered she was there.

He grinned. Swayed. And leaned in to kiss Marie. She put her finger to his lips.

'What do you think you get if you win your bet.'

His eyes widened.

'Madame,' he said. She'd lost count of the different ways he'd addressed her in his drunken state. He didn't follow up with anything else—he just kissed her finger. But then the lift reached its destination and shuddered to a stop.

He turned around and opened the gate. The corridor was dark. The floor looked as if it had been sealed and not used for many years, like the inside of a tomb.

'Is this the only route into the building,' she asked.

'All of the, the—' he burped. 'Oh! Excuse me,' he said and kept walking.

'All of the what?'

'All of the what, what?' he asked.

'That lift, why did we use that lift instead of the main entrance.'

'Because nobody knows this is up here. Besides, all of the stairs and what have you have been walled off.'

He led her down the corridor, past various individual offices resembling the same layout as the newspaper's offices.

'What's in these offices?' she asked, heading to one of the doors and turning the handle. Michael stopped and held the lantern up, spilling light towards her.

'Nothing but old news.'

She opened the door. From floor to ceiling were bales of newspapers.

'Why are there so many?'

'That's not all,' he said. Follow me.' He led her to the next room and pushed open the door. That, too, was filled with newspapers.

'Don't they sell any?'

'Not as many as the circulation figures used to show. The old publisher didn't want it to get out, so they buried their lies here. But that's not the best bit.'

He started towards a room she figured was at the front and centre of the building.

He dramatically swung the door open and went in. The storm lantern swung in his hand. He cursed himself, and as he steadied it, he burnt his fingers on the glass. He cursed again. 'Wouldn't want to set this off too early.'

Marie couldn't believe what she saw. She wondered if she was drunker than she realised.

The room looked like the inside of a barn. Bales of hay were stacked floor to ceiling.

'Not what you were expecting, eh?'

'It's been several years since I've rolled around in a hay barn,' she said. Michael grinned and started towards her.

'Oh no,' she said, stepping back from him. 'You need to tell me why it looks like a barn in here first.'

'Because hay burns, missy, so it does. And so does paper.'

'What, is this a story you've uncovered? Is the building's owner going to commit arson?'

'I told you. I'm a revolutionary miss. I don't just write the news. I create it too.'

'This is your doing? You did this.'

'Ay. We did this.'

'We?'

'Not you and I. Me and my friends.'

'You're going to set fire to this?'

'I thought you were a revolutionary Lafetee.'

'It's Vallette,' she said, reminding him of her name. Was he testing her, she thought?

'Yes. Of course,' Michael said. 'Madame Vallette.'

She couldn't work him out. He seemed to sway in and out of sobriety along with the sway of his body. 'What for? How does burning this building help the Irish cause?'

'Oh, it helps many missed causes, so it does. Many great causes.' He started walking towards her again. 'It helps my cause. It helps your cause. It helps the cause of all common people. It will fix society as we know it.'

'By burning down a newspaper's offices?'

He laughed. 'This building is home to many newspapers, don't you know? All spouting lies, along with the advertisers that mass-produce their superficial lies, and the whole lot... It's gonna burn.'

'You are anarchists?' Marie asked.

He stood proudly and said, 'Ay. So we are.'

'And burning this to the ground will do what?'

'You ask a lot of questions.'

'You bought me here. What did you expect me to do?'

'It is one of many acts that will compel the public into action. Make them believe those who seek to lead aren't fit and they'd be better off leading themselves.'

Marie shook her head.

'You think it's a laughing matter?'

'I don't think you can incite a change in society through a couple of acts of terrorism.'

'It is propaganda of the deed.'

'Quite the opposite. The people you want to change or convince will only take action against you.'

He placed the lantern onto one of the bales of hay. 'It won't. It will show the people the state and the upper classes are not almighty.'

'And their response will be more oppressive on the people you wish to free.'

'Ay. And the people will hate them for it. They'll revolt.' He suddenly turned to face Marie. 'Who are you, missy? You think you can ply an Irish man with drink and hope to get him drunk enough to get answers from.'

'I told you. I am Camille Vallette. So stop playing games pretending you're drunk.'

'Then what do you want?' He pulled a gun from his pocket and pointed it at her. Marie had never had a gun pointed at her before. She was surprised by how calm she felt.

'I can give answers. But I can take answers, too, so I can. You must know by now I can't let you leave. You've opened Pandora's box. For answers, there are consequences. And you've asked too many questions.'

'I still have one. Did you kill my sister?'

He looked at her and frowned as he tried to figure out who she really was.

'You're going to have to be more specific.'

'Killed many have you?'

'Did you kill Capucine Cadieux?'

Michael kept the gun pointed at her, stepped forward, and pulled the wig off her head.

'You're the sister, aren't you?'

'Yes.'

He threw the wig on the floor. 'I didn't kill your sister.'

'Your organisation killed her, though. For what? Those shitty ideals you've eluded to? Who was it? Voltairine?'

'Oh. You do know too much. It's a shame,' Michael stepped back and lifted his gun to her head.

'I wouldn't do that if I were you,' Charlie said from somewhere in the darkness.

'Who's there. Show yourself.'

'Did you really think you could get away with this?' Charlie asked.

Michael aimed past Marie, sweeping his gun from left to right into the darkness.

'Only a fool would reveal such a plan. Yet here you stand.'

Michael fired off a shot in the darkness. The flash was enough to reveal Charlie's silhouette to the right. He swept the gun's aim that way and fired off two more. The bullets hit bales of hay. Marie grabbed the man's arm. They struggled before he wrestled it out of her grasp, and he backhanded her with the pistol. The strike knocked her unconscious. She fell to the floor.

Without Marie in the line of fire, Charlie shot at Michael, who was lit by the lantern. The bullet hit Michael on his bicep. He spun around and threw himself behind one of the bales of hay.

'Agh. Bastard. Fucking bastard,' he shouted. Michael realised he would either die or they might reveal the anarchist's plot. So, he decided it was time to act. He reached over the bale and went for the storm lantern. Charlie took another shot, but he missed. A cloud of hay dust blew up as the bullet hit the bale.

The storm lantern was in Michael's hand. He pulled back and threw it towards the bales Charlie was standing behind. The glass broke as it hit the floor. Paraffin leaked and hit the flame. The floor lit instantly. And then the hay ignited. Charlie saw him in the flame light and took the shot. The bullet struck him in the neck. Charlie climbed up the bales and jumped over the flames. Marie was still on the floor, knocked out. He glanced at her as he ran past over to Michael. He found the man lying on the floor, clutching his neck. Choking on blood.

Charlie knelt beside him. 'Who are you working with?'

He struggled to breathe, struggled to swallow, struggled not to choke on the blood leaking and seeping into him and out of him. He stared at the ceiling and struggled to say something.

'What is it?' Charlie asked.

Was he even trying to say something? Was he just trying to breathe? It sounded like he said the or v. But it could just easily have been laboured breathe.

There was nothing Charlie could do to get a confession. The man would be dead before the flames got to him.

Charlie went over to Marie. The flames were spreading fast, and there was no way of putting them out.

He got down beside her and shook her.

The heat was intense.

'Goddamn it, Marie, wake up!'

He started dragging her towards the door. But one of the windows shattered from the heat, and the fresh air fanned the flames blocking their exit. Marie stirred and then startled awake as her senses alerted her to the danger. Charlie dragged her upright, and she stumbled into him.

'What happened?'

'McGarrity is dead,' Charlie shouted. 'And so will we be if we don't get out of here.'

Marie shielded her eyes from the heat with her arm.

'The way out's blocked,' he said, leading her to the window. He hit the glass with his revolver, and it smashed. He dragged the barrel of his gun over the shards, breaking them out of the window frame.

'We're gonna have to climb out onto the ledge.'

'Have you gone insane?' Marie asked, looking at the drop below. The building was six storeys high. Wooden panels on the walls spat and cracked as flames climbed. Marie climbed through the window. There were already people on the street below. She clung to the building as she stood.

'Hurry up, kid. It's getting a little warm in here.' Charlie said between coughs. Charlie climbed out and joined her on the ledge. He peered past Marie. 'Move along. I think we should jump from there.'

'Jump?'

'Across to that fire escape.'

Marie edged along the ledge. She cursed being dressed in the disguise, as the dress and the bustle took up too much of the limited space.

The flames came out of the window they'd just climbed out of.

'This whole building's gonna drop.'

Marie gripped every handhold on the building as she made her way to the corner. There was a six-foot gap from the ledge to the fire escape.

A crashing sound added to the cacophony as the roof caved in. Tiles slid over the edge. They both clung to the wall as slate nearly struck them.

Marie hitched up her skirt. 'Tell me I don't have to wear a disguise like this again.'

'We survive this. You do what you want.'

Marie leaned back and then threw herself across the gap. She caught hold of the iron railing as she landed. And pulled herself over onto the balcony. She turned to Charlie, who was still on the ledge above. As he jumped, the ledge broke beneath his foot. He fell across the gap. Charlie managed to grab the railing, but his feet missed the landing. He yelled in pain as his arm wrenched and took the strain of his weight. The weight of them jumping onto the fire escape shook it loose from its fixings. The iron structure tilted as if it were going to fall from the building. Charlie dangled. Marie balanced. She approached the railing and leaned over, trying to grab Charlie. The fire escape tilted further away from the wall. Charlie swung his legs up to the railing and hooked his foot between one of the struts. Then he pulled himself over onto the balcony.

'It feels like this whole thing will come crashing down,' Marie said.

'Why would it be any different?'

As they descended the first ladder to the balcony below, the one they'd been standing on broke free of the wall. They managed to descend to the next balcony before it crashed above them.

'Go! Go!' Charlie shouted, realising there was a chance the fire escape would collapse like a concertina. One by one, the balconies above them fell. The weight of each one falling onto the one below increased the speed at which they broke, snapped, and tore from the wall. Brick and mortar rained down on them. Pieces of rusted, snapped iron peppered their escape. One of the balconies fell from the pile and dropped past them, thudding into the street below.

They reached the lowest balcony and were about to take the ladder down on the street when the weight above crushed down, blocking their escape. Charlie grabbed Marie and pulled her down before she was crushed. Access to the ladder they were about to descend was now blocked. The tangled mass of iron above groaned.

'We'll have to jump down,' Charlie said. He stood as much as he could, squeezed through the gap, and lowered himself. Then Charlie dropped to the street below and rolled onto the cobbles. Pain immediately throbbed from his ankle as he stood, but he could put weight on it.

Marie followed by climbing through the gap and over the balcony. She tried to lower herself like Charlie had, but her arms weren't strong enough to take her weight. Marie fell back towards the street. He managed to break her fall as he half caught her, and she half fell onto him.

They both lay on their backs, trying to comprehend what had just happened and discerning what aches and pains were more than strains or sprains. Then, the balconies above grated and groaned. They both sat upright despite their pains.

Without needing to say a word to each other, they scrambled to their feet and ran clear as the pile of iron clattered and mangled onto the street where they'd been lying.

As they stood catching their breath and nursing their pains, somebody on the street ran over to a red, cast iron fire alarm call box, opened it, and pulled down the lever.

Charlie raised his eyebrows. 'Well, it's probably a bit late for that. Fire service ain't never gonna be able to put that out.'

The flames had already spread to the floor beneath the attic and emerged from the windows as the panes shattered in the heat.

'Merde,' Marie said, shielding her eyes from the glass. 'Merde.'

The next day, Charlie sat with his foot resting on his knee, rubbing his sprained ankle.

Marie paced about her art studio. 'Voltairine's behind it, Charlie,' Marie said. 'You've got to go and arrest her or something.'

'It doesn't work like that,' Charlie said.

'I saw her in the Mills-Parker Building. It adds up.'

'And you reasoned yourself that the next day, there was a notice in the paper for one of the suffragette meetings.'

'But, you said he was trying to say her name.'

Charlie shook his head. 'I can't be sure what he said. Or if he was even trying to say anything.'

Marie stopped pacing. She crossed her arms. Then she started pacing again.

'This is exactly why I wanted you to spy for me. Now, you need to infiltrate the suffragettes and determine if Voltairine or anyone else is involved.'

'I don't know how I can even be in the same room as her, let alone talk to her as if I don't know.'

'This is what it's going to take to bring them down. You can't let even a flare of your nostril betray you.'

'I do that?'

'Yes.'

'Really?'

Charlie nodded.

'Merde,' she said.

She placed her hands on the table. 'If I can control my facial expressions, then what? How do I get her to confide in me?'

'You flare your nostril.'

'You just told me not to.'

'Not at her, but so she can see.'

'For what reason?'

'For being displeased with the suffragettes' apparent lack of action. You need to become invested in the cause but frustrated enough to want to take matters into your own hands. You're going to have to be clever about it. But you must take direct action to further the suffragette's cause.'

'Direct action?'

'Small acts. Broken windows and the like in the name of the cause. Throw some rocks at the police. Get yourself arrested. She's got to think you mean it. Let her see you feel the sting of injustice.'

'This is all well and good, but even if I could convince her our beliefs align, if she was involved in Capucine's murder, well, will she ever risk revealing what she did?'

A knock on the studio's door diverted Marie and Charlie's attention.

'It's me, Joe.' Marie recognised his voice behind the door, so she let him in. He took off his hat as he crossed the threshold.

'What's it looking like?' Charlie asked.

Joe raised his eyebrows. 'The whole building dropped this morning,' Joe said. 'I've never heard of a fire spreading so fast or causing so much damage.'

'Well, that's what happens when it has some help,' Charlie said.

'It sounds like you took an awful risk, Marie, going with him,' Joe said.

Marie sat on the stool next to her table in the studio. She

knew she'd had a lucky escape and was fortunate to have just a sore arm. 'I'm just glad Camille Vallette perished in that fire, and I don't have to wear that disguise again.'

'So, did it help you find out anything?' Joe asked.

Marie and Charlie looked at each other.

'No,' Charlie said.

'Yes,' Marie said at the same time.

'Well, which one is it?'

'Charlie thought James McGarrity was trying to call for Voltairine as he died.'

Charlie shook his head. 'No. I didn't. It sounded like he said Vee, but he was more than likely trying to breathe his last breath.'

'And who do you think this Vee is?' Joe asked. 'Wait. Isn't that the suffragette—'

'Yes,' Marie said.

'What makes you suspect her?' Joe asked.

'Coincidence,' Charlie said. 'We've got a potential crumb of a lead, and Marie is trying to make it fit. Find a whole load of crumbs, and then maybe we'll have what is called evidence.'

'Don't patronise me, Charlie. You did exactly the same with the Statue of Liberty.'

'That's different,' Charlie said, pointing at her.

'Why do I get the feeling I don't want to hear this,' Joe said.

'I think they intend to attack the Statue of Liberty at the unveiling.'

'The unveiling the president is attending?'

Charlie nodded.

'They wouldn't dare.'

'You really don't think so? Heads of state all across Europe are dropping like flies to anarchists.'

'We won't be able to stop the unveiling. The whole world's

watching.'

'They need to think about doing something,' Charlie said.

'They won't cancel it, especially not on a hunch, no matter how good it is. Hell, I don't even think it would be cancelled if these anarchists sent a telegram saying they would do something.'

'Then what are we going to do?' Marie asked. 'If they successfully do something at the unveiling, they'll be close to achieving their aims.'

'I guess we'll just have to stop them before it gets to that,' Charlie said.

'Anyway,' Joe said. 'You're not the only one who has a lead. A friend of mine is a lieutenant colonel in the Seventy-First Infantry. They've had a problem.'

'Oh yeah, what?'

'It seems they've misplaced a whole load of gunpowder...'

'By misplaced, I guess you mean stolen.'

'There you go again, Charlie,' Marie said. 'Jumping to conclusions...'

Benedict and Voltairine met on the Brooklyn Bridge. He walked slightly ahead of her. 'Nobody has seen or heard anything from James McGarrity,' Benedict said. 'The consensus is he probably died in the fire.'

Voltairine was the last of the Black Veil to meet separately with Benedict since the Mills-Parker Building had burnt down the night before. They had always intended to raze the building and disrupt several newspapers and advertising agencies, but not as soon as this.

'I bet the fool set it alight when drunk,' Voltairine said.

'If he did perish, then it's a shame because the whole

building went down how he said it would.'

'A shame?' Voltairine asked, shaking her head. 'I told you he was a liability. They all are.'

'They have skills—'

'What good are skills if they blow the operation? He could've been arrested for all we know.'

'James wouldn't talk even if he was.'

'He craves notoriety,' Voltairine said and then sighed. Benedict's trust in the others was infuriating, yet she had to remind herself his foresight had started the operation. He had gathered and assembled them all. He had the vision to take action, whereas so many had only spoken and theorised about a society without rule. When she had been wallowing in pity and despair, wracked by a thirst for vengeance, Benedict had been the one to offer his hand and a chance to rise.

'What now?'

'We proceed as planned.'

'But McGarrity was our explosives expert. We need another one capable.'

'I have someone in mind.'

'If he was good enough, you would've recruited him instead of McGarrity. So, why didn't you?'

'Because in this line of work, capable men are very dangerous men.'

They held each other's gaze.

'Will this man get the job done?'

'Yes. Yes. I believe he will.'

It was just after midday when Charlie and Joe walked up to the gates of the barracks of the Seventy-First Infantry. Joe introduced himself to the guard at the gate and waited in the sunshine for someone to collect them.

Eventually, a man showed up, tall and athletic, dressed in the blue uniform of an infantry soldier. 'I'm Lieutenant-Colonel Wallace Hunter.'

'Joe Petrosino of the New York Police Department.'

'Charlie Blaine.'

They shook hands.

Wallace considered Charlie for a moment. 'You're ex-army, I was told.'

'I was a 'Lieutenant Colonel myself, Colorado infantry.'

'Oh well. We can't all be perfect,' Wallace said, grinning.

'Well, at least we never lost any explosives. At least not on my watch.'

Wallace's smile faded. 'That hurts. Even more so now, a cop and a fifty-third are investigating.'

'Don't worry, we're not here to investigate how explosives went missing from a base. Though you can be sure some people will want to know that, but not us.'

'What are you here for then? Why did they send you?'

'We need to discover who took them and why,' Joe said.

'I'd very much like to find out too,' Wallace said.

'Well, are you going to invite us in?' Charlie asked.

They walked silently until they arrived at the store, where an eager young guard was posted at the door. He saluted Wallace and looked past Joe and Charlie. Inside, light beams cut through the dust.

'Nothing looks out of place,' Charlie said. The store was stacked full of crates and barrels.

'That's what we thought. Until we counted the inventory.'

'What's gone?'

'Five barrels of black powder. Seven cases of dynamite.

One case of bullets.'

Joe whistled. Charlie rubbed his stubble.

'I was told you might know who took it. We'd very much like to recover it.'

Charlie shook his head. 'Well, here's the rub. We don't know who took it. But we have suspicions. I take it from what you said you have no idea who?'

'We have our suspicions too.'

'Anyone with anarchist tendencies?' Joe asked.

Wallace twisted his lips. 'No. But the same accent as you.'

'Italian?' Joe asked.

'Yeah, a couple of them have gone awol. It's why we checked our inventory.'

'Any chance of finding them?' Charlie asked.

'In New York?' Wallace asked.

'Not a chance,' Joe said.

'How long had they been with you?'

'About six months.'

Charlie narrowed his eyes. 'If they are with the same people we suspect, they've been plotting this for some time.'

'Plotting what?' Wallace asked. 'Enough with the dance. Who are they, and what do they plan to do with those explosives?'

'I said. Anarchists. And I have a theory,' Charlie said.

'Well, don't leave me in suspense.'

'They might be planning to blow up the Statue of Liberty.'

Wallace's eyebrows raised. 'I mean. Wow. I guess if you put anarchists and a whole load of stolen explosives together, and with an event like that coming up, you're gonna jump to that conclusion.'

'It would be such a jump if previous examples of their handiwork hadn't been as dramatic as that potential outcome.'

'And it's just you two investigating this? Sounds like you're going to need some help.'

That evening, Marie arrived late for the general meeting of the New York City Woman Suffrage Association to avoid having to make small talk with Voltairine. Marie had decided that if she couldn't mask her emotions, it would be best to let Voltairine believe it was because she was late and frustrated by what the speakers on stage spoke about. She sat next to the woman who she suspected was involved in killing her sister. Her hands were clenched in her lap, fingernails digging into her palms. Just their arms touching against each other made Marie want to stand up and accuse her in front of everyone.

She gritted her teeth and kept her gaze firmly on the stage. Matilda Joslyn Gage was flanked by several more senior members.

'Our plan, therefore, is to rally, march, and let our voices be heard,' Matilda said.

Marie squirmed in her seat. She crossed her arms. She sighed as they outlined the dates when they would rally. Voltairine glanced at her, but Marie didn't acknowledge the woman had seen she was annoyed.

'Are you okay, Marie? You seemed distracted.'

'This is exactly why I didn't wish to get involved,' Marie said.

'Why, what's wrong?'

'Capucine was always the diplomat. Whenever I fell out with my friends in the village, my sister would always come and calm me down,' Marie said, smiling, shaking her head at the memory.

'She always said you had an artist's temperament.'

Marie let her smile fade. 'We shouldn't have drifted apart like we did.'

'You had your art. She had this.'

'Mon Dieu. Only she could cope with this. They are frustrating. No? Do you not feel it?'

Voltairine smiled but didn't say anything. Marie wouldn't push it further. She could hear Charlie's voice in her mind, whispering to take small steps.

Voltairine patted Marie's hand. Marie smiled but wanted to slap her.

'Honestly, Vee, I don't know if I can become invested in the cause.' In adopting this different persona, there was something in the process of acting that focused her rage. 'I'll become too frustrated with them. I've come today for you. Through you, I feel closer to Capucine.'

'I'm glad. It is soothing to reminisce. I guess this is what you French refer to as true fraternity.'

Marie smiled again and tried to force as much enthusiasm as she could into her expression to expel the tears and anger welling inside. 'I think, in this instance, it would be sorority, no?'

CHAPTER 16

Joe, Charlie and Lieutenant-Colonel Wallace had interviewed several of the other soldiers who had known the two awol Italians. Information was thin on the ground. The only lead they had was that one of them was an avid baseball fan, and his father worked one of the gates into the stadium. At the weekend, a few days later, Joe, Charlie and a couple of Wallace's troops met outside the baseball stadium. They all wore civilian clothes. The smell of charcoal filled the air from the many pie carts cooking sausages and serving red hots on buns.

'Gate four,' Private Frazier said. Frazier was in his late twenties, wiry limbed, and though he had a fun sense of humour his mean stare showed his determination to catch the awol troops. 'He said all we had to do was mention his name to his father and he'd let us in.'

'Well stick to the plan,' Charlie said.

Frazier nodded and turned to his colleague, Private Doran, a broad shouldered Irish man. Charlie and Joe watched on as the two men stalked off through the crowd towards the gate.

'Surely he won't be so stupid as to show up here?' Joe said. 'He should be long gone.'

'He'll have either forgotten bragging his father can get anyone entry or it was just a lie to get them friendly.'

'No better place to be anonymous than amongst the many,' Joe said. Then his expression began to change. 'Look,' he said.

Doran rubbed the back of his head. The symbol to confirm

they had gained entry.

'Long shots do pay off,' Charlie said.

The two soldiers hesitated from going inside however. They stood to the side of the ticket booth away from the queue.

'What are they doing?' Joe asked.

'I got a feeling they're waiting for someone.'

Eventually a man skipped the queue strolling alongside it, and when he approached the booth he saw the two soldiers. It took him a moment to recognise them in civilian clothes. Then he ran.

'Farrelly,' Charlie and Joe said in unison.

The awol Italian soldier ran away, pushing and bumping into people. But unbeknownst to him, he ran towards Joe and Charlie.

'I got this,' Charlie said, stepping to the side. Farrelly saw the gap open between them and thought he had a route through the crowd. At the last moment, Charlie stuck his foot out and Farrelly tripped and hit the floor hard. His face took the full impact. People around them winced, but paid no other attention to the man as Joe casually helped him to his feet as if he was a concerned bystander. Farrelly quickly regained his wits, but then it was too late. Joe handcuffed him and he was surrounded as Private Doran and Frazier caught up with him. Farrelly tried to struggle free but realised it was useless.

'Looks like you're going to take a little trip with us,' Charlie said.

That same afternoon, across town, hundreds of women marched towards New York City Hall from their meeting point at the Battery.

Groups of people stood on the sidewalk, watching them pass by. Some pointed. Others laughed. Men, women, and even children rebuked them, spat in their direction, and mocked them.

'I had no idea it would be like this,' Marie said.

'People have no tolerance for beliefs that aren't the same as the majority,' Voltairine said.

'Capucine used to go through this?'

'Indeed.'

Marie saw it out of the corner of her eye. At first, she thought somebody had thrown a stone at her until it hit her on the side of the head. There was a sharp crack as the shell broke. She felt the rotten egg ooze down the side of her face. Pieces of shell clung to her hair. The smell made her wretch. She saw the person who'd thrown it laughing. It was a man old enough to know better. The people next to him laughed, too. The policeman near them smirked and did nothing.

Marie felt her temper rise. She began to pull away from the column of suffragettes, but Voltairine grabbed her arm and dragged her back.

'Are you not going to do anything about those bâtard's?' Marie shouted at the policeman.

The women around her gasped in shock at what she said.

'Marie!' Voltairine scolded her. She tugged on her arm, keeping her instep. 'Show some decorum. We should rise above it.' She offered Marie a handkerchief to clean herself with.

Marie gazed at her open-mouthed, surprised by her attitude. Voltairine held the handkerchief to her in reply, and she took it.

By now, the policeman Marie shouted at had approached

them. 'You'd be kindly reminded such language has no place coming out of a woman's mouth.'

'Well, if you—'

'She's sorry, officer. It's her first time on a march. It came as a shock.'

He scoffed at her. 'Clean yourself up. You stink.'

Marie wiped rotten egg white from her hair. A pile of blackened yolk sat in the handkerchief, and as the policeman walked away, Marie prepared to throw it at him. Voltairine slapped it from her hand, and it fell to the floor.

'Are you insane, Marie?'

'Those bâtard's threw that, and he comes and cautions me.'

'It's the way of things. You must grow a thicker skin,' Voltairine said, pulling her along, keeping her moving.

Another woman handed her another handkerchief.

'It's a good job you wore those clothes,' Voltairine said.

'These clothes?' Marie was confused. 'What do you mean?'

'Nothing,' Voltairine said. 'I just meant not your Sunday best. This is why I wore this old raincoat.'

'Because of this?' she said, pulling a lump of mouldy egg white from her hair. 'This has happened before?'

'Yes, of course. That and worse. Your sister once got hit by a stale fish. And it'll happen again today, you'll see. The closer you are to the front of the march, the worse it is. People can't wait to throw what they've brought with them. They get even more joy for hitting one of the leaders. Consider yourself honoured.'

'Doesn't it make you angry?'

Voltairine smiled and shook her head. 'Why give them more power over us? They already have enough.'

'I wanted to punch that bâtard in the face,' Marie said.

'You really are nothing like your sister. It really surprises me.'

'Capucine would've offered this side of her face to them,' Marie said, tapping the clean side of her head.

'And they would've apologised more than likely. Capucine always was capable of making people see things differently.'

Marie laughed and shook her head. Then she frowned on getting another waft of the pungent smell coming from her hair, and her mind made its circular route back to the death of her sister. 'Do you suppose she did that to her killers? Do you think they hesitated before murdering her?'

'You think it's two?'

'What do you mean?' Marie asked.

'You said killers, not killer. Have the police discovered something?'

'Oh,' Marie said. She realised she'd inadvertently let slip what Charlie and her had surmised. Marie knew she'd have to be more careful in the future. 'No, no. Sometimes my English slips,' Marie said. 'The police have no leads. At least, that's what I believe, though they always try to convince me they are a couple of steps from a breakthrough.'

'It must be frustrating?'

'It is...difficult.'

Marie could sense Voltairine was fishing for information. But why? Did she simply want to know, or was there more to it? Marie didn't know if she could live with this level of paranoia.

'One of the officers comes often to check on me. He is very kind. I think he tries to reassure me,' Marie said.

'Maybe he likes you.'

She'd taken the distraction. 'No. No, it's not like that,' Marie said, looking away, feigning embarrassment.

'It sounds like he cares for you.'

'Do you think?' Marie asked.

'Do you care for him?'

'Maybe. I...we're on a suffrage march and talking about men.'

'Well, it doesn't mean we hate them, Marie.'

'I know. I can't imagine Capucine talking like this.'

'Oh, she did.'

'On a march like this?'

'Generally yes. Of course.'

'She never talked about such things with me. Well, not so much anyhow. Did she tell you about Phillip?'

Voltairine hesitated from speaking. 'Yes,' she said and twisted her head.

'It's okay,' Marie said. 'I won't be offended. I guess we were not very close when it came to it.'

'She merely said she was courting somebody. She never said who it was, well, not his surname. I had no idea what he did.'

'Had it been long?'

'A few weeks, I believe.'

'Really?'

'We really didn't talk much about it. Whenever we met, it had to do with all this business,' she said, gesturing at the suffragettes.

Chanting struck up from the front of the march. Voltairine held her fist aloft and joined in with most of the other women. Marie walked along beside her, lost in thought. It felt strange to try and gather intelligence, as Charlie had called it. You had to be yourself to make it believable, yet twist the truth to get what you needed. The hardest part would be keeping track of the tales she had told. She'd reasoned it was like being an actor. She would need to remember her character, her backstory, and the lines she delivered. Every time she doubted whether she could do this, Marie thought about the justice her sister deserved.

CHAPTER 17

'Who are you and Vicario working for?' Joe asked.

'I work alone. For myself,' Farrelly said. He flexed his wrists where the handcuffs had been recently removed. He sat in a chair at a table in a claustrophobic room in the barracks.

'I bet you didn't expect to be back here so soon,' Wallace said.

Farrelly glowered at Wallace.

'Look, none of us has the time to get to the part where we start pulling teeth or breaking bones. There's always a deal to be cut in exchange for information,' Charlie said. 'Let's not waste days getting you to say what you'll tell us anyhow.'

'Go to hell,' Farrelly said.

Charlie sighed. 'I'm bored already.' He walked over to Farrelly, grabbed the man's hand, twisted his arm around his back, and applied pressure. Farrelly struggled, Joe protested, but then Charlie pushed harder. There was a crack. The man's arm broke, and he cried out in pain. He slumped back onto the table.

Wallace folded his arms across his chest and Charlie stalked around the table to face Farrelly.

'What are these anarchists planning?'

'I don't know who you're talking about,' Farrelly shouted. His eyes were bloodshot, his face red as he dealt with the pain.

'The anarchists you stole the explosives for.'

Farrelly shook his head. 'I didn't steal it for anarchists.'

'I thought you worked for yourself,' Charlie said. He grabbed the wrist of the man's broken arm. Farrelly feebly tried to resist. Charlie unholstered his revolver. He tossed it in the air, caught the barrel, and held it poised, ready to strike the butt down onto Farrelly's fingers. Wide-eyed, Farrelly pleaded.

'You might just get that arm fixed, Charlie said. 'But what good is it if you have no fingers left at the end of it.'

'I work for the Camorra. I don't know anything about no anarchists. I do what the Camorra tell me to do.'

'And what did they tell you to do?' Charlie asked, pushing down the man's wrist so the pain pulsed in the break.

'Steal the black powder.'

'And...'

'Take it to a warehouse, that's all.'

'What warehouse?' Charlie asked.

Not long after Charlie persuaded Farrelly to talk some more, Charlie, Joe and Wallace met outside the interview room.

'Well, there you go,' Charlie said.

'I'm not sure I approve of your methods, but they were effective,' Wallace said, raising his eyebrows.

There was a knock on the door. Then, in walked Private Frazier.

'Sir,' Frazier said and saluted.

'At ease, Private. So listen up. In short, Farrelly said he was working for the Camorra.'

Frazier glowered at the door Farrelly was behind.

'They're supposedly transporting the explosives out of Pier Seventy-Six,' Wallace continued. 'Vicario should be there.'

'And you know I'm the best shot in the company,' Frazier said.

'We need a man to scout out the Pier.'

'Wait,' Charlie said. 'We need to get down there and strike

them.'

'And we will.' Wallace looked at his pocket watch. 'In about three hours when it's dark. Private, scout out the pier and find out as much as you can. Then, when we arrive, your intel will allow us to take down the crew—'

'For arrest,' Joe said.

'For arrest,' Wallace confirmed. 'And we will reclaim the explosives. Does everyone concur?'

Charlie clenched his jaw and didn't say anything. Joe nodded, and Frazier saluted.

Matilda Joslyn Gage stood onstage in the meeting hall that evening. It was standing room only, and there was barely anywhere to do that. Even the women with seats stood as they shouted and clapped in solidarity with the white-haired woman onstage. 'As we have long since believed, it has been officially confirmed to us that no women will be allowed to attend the inauguration of the Statue of Liberty.'

A collective groan came from the audience. Matilda remained stoic as she waited for everyone to stop talking to the people they sat beside. Eventually, a hush descended across the room. 'I know it's disappointing, but it's not unexpected. We shall just have to highlight the fact so people will see how absurd it is.'

'Of course, if anybody has ideas for how we might protest, please speak up. We are open to suggestions.'

The usual suspects raised their hands and posited their usual ideas.

Marie and Voltairine glanced at each other. Voltairine went to speak but held back.

'What is it?' Marie asked.

'Nothing. It's silly,' Voltairine said, shaking her head.

'I won't tell anyone,' Marie said, encouraging her to share her idea.

'I was just thinking that if women are banned from setting foot on Bedloe Island during the ceremony, then we shouldn't.'

'We should not?'

'No. We don't even have to step on the island to make our voices heard. We could just sail right up alongside and do that.'

'From the water?'

'Yes, why not?'

'There's no reason why not. Thomas Moran said—' Marie realised she was about to reveal she had interviewed the artist while under her alter ego Camille Vallette. She coughed to hide her wince and struck herself on the chest to clear her throat.

'Moran the artist?' Voltairine asked.

'You know him?'

'I know of him. I read an interview with him recently in the newspaper.'

A chill ran through Marie. 'Yes. Yes, that one. Well, I presume it's the same one you read about. But he came in to do a talk at my art school,' Marie said, lying.

'And your point is?'

Marie shook her head. 'He said there would be a great flotilla. That's what he hopes to capture in his painting.'

Voltairine nodded slowly.

'But your idea is great,' Marie said, hoping to divert the attention away from Thomas Moran. 'If we could sail a boat through so many others and as close to the island as possible. They wouldn't see us coming. You should tell them,' Marie said, waving to the leaders of the organisation standing on the stage.

'Nevermind. It's silly.'

'It's better than anything else anyone is coming up with.'

'Maybe you're right.' Voltairine said, raising her hand.

On the stage, Matilda saw Marie waving. She cut off a woman who was taking far too long to make her point.

'Thank you, Anne. We will bear that idea in mind. Marie, is there is something you wish to add?'

'Voltairine does,' Marie said.

Everyone looked to Voltairine expectantly.

She nodded. 'Yes. I have an idea for what we might do,' Voltairine said.

'Please, we are open to suggestions.'

Voltairine edged along the row and out into the aisle. She smiled as she looked around at everyone in the hall. 'It is the sarcasm of the 19th century to represent liberty as a woman, while not one single woman throughout the length and breadth of the land is as yet in possession of political liberty. And if those great men,' she said sarcastically, 'will not let us join in their celebrations of that statue. Who is unfathomably none other than a woman. Then I say, like the great lady herself, who strides over the broken shackles at her feet, we too shall break free of the shackles of expectation they place upon us. We shall sail upon liberty and let them know that, indeed, we, too, are huddled masses yearning to breathe free! Imagine Matilda,' she said and pointed up at the woman. 'Imagine her not stood on stage, but stood on the prow of a boat, bullhorn in hand, leading a protest.' Voltairine looked at the women who were captured by the image she made. 'They've said women cannot step foot on the island, but they haven't said we can be stood mere feet away from it. It's a simple plan, so easy we haven't considered it. We charter a boat. We don't have to be on Bedloe Island to make ourselves heard.'

The women all began to smile and nod as they realised what Voltairine had proposed. Murmurings of approval went around the room.

'Well, it's certainly a bold idea to consider,' Matilda said.

The audience erupted with cheers, which turned into a wave of applause that quickly consumed everyone in the hall. It seemed the audience believed in Voltairine's idea.

Marie shook her head in admiration while also clapping in support. She wasn't sure she would be able to stay on the boat because Marie wished to storm Bedloe Island and claim the Statue of Liberty for herself and all women across the globe. There was no way this woman had killed her sister, she thought. She felt ashamed for believing such a theory. No, Voltairine had been her sister's friend. The two women had clearly supported and inspired each other in the suffrage cause. Perhaps the best way to honour her sister's legacy was to not find her killer but fight for what she believed in.

It was dusk as Joe, Charlie, Lieutenant-Colonel Wallace, and three of his men joined Private Frazier, who had been casing the pier.

The warehouse and compound at Pier Seventy-Six looked inconspicuous, like most of the others lining the banks of Manhattan Island. A gated compound led to the warehouse; a steel-framed, wooden shed, with sliding doors and filled with crates and men seemingly going about their work. Alongside the dock was a space to load and unload with a couple of hand-operated cranes running on tracks between the cobbles. There was no signage as to who operated from it; there was just one that read Pier Seventy-Six.

'I've been here since Vicario went in, and he ain't left.'

'You sure you didn't fall asleep, Private?' Wallace asked.

'No sir, no I ain't. Had my eyes on that yard the whole time waiting for that sumbitch.'

'There been much activity?'

'It's been quiet. Except one boat came, which they were loading up. I'd say they're almost done, but it's hard to tell.'

'And Vicario?' Charlie asked.

'I saw him reappear in the front yard. He seems to be overseeing things. Telling people what to do.'

'Did you glass where it came from?'

'The boat? Came from out Brooklyn direction, I'd say.'

Charlie's eyes narrowed. Both Charlie and Joe looked at each other.

'Fits with them being Camorra if so,' Joe said.

Frazier opened a notebook where he'd sketched a rudimentary plan of the pier and its building. They all gathered around to look at it. 'There's only one way in and out as far as I can see,' Frazier said. 'That's those front gates. You could potentially get to it from one of the other piers either side but you'd need to cross the quay between each pier.'

'How many men?' Wallace asked.

'Twenty-two,' Frazier said. 'At least five arrived on the boat. There are seven of them on the boat at any time loading the crates. There could also be more in the warehouse that haven't come out.'

'You seen anyone with guns?' Joe asked.

Frazier shook his head. 'No. If you didn't know, you'd say it was clean. Just a business going about its business.'

'Yet you're sure you saw this Vicario associate of Farrelly's?' Charlie asked.

'Yessir.'

Charlie looked at Wallace. 'Well, it's your men you're putting on the line. How do you wish to proceed?'

'Without a gunfight.' Wallace lowered the binoculars. 'You need answers, and we don't want this getting out into the public. This mission is strictly off the record. And I'd prefer to keep it that way. So, Doran, you and Hasting's go over the fence at the corner of the compound to the right to flank them. Frazier, you go over the same from the left. Jones, you come with me. We'll go to the front doors and see if we can't lure Vicario out. We incapacitate them as silently as possible. One by one.'

'All twenty or so men?' Charlie asked.

'One by one,' Wallace replied.

'And what about us?' Charlie asked.

Wallace took a deep breath. 'Frazier, is there a way to get to the back of the pier?'

Frazier bared his teeth and drew in a tight breath. 'Only from the river. If you had a boat, it looks open to all and sundry on the other side of those fences. You could berth right up, but you ain't gonna be able to do that.'

'We'll find a way across,' Charlie said. 'Come on, Joe.'

'You telling me you can walk on water now?' Joe asked as he went across the street with Charlie to the adjacent pier. The gates were locked for the night, so they climbed over.

They went across the compound and down the side of the warehouse. They could see the men loading crates onto the boat opposite, but nobody spotted them in the shadows.

'There's no way across,' Joe said.

'I'm gonna swim.'

Joe scrunched up his nose. 'Swim? And then what? Take them out with a wet fish?'

'I don't intend to stop them.'

Joe's brow knitted. 'Care to inform me what you intend to do then?'

'I'm gonna let them take me to wherever they want that tub to end up.'

'You're gonna swim after it?'

'No, I'm gonna go board it. Hide and then sail to wherever it goes.'

'Well, you're forgetting, it ain't sailing anywhere. Not if Wallace has his way.'

'But if they get spooked, they'll float away as quickly as possible...'

'You're gonna need a diversion,' Joe said.

Charlie nodded. 'I'm gonna need a diversion.'

Joe watched as Charlie descended the ladder attached to the dock wall into the water and swam across the quay to the boat. Cargo netting hung over the side. It was barely within reach from the waterline, but Charlie managed to grab it and climbed up onto the deck.

When he was clear, he thumbed up at Joe.

Joe thumbed back. He wasn't convinced by Charlie's plan, though he could see the reasoning behind it. Wallace's sole concern was to reclaim the explosives and apprehend those responsible. Charlie was focused on discovering who was behind the anarchist conspiracy and what they planned next. Joe hoped both outcomes could be achieved. He took Charlie's revolver from the holster and belt Charlie had left with him. The Colt was a lot heavier than his own gun. He aimed it across the quay to the boat and fired off a couple of shots. 'New York police,' he shouted. 'Stop what you're doing.'

'There's nobody called Vicario here,' the man Lieutenant-Colonel Wallace spoke to at the front gate said. He heard the gunshots ring out from the adjacent dock. His eyes grew wide. He cursed at Wallace and Private Jones, then shouted something in Italian as he returned to the compound. Three men appeared at the doors to the warehouse. They lifted their rifles and fired at Wallace and Jones. Wallace pushed Jones, and the pair split up, running in opposite directions away from the gate.

Bullets pinged off the railings, and then more bullets traced after them, but the pair made it safely away. Wallace caught his breath. His heart pounded. What the hell had happened? He was sure he'd heard Joe Petrosino shouting from the adjacent dock following the initial gunshots. His men had now opened fire from beside the crates inside the compound. He grabbed hold of the mesh wire and started climbing over the fence.

Charlie snuck up behind one of the men on the boat and punched him in the side of the head. He wasn't knocked unconscious like Charlie had hoped. The man fell forward onto a crate but quickly turned around. He rubbed the side of his head and then looked at Charlie. Charlie smiled and shrugged. Then he launched himself at the man, swinging another punch. The man leaned back, and Charlie's knuckles skimmed his chin. Then the man swung a punch and his fist connected with Charlie's jaw and it felt like a brick. Charlie's knees buckled, but he managed to stand and stagger back.

'Shall we call it a draw?' Charlie asked.

The man charged forward. Charlie sidestepped and stuck his foot out. The man tripped and head-butted the taffrail on the boat and crumpled onto the deck. Charlie winced. He didn't expect it to be that easy. There was shouting coming from further down the boat. A crate was dropped onto the deck. The crane's hook was disconnected and swung overhead. The engines had been stoked on the boat, and the water was churning beneath. Charlie knelt beside the unconscious man, found a box of matches, cigarettes and a knife. Then he picked him up and dumped him overboard. Then he found some crates covered in tarpaulin, loosened the straps and crawled underneath. Fighting continued in the warehouse and pier as the boat was unmoored and pulled away from the dock wall.

Wallace and his men overpowered the Camorra's dock workers, with only Private Doran taking a bullet to the leg. As Wallace finally reached the dockside, the boat was already heading into the bay.

He spotted Joe stood across the water on the adjacent pier. 'What the hell happened to being quiet?' Wallace shouted. 'I take it that was you shooting?'

Joe looked sheepish. He readjusted Charlie's gun belt slung over his shoulder.

'Wait, where's Charlie?'

Joe pointed at the boat.

'On there?' Wallace asked.

'He had someone sneak up on him when he boarded,' Joe lied. 'I had to alert him.'

Wallace sighed and folded his arms. 'Well, I hope he knows what he's doing.'

Charlie peered from beneath the tarpaulin. At least nine men had escaped with the boat, and they were all standing near the helm arguing and discussing what had just happened.

Beyond the stern, Manhattan Island was already shrinking into the distance across the bay. He could sense the course they had taken and where they were headed; Bedloe Island and the Statue of Liberty. He couldn't hope to arrest all of the men or stop them. He knew the odds. Charlie was outnumbered and death was likely. He could, of course, let them carry on with their plot. Surely, they were seeking to hide the explosives within the pedestal building or somewhere within the statue's structure. But what if they weren't going to wait until the opening ceremony? What if their plan was to blow it up now? There was only really one thing Charlie intended to do. No explosives heading anywhere was the best outcome.

He edged backwards and crawled from under the tarpaulin out behind the crates. He reached up and grabbed the crowbar the Italian docker had intended to hit him with.

He peered around the crates. The men were all still distracted on the helm. The sound of the boat's steam engine and the water hitting the hull was enough, Charlie hoped, to drown out any noise he was about to make. He jabbed the sharp end of the crowbar into the barrel lid and started levering and breaking the wood until he opened it up. Sure enough, it was black powder inside. Charlie twisted his lips and took a deep breath. He checked again to see that none of the men had been alerted to his presence. They hadn't been. So he twisted the barrel out from between the others and carefully eased it onto its side. He tipped a pile of powder amongst the other barrels, and then he poured out a line of powder leading away from it. He knew the men would see it once it was lit. But he knew they wouldn't have time to douse the racing sparks and flame once it was on its way.

Now, he went out into view of the men. He dragged the barrel along, spilling the black powder. A searchlight hit him. He froze. The men started shouting from the helm. He lifted the barrel upright. Someone shot at him. But they were instantly shouted at, and no more bullets were fired. Charlie fumbled out the book of matches. He struck one, but it instantly fizzled out. He struck another match, but that also went out. The third match lit and stayed alight long enough to catch the black powder. The spark hissed and flared into a bright flame that began to chase back down the powder trail. The men were already heading along the deck towards him.

'Shit,' Charlie said. He wouldn't have time to see if the men would get a chance to extinguish the flame. He threw the knife and it hit one of the approaching men in the shoulder.

Charlie then got up from behind the barrel and jumped over the rail. He hit the cold water hard and went as deeply as possible under the surface.

There was a moment of calmness. The sound of the boat's engine was muffled as it sailed past above. Bubbles in the water surrounded him. Then, the darkness was filled with light. He heard the blast. He felt the blast. His held breath was pushed out of him. Debris started hitting the surface above. He couldn't hold his breath longer. He surfaced into carnage. The heat from the burning boat was intense as he turned to face what he'd created. Wood and metal continued to rain down. A severed arm hit the water in front of him, floated and then sank. The boat barely existed. The deck and everything that was on it was obliterated. The burning hull bobbed, taking on water. The Statue of Liberty reflected the blaze. Charlie grabbed hold of a floating piece of wood and began kicking his legs, heading toward Bedloe Island.

CHAPTER 19

Marie yawned. She was sat in the window seat with her sketchbook propped up on her knee. Clouds drifted past the moon, which had finally cleared the rooftops. She pressed harder on the pastel crayon, adding a deep, long shadow of copper to a close-up portrait she'd created of the Liberty statue. She knew she'd regret working in gaslight when she saw her pastel sketch in daylight, but the act of creating distracted her from what might be happening with Joe and Charlie.

As she started smoothing the shades with her finger, there was a knock on the door to her studio. She looked up from her notebook and towards the door. She looked at her watch. It was twelve-thirty. She wasn't expecting Charlie or anyone else. She tiptoed over to the door and looked through the spy hole.

'I wasn't expecting you tonight.' Marie said, letting Charlie in and closing the door behind him. 'How did it go?'

Charlie groaned and waved his hand. 'You got anything to drink in here?'

'You're all damp. What happened? Where's Joe? Is he alright?'

'Joe's fine, kid. He's fine,' he said taking off his wet shirt.

Marie found a bottle of bourbon, took it to the table, and slid it over to Charlie. He went to take it, but she kept hold of the bottle's neck.

'What happened?' she asked.

Charlie relented and told her what had happened. He drank four long glugs straight from the bottle and smoked his pipe as he recounted the night's events with a blanket wrapped around him. Charlie shrugged, 'Then Joe came out to the wreckage on a police boat and found me waiting on Bedloe Island.'

Marie raised her eyebrows. 'You are certain it was headed for the statue?' she asked.

'Definitely.'

She frowned. 'How does it feel? I mean, how do you cope with killing so many people?'

Charlie held eye contact with her. His face was expressionless. 'For the greater good, Marie. For the greater good.' He took another swig of bourbon.

'But Charlie. You killed—' she could sense he wasn't saying what he truly felt. 'I mean, regardless. I hope the price isn't too much of a burden?'

'People who get into that line of work ought to know the potential consequences of making others' lives miserable.'

'To live by the sword goes both ways, Charlie.'

'I know what I'm doing.'

'What motivates you to do this?' she asked.

'I prefer to be on the side that brings justice.' He took another swig of bourbon. 'Tell, me about you anyhow. How did the suffragette talk go?'

Marie smiled and nodded. 'The authorities are not letting women attend the ceremony.'

Charlie tried to rub the tiredness from his forehead. 'The statue's ceremony?'

'Yes.'

He shook his head. 'Fancy not letting women attend the opening of a statue of a woman called Liberty?'

'Ironic, isn't it? Well, the suffragettes plan to charter a boat for a protest.'

'So they should.'

'If the authorities asked you to stop the boat, would you?'
Marie held Charlie's eye contact.

'Not unless the boat they're chartering is the one I sunk.'

'Well, I'm glad you're a noble man, Charlie Blaine.'

After sleeping at Marie's studio, Charlie woke early and headed downtown to City Pier A, where the NYPD's harbour department shared a building with the New York City Board of Dock Commissioners. The time on the clock tower was eight thirty when he went in and found Joe Petrosino.

'You look rough,' Charlie said. 'Did you not manage to sleep?'

'Got a couple of hours in one of the rooms out back.'

'And Wallace?'

'He's gone. Luckily for you.'

'Did he calm down?'

Joe smiled. 'Eventually. It's a good job the mayor wants to keep a lid on the whole thing.'

Joe led Charlie to a desk, where a rookie officer sat with his shirtsleeves rolled up and his hair ruffled. 'This is Henry,' Joe said. 'He's a good kid.'

He was probably only a couple of years younger than Joe. But he let it slide. Charlie shook his hand. 'Joe had you up all night working on this?'

'Sure has, but that's just fine. This case is just grand.'

Charlie looked at Joe, concerned that he'd revealed too much.

'He knows what he needs to know. But we're gonna need their help.'

'From how excited you look and that wad of papers, it

looks like you have something you're eager to share,' Charlie said to Henry.

'Sure do, sir. The dock is currently leased out to one Campania Ice Merchant.'

'You've got an address?'

'And a name. Tony Gallucci. Over in Navy Street Brooklyn.'

'And the odds of that company existing?' Charlie asked.

'Slim to none,' Joe said. 'But after last night, they'll be pissed. The Camorra don't like being challenged.'

'You really think the Camorra are behind this?'

'There's Italian involvement. It'll be the Camorra.'

'Somehow, I don't think the Camorra have a vested interest in anarchism,' Charlie said.

'Me neither. But if there's an angle to be worked, they'll exploit it somehow,' Joe said.

'We've wasted a lot of effort for there to not be a connection, Joe.'

'I don't think the Camorra care about either side of the debate. Suffragettes. Anarchists. Whatever. But if there is a way to take advantage and make a profit, you'll be sure they're at the heart of it. Wanna take a trip to Brooklyn and see how pissed they actually are?'

It was a sunny day, but it felt like a dark cloud hung over the Brooklyn neighbourhood with the energy of a brewing storm.

'Is it just me or do you feel that?' Charlie asked.

'Tension?'

'Yeah.'

'Everybody's mood is dictated by their mood. Like having an ill-tempered father.'

Charlie growled, acknowledging what Joe had said. They went across the street to a Camorra-run cafe and sat outside in the warm, drinking coffee and watching the comings and goings.

'The boss here's called Giuseppe Alfano,' Joe said. 'He not only owns this joint but is the capo of this particular clan of the Camorra.'

'So, if they're not political, why get mixed up with a political situation?'

'Money. Friends in high places give them that. And if they don't, they'll just go to the other side. Political mercenaries, you might call them.'

An overweening man put his foot on the wall near them and tied his shoelace. He paid no attention to anyone but his own reflection in the window. He smoothed his hair, adjusted his collar, and walked inside the cafe.

'Alessandro Parretti. Cocky shit by all accounts,' Joe said eyeballing the man as he went inside.

'I never would've guessed,' Charlie said. 'How'd you know so much about these guys?'

'I think they're a stain on good Italian people. Good Italian American people. Those in charge won't let me do anything about them.'

'Because they're on the payroll?'

'Let's just say I'm not entirely comfortable letting them know the case has taken this turn.'

Charlie watched as Alessandro Parretti left the cafe carrying a parcel under his arm.

'Well, I don't have time for this,' Charlie said. 'Maybe it needs the touch of someone who hasn't got the restraints of someone in your profession.' Charlie stood. 'Wait nearby. I'll be back soon.'

Charlie went in the direction Alessandro Parretti had gone and followed him from a distance. They'd walked a couple of blocks when Alessandro suddenly turned down an alley. Charlie followed after him. But halfway down the alley, Alessandro stopped and faced Charlie. The young Italian held a knife.

'Alright, pal, what do you want? A belly full of blade?' Alessandro asked.

'Don't think that's happening anytime soon,' Charlie said, drawing his gun.

The young man's eyes narrowed. He spat his toothpick on the floor.

'I want to know what all the commotion is about,' Charlie asked.

'What are you, the busy police? People working, what do you think they're doing?'

Charlie stalked towards him with the gun bearing down on him. 'Has your boss sent you to get some ice for the cafe?'

The penny dropped, and Charlie could see the realisation in Alessandro's eyes.

'I guess you'll be going to collect it from the warehouse, but I didn't see much ice there.'

'It's been a warm week. It must have melted.'

'The only thing that melted was your boat. And several of your colleagues. I don't give a fuck that you guys are pulling whatever job it is. I just want to know who you're working for.'

'Are you a cop?'

'Do cops dress like this?'

He tilted his head to the side and regarded Charlie's attire. Then he sneered. He scratched the dimple at the corner of his mouth and said, 'I don't know the client, but I can take you to people who do.'

'Yeah? I bet you can.'

'That's all I'm offering.'

It was Charlie's turn to consider the man. Then he looked down at his gun and then back at the man who looked unconcerned.

'Are we going or what?' Alessandro asked.

'You pull anything, and I pull the trigger.'

Finally, Alessandro frowned. 'What? You actually wanna go see the boss?'

'Only if the organ grinder actually has got something to say. Because the monkey sure doesn't.'

Alessandro grinned and laughed. 'Oh, he'll have plenty to say, alright.'

Joe stood on the porch of the sweet shop, open-mouthed, nearly letting liquorice spill from a paper bag as Charlie marched Alessandro Parretti back down the middle of Navy Street with a gun pointed at his back.

'Hey Franco,' Alessandro called out to one of the waiters serving customers at a table. 'Get Giuseppe out here. I got a man who wants to talk about ice.'

Everyone in the street stopped going about their business and gawped at what was happening. It was a little while before Giuseppe came out, but when he did, it was as if everyone in the street, even those who sat at tables outside the cafe, obeyed some silent command and left. Within less than a minute, the usually bustling street was deserted.

Giuseppe Alfano, the boss Alessandro had called for, walked casually onto the street, flanked by four men.

His clean white shirt sleeves were rolled up. His hands were in his pockets, and his well-polished shoes, as shiny as his slick-backed, well-oiled hair, glinted in the sun.

'Got yourself into a spot of bother there, Leo'

'No. Just got a man who likes conversation.'

'I believe you boys like transporting products that have a habit of transforming beyond their form. Artichokes get eaten and turned into shit. Ice melts and turns to water. And gunpowder. Well, it sets fire and burns, doesn't it?'

'What? Are you a scientist? Who the fuck are you?'

'Never mind who I am. I want to know who you're working for?'

'You come to me, call me out on my street and ask me to rat on myself? You never dealt with our type before, have you?'

'I've dealt with plenty like you.'

'And what type is that mr know it fucking all?'

'Those that prey on the weak. Those that stroll and strut not actually having to do anything because everyone's too scared of what they might do.'

'It sounds a lot like you're calling us bullies.'

'Do you know what the name Comanche means?' Charlie said.

'Enlighten me.'

'It means anyone who wants to fight me all the time. You see, I grew up learning how to fight the Comanche because, unlike you sons of bitches that only know how to smash a couple of windows and scare shopkeepers into paying you protection, the Comanche smashes your bones like glass with his tomahawk. And while you're on the floor, unable to move, he comes at you with his knife. And he takes the scalp right off your head while you're still alive.'

'You don't look much like a native.'

'No. No, I'm not. But now I get to the point of why I refer to my dealings with Comanches. You see, like you, they appear in small groups, and everyone's scared of them, but that's where the similarities end. But...' Charlie said, raising his hand and wagging his finger like a priest on Sunday. 'But, my method of dealing with you both remains exactly the same. You see, my father raised me shooting. Shooting fast. Shooting accurate.'

'Let me share a cultural curiosity and translate a word for you, mr?'

'Blaine. Charlie Blaine.'

'Omertà. Omertà, Mr Blaine, in Italian, means importance in the virtue of being silent. Especially to outsiders.'

'I thought you might say that.'

Charlie kicked Alessandro in the back of the legs. He dropped to his knees, and Charlie shot over his head.

Three of Giuseppe's men were dead without reply. The last man standing of Giuseppe's men shot at Charlie, but Charlie had dropped to his knee and put a bullet in the man's ribs. Giuseppe scrambled on his hands and knees over to retrieve a gun from one of his dead men. Charlie shot him in the knee. He screamed out in pain.

Giuseppe tried to reach out for the gun.

'Unless you want the other knee taken care of, I suggest your hand stays where it is.'

Charlie grabbed a fistful of Alessandro's oily hair and dragged him over to Giuseppe.

He pointed his gun at the boss. 'Who you working for?'

'Omertà.'

'And I told you what Comanche means,' Charlie said, then struck Giuseppe across the face with his gun. His nose split. Blood gushed.

'You fucking, mother fucking—'

Charlie hit him again.

Giuseppe's eyes went wide.

'Anarchists,' he eventually said quietly.

'Speak up, I can't hear you.'

'Anarchists. They call themselves the Black Veil,' Giuseppe said, and then he spat blood on the floor.

'Anyone in particular?'

'We don't know their names.'

'You expect me to believe that?'

'He said—'

'What, are you his parrot?' Charlie said, kicking Alessandro in the stomach. 'Am I an ornithologist now? I got myself a parrot and a canary? Start singing.'

'You got company,' Joe said from the porch of the sweet shop.

Charlie looked up. A gang of men carrying various weapons, including shotguns, headed down the street.

'Bastards won't shoot unless they've come to take care of this rat. It's a good job I didn't shoot your other knee after all. On your feet.'

Charlie grabbed Giuseppe by the scruff of the neck and hauled him to his feet. He held the gun to the man's head. The gang stopped.

Charlie edged back, dragging the hobbling Giuseppe. Joe came up alongside him and held his gun pointed at the gang. Alessandro crawled away across the cobbles to the cafe.

'I'd cut your losses with the anarchists now if you want to keep the rest of your empire intact. Tell me where I can find these anarchists, or I'll tell everyone watching that you're a stinking, squealing little snitch.'

Giuseppe spat out blood, and it dribbled down onto his shirt and mixed with the rest of it. 'Meetings were held in the Mills-Parker Building, but it burnt down.'

'Alright, one more thing—'

'We gotta go, Charlie,' Joe said. They had backed up into the entrance to an alleyway and had a clear escape route.

'Did you intend to blow up the statue?'

'Yeah, and I wish we had.'

The sound of Charlie's gun firing echoed down the alley. Giuseppe fell on his face into the street.

Both Charlie and Joe turned and ran. Bullets struck the walls at the entrance to the alley.

'What the hell, Charlie, did you kill him?' Joe asked as they ran.

'Shot him in the back of the knee.'

A short while later, after navigating the streets, Charlie and Joe stopped running as they approached the Brooklyn Bridge. A crowd of suffragettes stood waiting to march.

'Let's try and avoid those.'

'Jesus, Charlie,' Joe said as he caught his breath. 'Do you realise what you've done? You just cut the head off the snake.'

'Good. I don't like snakes. It's about time the East Coast got some Western-style justice.'

Four women had apparently joined the New York City Woman Suffrage Association because of the march a couple of days earlier at the town hall. It didn't seem like many to Marie, yet Matilda Joslyn Gage had spoken of it like a great victory. And so they had decided to march again, hoping to find more support. Marie already knew what she aimed to do that day. After getting egged in the previous march and seeing little progress made regarding the investigation into her sister's murder, Marie would be seen to be letting her frustrations get the better of her. Hopefully, this would draw out the more extreme factions within the suffragettes.

It was a sunny midday as another hundred or so suffragettes gathered in Brooklyn to cross the bridge to Manhattan. It surprised Marie that there were a couple of men in the group. They seemed to be the type of men who wanted to gain favour with some of the women either romantically or to be seen as progressive. Which usually meant they wished to be romantic either way. She wondered if this role as a spy was making her cynical. Had she always been naive up until this point in her life? She'd always taken people at face value for who they appeared to be and what they said they were. But now, as she stopped and observed people, she began to think differently. Perhaps everyone led a double life, really.

As they waited to begin, Marie targeted Amelia, the receptionist from the Astor library who had escorted her to the New York City Woman Suffrage Association meeting when she was trying to locate her sister.

'Do you think they're capable of making a change? How

many weeks go by with just marching and talking?' Marie asked.

'You think there should be more action?'

'Maybe,' Marie said, pausing to think about what she meant to say. Really, she knew exactly where she wanted to steer the conversation. 'I'll be as old as Madame Gage by the time anything happens, even if it does.'

'Some believe a more direct approach would yield better results.'

'Direct action? Like what? Going to vote? Imagine if we all placed a ballot regardless of whether we were allowed or not.'

The young woman looked excited by the prospect. 'I like that idea, Marie. But no, when I say direct action, I mean violence. Attacks.'

When Amelia spoke of such action, her eyes widened with excitement as if she were trying to sensationalise the idea. She looked like an excited gossiper rather than an anarchist. Marie feigned a look of surprise. 'Really? Attacks on who?'

'Politicians, the wealthy. Antis. Attacks on buildings and infrastructure. Acts of disruption.'

'It sounds like the reign of terror,' Marie said, thinking about France's struggle during the Revolution, which she'd learned about in school.

'You don't think it would help the cause?'

'Do you?'

'Somewhat...'

'Really?'

'Imagine if I just climbed over that railing on a Monday morning,' Amelia said. 'Imagine me standing in front of one of the cable cars and stopping all those people from getting where they wanted to go.'

'You'd probably get crushed. I don't believe those car-trains have drivers.'

'I'd make the papers. Imagine the publicity.'

'Wouldn't it annoy people, though? People are less likely to support us if you disrupt their lives for the worse.'

Amelia's excitement waned.

Marie looked into the distance, feigning thought. 'It should be those who have power who are targeted. Those who wish to lose it by us having the vote.'

Amelia's enthusiasm returned faster than a steam train. 'Politicians. Merchants. Bankers. The Police. Industrialists.'

Marie nodded. 'The more disruption they faced. The more money they lose. We should squeeze them by their—'

'By their what?' Voltairine had spotted Marie and Amelia in the crowd and joined them.

'Oh, nothing, we were just getting over-excited.'

'Excited about what?' Voltairine asked as she leant into the two younger women and whispered. 'Squeezing a man's testicles?'

Their eyes grew wide. Then, the three of them burst into laughter.

'I dare say that is not going to get us the vote,' Marie said.

'With the right man, it might,' Voltairine said.

'We are hearing a side to you today that I didn't know existed.'

'We all have our secrets, Marie,' she said, linking arms with her. Come on, ladies. They're due to start. Let's see if we can assume a more senior position at the front of the group.

The trio began going through the crowd to where the Association's leaders stood elevated on the boardwalk in the bridge's centre.

Matilda Joslyn Gage held a banner aloft with the

Association's logo embroidered upon it. 'Come, women. Let us march over the Hudson's waves and hear us sing over the city.' She started singing, and the crowd began to join her.

'I thought you said being at the front makes one prone to getting hit with more eggs and flour than it would take to bake a cake,' Marie said to Voltairine.

'Indeed I did, didn't I? Then it's a good job we're on the bridge and not on the street. I doubt they'll be able to reach us from the sidewalks.' She glanced sideways at Marie.

'Why, you wily thing...' Marie said.

'You should be our General with a strategy like that,' Amelia joked. 'I'd follow you with that level of thinking.'

They'd made it a quarter of the way across the bridge when four policemen approached them. They held batons and spaced themselves abreast of the walkway blocking the suffragette's route.

One of the policemen in the middle raised his hand, prompting those leading to stop before them.

'I'm afraid you'll have to turn back, ladies,' he said.

'On what grounds?' Matilda asked.

'On the grounds that I said so.'

'And if we don't?'

'Let us not get to that stage,' he said, twisting the baton in his hand.

Matilda went to the other leaders, and they began to converse.

'Look at that bâtard smirking,' Marie said, nodding towards the policeman.

'Just because you say it in French doesn't mean we don't know what you're saying.'

'Well, they are. So smug.'

'What do you think they'll do?' Amelia asked.

'You've known them longer than I have,' Marie said.

'They'll back down,' Voltairine said.

Marie tutted. 'They'll never get anywhere if they back down.' She could sense Voltairine studying her.

'What do you think, Vee?' Amelia asked.

'I think we're about to find out,' Voltairine said.

Matilda stood alongside the other leaders. 'We respectfully agree not to march.'

Marie sighed. Voltairine took a deep breath.

'But,' Matilda continued,' it is such a nice day, and we all live mainly on that side of the Hudson, that we shall walk across, not march.'

Marie's eyebrows raised. She smiled at the woman's move.

'You see,' Voltairine said. 'Sometimes a heavy hand and a rash temper are not the right tools for the job.'

Marie continued to smile. 'I guess I still have a lot to understand about the workings of the cause.' She linked arms with Voltairine, and they began strolling alongside the other women.

However, when they reached the policemen, the officers braced and raised their batons above their heads. The nervous ones looked to the one who had so far done the talking.

'We asked you politely. Now, let's not make a scene.' He prodded Matilda's shoulder with the baton.

Matilda and the other women stopped. He leaned in towards Matilda and whispered something in her ear. Matilda, who was usually a ferocious-looking, fearless woman, faltered.

She immediately turned around and ushered the suffragettes to head back the other way. They went past Marie, Amelia and Voltairine, who stood there trying to imagine what had been said.

Word spread that they should all walk back the way they'd come.

'I've never seen her change like that,' Amelia said.

'We should do as instructed,' Voltairine said.

As the suffragettes moved away, Marie remained in the centre of the walkway. She stood facing the policemen.

Marie took the cardboard box out of her satchel and turned it over in her hand. The four policemen were opposite. Their spokesman smirked. The others stood taller as if they'd gained confidence from not having to go through with their threats.

'Marie,' Voltairine shouted. 'What are you doing? Come on.'

Some of the women turned to look at what she was doing. Marie smiled devilishly and weighed the cardboard box in her hand. She could feel the paint swishing about inside the pig skin in the box.

Voltairine pushed her way through the crowd, heading towards Marie.

'Votes for women,' Marie screamed at the top of her voice. Then she launched the cardboard box containing the pig skin full of paint. It seemed to fly through the air in slow motion before it hit one of the policemen, who lifted his arm to block it. The pig skin exploded on impact. Gold paint erupted, covering several of the policemen.

One of the policemen sat stunned on the floor. It took him a brief moment to realise it was paint and not his own blood covering him, and then he stood. His grip tightened on his baton, and then he ran at Marie. Marie tried to edge backwards, but the crowd was dense and unwittingly blocked her escape. He swung the truncheon at Marie and hit the back of her leg above the knee. Her leg buckled from the impact, and then the punch swung in and connected with her chin. First, her vision went blurry. She spun around and blacked out before she hit the floor.

When she came to, Marie found her vision slowly coming into focus on the wooden slats of the decking she lay on. She felt the pain throbbing in her head. She went to hold her head but discovered that she couldn't move her arms. The cold steel of the handcuffs dug into her wrists.

CHAPTER 22

'Are you okay, Marie?' Joe Petrosino asked later that day. He was dressed smartly in a police uniform, the buttons on his black jacket polished and glistening.

'I'll live,' Marie said, sitting on the chair holding the ice pack to her chin. A table and a few chairs filled the interview room. Charlie leant against the wall, smoking his pipe.

'I'm sorry they were so heavy-handed,' Joe said. But you'll understand we couldn't risk telling them the real reason behind your actions.'

'Don't worry. Their violence probably helped the cause more than you realise.'

'They were given orders not to use excessive violence against suffragettes however.'

Marie rolled her eyes.

'After a bomb was thrown at the police during the Haymarket incident, they're all a bit jumpy,' Joe continued.

'Are you trying to defend them, Joe?'

'No. Of course not. I'm embarrassed.'

'Well, you'd think they could discern the difference between a bomb and paint? Maybe he just felt ashamed and couldn't control himself?'

'Maybe you're getting too involved in the suffragette cause,' Charlie said.

'Too involved? You're the one that told me to do this,' she said, feeling betrayed by Charlie. She watched him, hoping he would smile and show he was joking, but he didn't. 'It seems to me that the rise of anarchy and the call for suffrage is related to one thing.'

'What's that?' Charlie asked.

'Inequality. Maybe you should do more about the crimes committed by those in power in this city. In this country.'

'I'm pulling you from this operation.'

'Wait a minute, Charlie,' Joe said.

'She's forgotten why she's even doing this. You've gotten too involved,' Charlie said, pointing at her.

'Forgotten?' She laughed in disbelief. 'I haven't forgotten my sister was brutally murdered, and her body hung in front of me.'

Marie and Charlie glared at each other.

'Marie, we're just concerned,' Joe said. 'It's a lot to deal with after what happened.'

'I told her, Joe, all she needed to do was gather information. I didn't think she'd become so invested.'

'Well, maybe you're both not making enough progress. I'm having to take matters into my own hands.'

'She's right, Charlie. Liberty's unveiling is approaching, and we're no closer to discovering who's behind all of this.'

'I know. Don't you think I don't realise that?' Charlie said, shaking his head. 'Look. The suffragette angle isn't the only one we have.' He looked at Joe for support.

'This is your gig,' Joe said to Charlie.

Charlie looked around the clinical room. 'Maybe this isn't the best place to talk, and maybe today isn't the best day to do it either?' Charlie said. 'But I don't think the suffragette angle is one we can afford to pay so much attention to any more.'

In a building midway down 5th Avenue, Voltairine looked around the chic office that Benedict had arranged for the

Black Veil to meet at. The setting sun cast an orange glow through the tall windows. It was a world away from the darkened, draughty space they had used to meet in the attic of the Mills-Parker Building. Clément Duval paced around the room as he always did. Five other people, including Voltairine, sat at the table. They comprised of people from all walks of life and many nationalities. They permeated various levels of society, and all had the same goal. Annihilation of the state. The number of members sitting around the polished oak table had also decreased. James McGarrity had never appeared since the Mills-Parker Building had burnt down. He was presumed dead. Giuseppe Alfano had failed his mission, and the boat had blown up in the bay. He had blamed another Camorra clan for the explosion, yet the word on the street was he'd been shot but was still alive. It seemed like an impending civil war between the Italian crime syndicates was having an adverse effect on the anarchist's plan. But all was not lost.

'Rest assured,' Benedict confirmed. 'It is not a setback. Our plans will proceed as intended. Alberta has already found a replacement for Mr McGarrity.'

'Indeed,' the older American woman called Alberta said. 'And there's no doubt he will pass the test of trust. We should be able to proceed without too much delay and keep to our initial schedule.'

Clément stopped pacing. 'You all recognise I'm an advocate of action?' he said and waited for them to agree.

'Of course, we recognise that,' Benedict said in a friendly manner.

Clément nodded. 'I do not believe we should continue this path of destruction.'

'We must destroy to rebuild,' Voltairine said.

Clément waved away what she said. 'We must inspire the people with our acts.' He looked around the room, gauging their reaction. A couple of people nodded.

'You have us on the edge of our seats, Clément. Please, tell,' Voltairine said, sarcastically.

'We exploit the inequality within the city. The rich are filthy rich, and the poor are desperately poor. So herein is my plan. An age-old plan. We will steal from the rich and redistribute the wealth to the poor.' He clapped his hands together, spread his arms wide and waited for their response.

Benedict leaned back in his chair and steepled his fingers.

Clément looked for support around the room. His smile began to twist into pursed lips.

Voltairine shook her head. 'It's not something we can do.'

'Why not? Such acts have always inspired nothing but love and admiration among the people.'

'Which is why we must avoid such acts,' she said.

'There is a danger, Clément, we might draw attention to ourselves,' Benedict said. 'We do not wish to become heroes or martyrs for a cause because, believe me, they will do everything in their power to turn us into villains. This is why we remain in the shadows.'

'But the people will love us for our deeds,' Clément said.

Voltairine shook her head. 'Why now do you question our plan? Yes, we must commit acts that expose the authorities as being useless. We must show them they are unfit to govern and protect the people. Yes, we must highlight the inequality.'

'Then why do you oppose my proposal? We want the same thing, do we not?'

'Of course we do. But we differ in our method of achieving these goals,' Benedict said.

'You agreed to our plan,' Voltairine said. 'We do not intend to deviate from it now at such a late stage. The inauguration draws ever closer.'

'This is ridiculous!' Clément said. 'Why do you always get to decide?' Clément thumped his hand on a cabinet. 'You are dangerously close to acting like you are the authority.'

'Clément, my friend,' Benedict said. 'You must understand why we have to collectively make decisions?'

'Collectively, yes. But it always seems to be what you and Voltairine want. It is becoming a tyranny of a tiny majority.'

Benedict leant forward. 'If we did not have a consensus, then we'd have...'

'What? Anarchy?'

'You misconstrue what I say.'

'Do I?' Clément started walking to the door.

'Where are you going?' Voltairine asked.

'To the tavern.'

Clément went through the door and slammed it behind him.

'Let him go,' Benedict said.

'He is a threat. I don't trust him. He will get drunk and start shouting his mouth off,' Voltairine said.

'Elias. We all know he trusts you,' Benedict said. 'Go and be a good friend to Clément. Lend an ear for him to grumble into, and make sure he doesn't say anything anyone might hear.'

'Ay. It might be for the best,' Elias said. The quiet Dane wearily pushed his chair out from under the table, headed for the door, and left the room.

'Everyone knows the penalty for betrayal,' Voltairine said when the door closed.

'Don't dare question our commitment,' a first-generation

American-Austrian called Lena said. 'We all risk a lot.'

'All he is arguing for is more direct action,' Alberta said. 'None of us think that is a bad thing.'

'No, none of us do,' Voltairine said. 'But if we all start randomly committing acts and one of us gets copped, that becomes a risk to us all.'

'You've got to see how being controlled by a higher, let us face it, authority such as ourselves can wind up a man who believes in the cause so vehemently like Clément does,' Alberta said.

'The sooner the day comes, the better,' Lena said.

'But that is not the denouement of our project, is it?' Voltairine asked.

'No,' Lena agreed. 'It is merely the spark that lights the firework.'

Everyone in the room exchanged glances with each other. Benedict drummed on the table with his fingers. 'Well, maybe, believe it or not, Clément has the right idea by going for a drink. Shall we adjourn for today?'

Nobody replied. Voltairine looked to Benedict. There was something she wanted to raise with the group, but she knew there was probably a better time.

Everyone started to stand or turn to talk to the person next to them. By the time everyone had eventually left, Voltairine was still sitting in the chair at the table, lost in thought. She would love to unleash nothing but act after act in the name of their cause. But she knew the public would soon fear them, and the authorities would label them terrorists like what had happened in so many countries across Europe.

'You look like you could use a drink, too, Benedict said. 'You carry the weight and worries of us all.'

'I do what I must. For the cause.'

'It's taking its toll. Learn to share the burden.'

'I would if everyone else would learn to accept it. They're all either giddy with their increasing power or completely losing sense of what we aim for. Clément is like a bad gambler that's had a little success but doesn't know when to quit.'

'Elias will take care of him. Now go, get some rest.'

Voltairine stood and lingered by the window. Across 5th Avenue, Central Park was bathed in the blue evening light following the sunset. 'Capucine's sister is becoming quite the revolutionary,' she said.

Benedict remained sat at the head of the table. He steepled his fingers.

'Really?'

'She was arrested for throwing a paint bomb at the police while we marched.'

Benedict's eyebrows raised. 'She did?'

'Though I doubt without her sister's death she would've become quite active with suffrage.'

'You sound suspicious of her?'

Voltairine turned around and perched on the windowsill. 'Marie?' Voltairine laughed. 'God, no. No. Not at all. She cares mostly for her art. She's actually quite good.'

'So why is she suddenly involved?'

'Because she has an artist's passion and wants to feel like she's doing something to honour her sister. She doesn't suspect a thing.'

'So you like her then?'

'Yes. Maybe I do. Like many artist's she's a freethinker. She might have been a motivated advocate of the cause.

'You don't think she'd join us?'

'Join us?' Voltairine laughed in disbelief at his suggestion. 'Wait. You're being serious?'

'Of course. If the injustice of her sister's death rages within her, she could be a useful ally. Grief is a powerful motivator, as you know.'

Voltairine understood what he meant. Her grief had brought her to seek revenge. At first thought, it seemed like a ridiculous idea. But it also made sense. Marie seemed impressionable to a degree but was also fuelled by a strong sense of injustice. Much like she had been. An uneasy thought took hold of Voltairine. Had Benedict groomed her, too? Had he used her pain or merely showed her a path. She shook her head. Now was not the time to ponder such thoughts.

'What is it?' Benedict asked, holding Voltairine's gaze.

'I was thinking of the ways we could use her.'

Benedict leaned back in his chair. 'There are many ways she could be useful.' He began to smile.

CHAPTER 23

Several blocks away in the Lighthouse tavern, Elias found Clément drinking heavily and chatting to a bawdy woman.

'So!' he bellowed, pointing at Elias in the doorway. 'They sent you.'

A few people in the tavern turned to see who had entered, but they were unimpressed and turned back to their conversations or drinks.

Elias clapped Clément on the shoulder.

'Are you here to enforce their will?'

'Bollocks. I'm here to drink,' Elias said.

Clément's frown turned into a broad smile, and then he slapped his hand on the bar. 'Barkeep, two more ales.'

'Hey, what about me?' the woman trying to drape herself over Clément asked.

'Have you got a good-looking friend with you tonight?' Clément asked.

'I'm here on my own.'

'Then fucking leave!' he shouted.

The woman's smile faded along with her presence.

'Take your goddamned perfume with you too,' Clément said, waving the lingering scent away with his hand. As the barman placed a tankard on the bar, Clément knocked it over.

'You'll be paying for that one,' the bartender said.

Elias placed some coins onto the bar. 'And one to replace it. And a growler, too.'

The bartender eyed him, took the coin, picked up the tankard, and refilled it from a barrel. He placed it and the ceramic growler onto the bar.

'Those bâtard's are playing a dangerous game,' Clément said as Elias handed him the tankard.

'Don't consider our allies as enemies,' Elias said. 'We all want the same outcome.'

'This country will never become anarchist. Not with those trying.'

'Don't lose sight. We have as much influence as them, do we not?' Elias said, quietly hoping Clément would talk in the same hushed tones.

But he did not, and he laughed loudly. 'Every single thing is dictated by Voltairine and Benedict. They think themselves to be our betters, our rulers.'

'What is it you crave for then?'

Clément's eyes narrowed. He grabbed his tankard from the bar and pulled on Elias's arm, taking him to a table.

Clément leaned over the table, nearly burning his beard on the candle's flame. Elias moved it to the side.

'Action. Action is what I want, Elias,' Clément whispered.

'What kind of action?'

'Redistribution of wealth. I want to make that happen.'

'How would you?' Elias asked, wishing he'd bought more alcohol.

'A friend of mine who is a chimney sweep goes to a woman's house. She is a heiress. Lives alone in this massive house full of...full of things. It's unfair that one person has so much while so many have so little.'

James was nodding. 'This is true.'

'I want to take what this woman has. It would be an easy job. I want to take all her fine jewellery and give it to the people.'

'Voltairine and Benedict won't like this.'

Fuck them! I will do it in the name of the Black Veil,' he said, waving his arms wide again. His tankard flew across the tavern, hitting the bar before spinning on the floor.

Elias rolled his eyes. But then the bartender, talking to some patrons away from the bar, saw what had happened. He came at Clément from behind and wrapped his arms around him, enveloping him in a bear hug. He lifted him off the stool. Clément kicked his legs and tried to squirm free of the man's grasp. It made no difference. The bartender carried him across the tavern and threw him out through the doors. Elias raised his hands in surrender when the bartender turned on him.

'You keep him the fuck out of here. Else I'll be dragging my shotgun out of retirement. You hear?'

'No problem, sir,' Elias said, placating the bartender.

James went outside and found Clément picking himself up off the cobbles.

'Clem,' he said, putting his arm under the man's arm to keep him upright.

'That son of a bitch is going to get it,' he said, pointing at the doors he'd flown out of. Then he shouted, 'I'll blow the whole fucking building to rubble.'

He started lunging towards the tavern's doors. Elias pulled on his arm, and they veered off to the side of the building.

'You have got to go home and sober up. You put too much at risk.'

'He. He. Bâtard. Fuck made a laughing stock of me.'

Elias pushed him away from staggering towards the door. But he hadn't seen the flick knife Clément had fumbled from his pocket. Clément lurched towards the entrance again. Elias stood in his way. The blade slipped easily into Elias's belly. Neither man realised what had happened at first. They stood apart. Elias felt the pain. He grabbed his stomach. Blood poured out of the cut. In Clément's hand was the blood-smeared knife.

Clément had killed many people, but he hadn't meant this. Elias collapsed onto the floor.

'I'm. I'm sorry, El,' he said, folding the flick knife. He saw the blood on his hand. Somebody came out of the tavern. Clément started edging back from the scene. And then he turned and ran.

CHAPTER 24

Marie woke shivering. She'd kept her window open to let the sounds of the city enter in the morning. It made her feel less lonely. It would be cold in Paris, too, she thought. Of all the places you could go in the world. You should've chosen somewhere warm. Where else is there for art, though? She swung her legs off the side of the bed and sat up. She felt giddy. The bruises on the back of her legs throbbed where she'd been struck by the truncheon.

She ached all over. She stretched her arms and twisted her wrists where the handcuffs had been fastened too tightly. She stood and lit her stove. As she prepared some coffee, there was a knock on the door to her studio. She sighed. Charlie was the last person she wanted to deal with.

There was another knock on the door.

'I'm coming,' she shouted. Her voice was raspy. She downed a glass of water. She was running low and needed some more from the pump. She picked up her bucket. She would send Charlie and buy herself some time to get dressed.

She went over to the door, pulled the bolts across, turned the key in the lock, and opened it. 'I don't need another lecture—'

Voltairine stood there.

Marie was surprised. 'Vee,' she said.

'Are you not going to invite me in?'

'Ummm, yes. Of course.' Marie stood was worries something was left on display in the studio that might reveal their investigation.

'Well?' Voltairine said.

Marie shook her head. 'Yes. Of course. Come in,' she said, stepping aside. Voltairine entered the studio but didn't look around the room. She looked at Marie.

'How are you feeling?'

'Sore,' Marie said, putting the bucket on the floor.

'Well, I hope you've learned your lesson.'

Marie frowned. 'What?'

'You shouldn't have done that,' Voltairine said.

Marie took a deep breath. 'I've been lectured to by the police and my uncle most of yesterday,' she said, lying about Charlie's identity.

'And?'

'And what?'

'You know not to do anything like that again?'

Marie glared at her. 'Who are...' she took a deep breath rather than finish the sentence. 'Are you concerned about my well-being or what our beloved leader's reaction might be?'

Voltairine's demeanour changed. She reached a hand out to Marie, who folded her arms.

'Of course, I'm concerned. It just all happened so quickly. One moment, you were next to me. Then, you threw the paint. The next moment, the police were arresting you.'

'I'm aware of what happened. I have the bruises to show for it. I just couldn't stand marching, chanting, doing... nothing. Then, when they stopped us from walking, who will remember a march? What newspaper will print a column on the front page about a march?'

'You're right. Gage and the other leaders are not happy. Some of them were proposing to expel you from attending future meetings.'

'Then let them.'

Voltairine frowned. 'How do you go from not caring about the cause to suddenly wanting to fight for it?'

'I told you. I knew I'd find it frustrating, so I never got involved.'

'So, you'd rather do nothing or get arrested? You must see that is extreme?'

'Not as extreme as I'd like.'

Voltairine shook her head. 'Maybe it is not extreme, but more immature. Marie, you have a lot of explaining to do if you decide you don't want to be expelled. And I really hope you do explain yourself because it would be a shame to tarnish your sister's reputation.'

They stood silently for a while, neither one looking in the other's direction.

'Your sister and I were involved in a cause beyond the suffragettes,' Voltairine eventually said.

Marie's gaze shot up from the floor. She studied Voltairine's face.

'That is why we, I, do not let my emotions get the better of me. That is why your sister didn't let her emotions run wild.'

'What do you mean,' Marie asked. 'I don't understand.'

'Capucine and I believed in the suffrage cause, but like you, we didn't believe it did enough.'

'What are you involved in?'

'What do you know of anarchism?'

'Anarchism?' Marie asked. Her brow was furrowed in confusion. 'You're saying Capucine was an anarchist?'

'You say it like it's a dirty word.'

'I don't. I'm not. Capucine wasn't violent.'

'Violence? You think it's all about violence?'

'The Haymarket Riot was violent—'

Voltairine laughed, waving the suggestion away. 'Do you

think those who rule us do so out of the goodness of their hearts? Or do they do it to obtain, grow and keep power? To profit at our expense.' She began pacing around the room as she spoke. 'Those who govern would portray us as violent, and yes, there are people who would use more revolutionary tactics—'

'Is this why my sister died? Because she was an anarchist?'

'The police, of course, wouldn't tell you the truth.'

'And you know the truth. Who killed my sister?'

'The authorities. The institutions. The state.'

'You sound like a conspiracy theorist.'

'Capucine and Phillip Moses were murdered by our rulers. Of course, indirectly. It's not like they would do the deed themselves. But their minions, their foot soldiers. They killed them. As a warning.'

Marie held her head in her hands. She sat shaking her head as Voltairine let her comprehend what she said. Eventually, Marie dropped her hands from her face. 'Why?'

'Because they fear to lose their power.'

'And my sister, and you, you held enough power to make those already with it fear you?'

Voltairine paused from answering. She ran her tongue along the inside of her top lip as she considered Marie's question. 'It would seem so.'

'Why are you telling me this? Why now? Why not before?'

'Over twenty years ago, the building of the Tweed Courthouse commenced. Apparently, it cost three hundred and fifty thousand dollars to carpet the courthouse. Another contractor was paid one hundred and thirty thousand dollars for two days of work on window frames. Do you understand what I'm saying, Marie? Only five years ago, it was finished. Can you imagine the amount of money that exchanged hands during that period? I won't bore you with the details, but political organisations like Tammany Hall and its leaders such as William Tweed, who oversaw the courthouse's construction, added even more money to their millions. They embezzled over three hundred million dollars, assisted by a ring of political allies. These people still control this city. And more people like them sit in every city. Even Washington D.C.'

Marie shook her head. 'It's wrong.' Her words were barely audible.

'The United States wasn't like Britain or France, where its wealth was passed from generation to generation. People came here, and they stole, and they grabbed, and they took what wasn't theirs. They leave nothing but wreckage of lives in their wake while the dollars in their banks accumulate beyond even the wealth of lords or princes.'

Marie's breathing had grown deeper as she became more angry. Her countenance had glowered as she heard the injustice.

'My father died fighting against injustice in the Paris Commune,' Marie said. 'You say my sister died the same way?'

Voltairine nodded. 'Marie. You have to be disciplined. We cannot take the fight to them directly. They court the public's opinion. They have the power to influence how they think.'

'If people knew they killed Cap.'

Voltairine shook her head. 'If you can control your desire for revenge, which you will get. If you can find patience, we can take them down. Will you continue your sister's work?'

Marie did not give Voltairine an answer. Voltairine had not

pushed her for one. She told Marie to come to her with an answer when she was ready. Then she left.

Marie walked over to the window in her studio and waited. By the time Voltairine walked down the two flights of stairs and came into view on the street below, Marie had calmed somewhat from wanting to smash her studio to bits. She took a deep breath, slumped down the wall, sat on the floor, and put her head in her hands.

Had everything Charlie said been a lie? Had he used her? Was he working for them? Yes. He was their agent. He'd never denied working on behalf of the government. Thoughts and questions swirled in Marie's mind, making it impossible to think clearly.

'Fuck them all,' she said. Fuck Charlie, she thought. Fuck Joe. Fuck the suffragettes, fuck the anarchists. Fuck Voltairine. Fuck New York. She pictured her grandfather's farm. Damn it, Capucine. Why did you have to sell it and bring me here? You could spend a whole day on the farm and not see anyone. Not like here. The city felt claustrophobic. She still hadn't made good on the promise she'd made to herself at her sister's funeral: to go and scream at the sea.

She stood up, tore off her artist smock, and replaced it with her coat. She grabbed her satchel of art supplies and locked the studio behind her. She considered taking the steamship to Coney Island as she went down the street.

CHAPTER 25

The house was a tall brownstone on Murray Hill. The kid who'd been sent as a runner led Joe Petrosino right to the front door. Joe tipped and sent him on his way. The boy ran off, only as far as across the street, where a couple of his friends lingered. The kids were poor, and it was a prosperous street, so there was always a hustle to be made and errands to be run for people who could afford not to run them for themselves. The kid had said the policeman who'd sent him had told him there'd been a break-in.

From the outside, nothing looked out of place. No windows were smashed, and the front door looked fine. Joe knocked, and it was opened immediately.

A policeman stuck his head through the gap. 'You officer Petrosino?'

'Yes, I'm Joe.'

'I'm Nick,' he said, looking the short man in his uniform up and down. Then he ushered him inside.

'What gives? Why can't you open the door?' Joe asked as he slid through the gap. 'Oh,' he said.

'Maybe I should've warned you.'

'Maybe you should've,' Joe said. 'I might've ended up like him with the surprise. Fancy letting a man walk in on a dead body. And one of our own.'

'So, what's going on? Why'd you call me in on this?' Joe kneeled beside the body of the policeman. He didn't know him, but he sighed and made the sign of the cross.

'You know Henry Bull, right?'

'Right?' Joe confirmed.

'Well, he said you were on the lookout for anything suspicious. Said you were working a case and trying to link up anything that was revolutionary.'

'Revolutionary?'

'Yeah, that was the word he used. Anything to do with troublemakers, rabble-rousers, anarchists. That kind of thing.'

Joe frowned. He felt concerned it was becoming common knowledge he was investigating this kind of thing 'Got any witnesses?'

'We've only got one, the lady of the house who was involved. She interrupted a break-in, confronted the robber—'

'She sounds brave.'

'British. There's a difference. And she's no exception.'

'She got that whole taking charge attitude going on. Know what I mean?'

'Yeah, I get you.'

'Well, she shot at the robber, which alerted him,' he said, pointing at the dead policeman. Then the robber took off into the night with his swag.'

The policeman placed his hat back on. 'They're through here, Joe.'

Joe stood. 'Did you know him?'

'Well, you know everyone, don't you, as a colleague, that is, but I didn't really know him.'

'Lead the way,' Joe said.

The policeman led him over to a parlour where the door was closed. He knocked on it and awaited a response. Joe raised an eyebrow at the man's subservience and pushed it open without invitation.

A woman stood by the window. Her head shot around on hearing Joe's unceremonious entrance.

'Excuse us, ma'am. This is—'

'Joe Petrosino of the New York Police Department.'

She looked him up and down.

'You're Mary Leiter, I presume?' Joe asked.

'Yes.'

'I understand it's been quite the eventful night for you?'

'Considering an anarchist broke in. They stole a ridiculous amount of jewellery and nearly set fire to my house and killed a policeman in my entrance hall, then yes. I do believe you might refer to it as eventful.'

Joe ignored the comment and walked over to her. 'Miss, you just referred to the perpetrator as an anarchist. Can you enlighten me as to why you called him that?'

'I just told you my jewellery has been robbed. Heirlooms that have been in my family for generations and your pressing concern is what he might be?'

'Miss, if—'

'Ma'am,' she said.

'Ma'am. If you'd indulge me with an answer to my question?'

'Because he damn well bloody said he was an anarchist.'

'So you spoke with him?'

'I tried to damn well shoot him with my grandfather's pistol used at Waterloo. But the degenerate took a glancing blow to his cheek and came for me. Unlucky I couldn't add to the tally of French men that gun has downed.'

'He was French?'

'Aren't all anarchists?'

'It would seem not, miss, ma'am.'

She glared sideways at him.

'So,' Joe said. 'Did he announce he was an anarchist? How did it come out.'

'Indeed, he did announce. Was ranting on and on in French, shouting Vive le voile noir.'

Joe frowned, not being able to translate.

She sighed and said, 'The black veil.'

'My God,' he said and started laughing. He walked back towards the door as if to leave, then stopped.

Mary Leiter wore a look of incredulity.

'Have you quite finished looking so ecstatic? Does that mean something to you, officer?'

'Mean something? No. No. Not at all. But I have a feeling it's going to mean a lot.'

An hour after leaving her studio and walking downtown, Marie bought passage from the man at the ticket office and waited patiently in line on the ramp to the ferry.

By the time she boarded, at least a hundred people had also set sail. She ignored them all, sat on a bench on the top deck, and gazed out at the bay as they departed.

The waves slapped the hull. The engine chugged steadily. And so, the steamboat took the same route it took there and back twice a day across the bay, through fair weather or bad weather, with a deck full or light of passengers, passing the piers jutting out of Manhattan like a porcupine's needles, in view of the people commuting across the colossal Brooklyn Bridge; Marie sitting with a rucksack between her feet, a sketchbook on her knee, pencil hovering, timing her graphite mark with the roll of the boat, feeling the cool breeze mix with the warm sun on her face and happy to be leaving behind the city for a day.

The steamship passed Bedloe Island. Marie gazed at the newly constructed statue, glistening in the sun, sailcloth hanging from its crown and hiding her gaze. Marie remembered thought again about visiting the statue while on display in Paris. She felt proud of the statue because it had come from her home country.

It took the steamship a couple of hours to reach Coney Island. Once there, she composed herself and bought supplies: beer, bread, and cheese. Then she found someone taking their cart east, hitchhiked most of the way, and walked out to Plumb Beach. She had once visited here with a friend to paint, so she knew what to expect.

The beach was deserted. Marie dropped her jacket and satchel in the sand. She took her boots off and felt the first sense of relief since she'd started the journey as her toes sunk into the sand. She went the short distance to the shoreline and didn't stop walking until she was two feet deep into the sea. There was no current. The water was calm, cool, clear, and far away from the filth and pollution of the city. The sun beat down on her upturned face. Then she took a deep breath and screamed into the sky. All of her muscles felt looser for the first time in weeks. She stood there for a while, breathing in the salty sea air. Then, eventually, she went back to her belongings, collapsed into the sand, and lay there. Gulls glided overhead. She let the sand sift through her fingers, feeling the grains fall, revealing shells, so perfect it felt like an unbelievable mystery how something so tiny could exist, let alone have a function. As the sun dipped below towards the horizon, she gathered wood for a fire, arranged it, and lit kindling with a match.

Only now did she dare to let herself consider the question of which side had killed Capucine and why. It had blindsided her with the thought she had willingly accepted Charlie's story. But was Voltairine lying? Could Capucine have been an anarchist? Had Capucine being older when their father died had more of an impact on her? Might his death at the hands of the French authorities have struck a spark within her sister that had grown into an inferno? She stared into the flames dancing in front of her in the fire on the beach as she wrestled with the thoughts. Her gaze drifted to the waves gently breaking on the shore and then to the moonlit horizon.

Maybe she should just leave and let them all kill each other. She was leaving for Paris anyhow. Why not go sooner?

Marie lay down on her side next to the fire and pulled a blanket over her she'd brought. The stars shone brightly. It had been so long since she'd seen them. She wondered if there really was a place up there where Capucine now resided. A piece of wood on the fire spat and crackled. Marie knew she couldn't leave New York without knowing the truth. But what would happen if she did find out who killed Capucine? What would she do? Would only a death in return bring justice? Was she capable of looking someone in the eye and killing them?

In the warm glow of the fire, as sleep took her into its fold, Marie's mind kept saying I'm sorry, Capucine. I'm sorry, Capucine. I'm sorry...

Joe was giddy. He went to Marie's studio hoping to find her and Charlie and to tell them the news.

Charlie opened the door.

'Charlie! I'm glad you're here,' Joe said, walking enthusiastically into the studio and clapping him on the shoulder. 'I've been dying to get here all day. You won't guess what's happened.'

Charlie waited in the doorway and looked out into the gloomy corridor. 'Where's Marie?'

'What do you mean, where's Marie? Is she not here?' Joe asked, looking around the room.

Charlie shut the door. 'No. No, she's not.'

'Were you expecting her to be here when you got here?'

'No. Sometimes she's here, sometimes she's not. You know how it is.'

'Well, I guess she's her own woman,' Joe said.

'Yeah, but. She is. She just hasn't disappeared like this before without saying.'

'You're worried.'

Charlie swallowed. 'No.' He checked his watch. 'It's just late. So why are you here?'

Joe regarded him for a moment. 'Oh. Oh. So get this. Some rich heiress over on Fifth and Sixth nearly had her house burnt down in a burglary last night. A cop was walking by and heard her nearly shoot the head off the robber with a pistol from the battle of Waterloo.'

Charlie raised his eyebrows.

Joe continued. 'He sees the fire through one of the windows, hears the crack of the pistol and enters to save the woman's life. But in the process, he gets himself stabbed. Two, three, four times. By now, there's quite a commotion. Servants wake. People start coming out of their houses on the street, so the robber flees into the night with a whole loot bag full of heirlooms and jewellery.'

'I'm guessing there's some link to our case?' Charlie asked as he paced the room.

'Damn right, there's a link. A bully of one at that. The robber claimed he was an anarchist. While he was stabbing the policeman, he was shouting all kinds of slogans. Down with tyranny. Death to authority. Hang on. You're gonna love this,' he said as he opened his notebook to the page he wanted. 'Vive le Voile Noir,' he read out aloud.

Charlie stopped pacing. He looked up at Joe. 'Long live the Black Veil?'

Joe nodded. 'Long live the Black Veil.'

The next day, Marie returned to her studio. When she entered, Charlie was smoking his pipe in the open window. 'Where the hell have you been?' Charlie asked, standing and putting his hands on his hips.

'To the beach,' Marie said.

Charlie's eyebrows raised as he stalked over to her. 'Did you not think to let anyone know?'

'Not particularly. No.'

'You've been there all night? I thought they'd gotten to you.'

'You can just say you were worried for me if that's what it is?'

'Are you after attention—'

Marie slapped him across the face. They stood glowering at each other. She looked for the guilt in his eyes, for anything in his soul that might betray him. There was nothing. 'Charlie, I don't know what you believe to be the case here, but I'm not beholden to you or anyone. I come and go as I please. I don't work for you. You don't pay me a wage. And if I need to follow a cause like suffrage or just go to the beach, then I will follow my heart to its conclusion. Is that understood?'

Charlie rubbed the sting from his cheek. 'I thought you wanted to catch your sister's killer?'

She slowly shook her head. 'Yesterday, Voltairine stood right where you are, Charlie. She stood there and patronised me. She told me I shouldn't have acted so immaturely and I was damaging my sister's reputation in the suffrage movement.' Marie didn't feel angry like before she'd gone to Plumb Beach. Now, she felt determined. 'Whoever killed my sister, I will find them. And they will pay dearly for their actions.'

Charlie stared at her. Eventually, he nodded. 'I'm sorry, kid,' he said and held his hand for her to shake. She took hold of it and shook it.

'I understand what it is to want revenge and not be able to get it. We'll get to the bottom of this conspiracy. And when we do, those anarchists will swing for their crimes. Mark my word.'

'If it was indeed them.'

'You suddenly don't think it was?'

'I'm open to ideas. I'm open to facts,' Marie said.

'Well, here's a fact. The anarchists are called the Black Veil.'

Marie nodded as she took in the information. 'Well, I hope that brings the investigation one step closer to an end.'

Charlie nodded. 'Well, we have a lead. A member of the Veil has gone rogue.'

'Rogue? How?'

'An apparent member robbed a house, and one of the servants tailed him but lost him somewhere in the Five Points.'

Marie's lip curled. 'That place?'

'Thought it would hold fond memories for you.'

She looked at him with a stony expression.

'It's where we met, after all,' Charlie said.

'And I thought you'd killed my sister.'

Charlie regarded her for a moment, then said, 'Well, I think we should pay a visit to our favourite part of New York and let's find out if we can't learn a thing or two.'

Marie sighed. 'It's not the kind of place that's forthcoming with answers.'

'You only get no responses if you ask questions,' Charlie said.

Marie looked puzzled.

'So,' Charlie said. 'We're not going to ask questions...'

When they arrived at the centre of the Five Points, where the four streets came together, a commotion was ahead. A crowd stood facing a wall, and more people were running over to join them. A man stood above the crowd with his arms outstretched, wallowing in the adoration and attention he received. Marie and Charlie looked at each other. Then, they both started over to the melee.

'And I quote,' the man shouted in a strong French accent. 'Whoever lays his hand on me to govern me is a usurper and a tyrant, and I declare him my enemy.' He then threw a piece of jewellery into the air. It flew towards Marie, and she lifted her hand to grab it. But a man jumped up on the back of someone in the crowd and plucked it from the air.

'What are we going to do?' Marie asked.

'Question him, of course,' Charlie said.

'I thought you said questions don't lead to answers? Do you mean lean on him until he talks?'

'No. Why don't you channel your alter ego Camille Vallette and see if you can't remember how to be a journalist.'

'What? Ask him about art?'

'Go get that scoop.'

Marie frowned. 'Interview him?'

Charlie simply raised his eyebrows and walked away.

Marie took the notebook from her satchel, raised it above her head, and waved it to get the man's attention. 'Monsieur,' she said, speaking in French. 'I am a journalist! Monsieur,' she shouted again, waving her notebook in the air. 'I am Camille Vallette of the New York World. A quote for our newspaper if you'd be so kind.'

The man heard Marie and eyed her suspiciously. Then, after throwing the remaining pieces of jewellery into the crowd, he jumped down and over to Marie as the people parted to let him through.

'Can I ask what the reason for such a generous display is?'

'Redistribution of wealth,' he said.

'You are redistributing your wealth, monsieur?'

He smiled. 'No, Mademoiselle, I am the same as these people. I am redistributing the wealth of those who monopolise us.'

'Stealing from the rich to give to the poor? Are you the French Robin Hood of New York?'

'I am not Louis Mandrin, Mademoiselle,' he said with a devilish smirk.

'Louis Mandrin was inspired to steal from the state because they killed his brother and his friend,' Marie said. The story of the highwayman Mandrin robbing the King's tax collectors had been one of her favourite stories her grandfather had told her as a child. Though she has always liked Robin Hood had Maid Marian, Mandrin's tale had been propelled by grief. She had liked the romanticism of both stories. 'Do you have a tale of inspiration equally as tragic as Mandrin's?'

'Look around you, do my brothers and sisters not suffer a fate worse than death? While those in authority are paid for letting us live in such squalor? We should remove authority over our life.'

'As a champion of the oppressed, what political disposition would you class yourself as?'

'I am an Anarchist,' he said, puffing his chest out.

'Are you working on behalf of yourself, or do you have a band of merry men?'

At this point, the crowd began to lose interest and thin out as people walked away with no loot left to be shared. He raised his arms above his head and shouted. 'Do not allow yourselves to lose sight. No sooner is God going to help your position than the landlords of this town. Rise up with the Black Veil.'

A few people who had been lucky enough to grab some jewellery cheered, and an equal number of people groaned. Seemingly forgetting his interview with Marie, the man pushed off through the crowd.

'Monsieur, your name, please. Monsieur!' Marie shouted after him as he went.

'Clément Duval, founding member of the Black Veil,' he shouted, pumping his fist in the air.

'Well done, Frenchie,' Charlie said when he rejoined her. 'He's either crazy or wants to be infamous. It'll be interesting to know if Joe's records match that name.'

'I think he wants to be infamous,' Marie said.

'What makes you say that?'

'My journalistic instinct.' She stared in the direction Duval had gone. 'I had a feeling he was making a statement. He was so keen to tell everyone he was a founding member. Why advertise it? Why now?'

'Perhaps this anarchist Black Veil organisation was too authoritarian for an anarchist.'

'Exactly,' Marie said. 'I think the anarchist has gone rogue.'

Rain fell heavily the next day. Despite this a crowd had gathered. They left it attached to the noticeboard in the centre of the Five Points. Nobody wished to remove the grim souvenir. Everyone just stood and stared. As word got around about what had been nailed to the noticeboard, more people came to look. Soon, the crowd was at least ten bodies deep. All looked at it in hushed silence.

Marie and Voltairine walked together through Central Park. The leaves were yellowing, and the chill in the air had returned following a mild couple of days. The sky was overcast and threatened to rain again , so most people had retreated from the treelined paths, allowing them a level of privacy to speak openly. Voltairine didn't seem surprised Marie wanted to take her sister Capucine's place within the anarchist organisation.

'We are known as the Black Veil,' Voltairine told Marie, who nodded. 'A collective name for collective acts of propaganda of the deed to further the cause of anarchism,' she explained. 'To determine what level of involvement within the organisation you will take, you will be required to undertake an initiation. The greater the act, the more trust you will earn. We will also be able to determine the scope of what we might accomplish with you.'

'What did Capucine do?'

'I don't know. We are not told what the other members before us have achieved.'

'Capucine was in the group before you?' Marie was surprised. She'd presumed Voltairine had recruited her sister.

'Yes, she was. To join the Black Veil, we are required to have a sponsor. Someone who will be accountable for our actions until we are fully accepted. Your sister recruited me and was my sponsor. She was accountable for me. As I will be for you.'

'Accountable? In what way?'

'Accountable for choosing the right candidate. Only the most serious and committed people should be granted an opportunity to join the Black Veil. Choosing an uncommitted candidate would put the whole organisation at risk. Candidates must prove their commitment to the cause.'

'But what should I do?'

'Anything that sums up your aspirations.'

'Could be anything, though. What is too much? What is not enough?' Marie asked.

Voltairine shrugged. 'I cannot say. To do so would be to influence your ambition.'

'I was arrested for throwing a paint bomb. Doesn't that prove my commitment?' Marie asked.

Voltairine smiled patronisingly, causing Marie to laugh.

'That's fine,' Voltairine said. 'Your ascent will be determined by the limit of your actions. Your actions should reflect the injustice you feel in your heart.'

Marie's laugh faded as her face turned stony. 'If I knew who killed my sister, I would kill them. Would that be enough?'

'The bourgeois, the authorities, the ruling class are responsible for your sister's death, Marie. There are plenty of them to...' Voltairine tilted her head. 'To get your revenge from.'

Marie walked away and then stopped. She turned to face Voltairine. 'I can imagine the authorities killed Capucine. After seeing how the police reacted to the paint bomb, it wouldn't surprise me. Not if they knew what she was doing.'

'Then imagine how they'd react to a real bomb?'

Marie shook her head. 'The night I found my sister, I saw a man in the fly tower above the stage. I swore he was the killer, but Joe, he told me he wasn't, and I believed him. Joe didn't want me to search the theatre. He wanted me to stay with him. I couldn't admit it to myself afterwards, but I felt he didn't want me to miss seeing them hang. I was welcome of his presence, clouded by it. I just wanted someone with me. I should've listened to my instincts.'

'If your instinct tells you Joe was involved in your sister's murder somehow, maybe you should listen to it.'

'He was too kind to me. He's given me more help than any policeman should ever have done. He's the only one investigating her murder. But in hindsight, I feel like he wants something from me. Information. I don't quite know. Like I said, he dismissed any notion of that man on the fly tower being involved. What if they were in on it together?'

'It is incredible how clear the truth becomes when the veil of normalcy is lifted, Marie. They hold positions of power and responsibility, purporting to protect and serve the people. Yet they do it for their own gain.'

Marie's breathing was short and shallow. She felt tense and full of anger. 'If I kill him, would that be enough?'

'To join us, Marie? It would be more than enough.'

A scream grabbed their attention, and they looked to where it had come from the boating lake.

Like a ghost ship appearing out of nowhere, the rowboat had gently drifted across the water, silently moving without propulsion. Most people rowing on the lake avoided the boat, believing it was astray and not wanting to bump into it. Just as the boat manager sent a boy down the jetty to go and retrieve it, a young couple, bad at rowing, drifted too close to the row boat. It was the young woman who had screamed. The young man stood in shock and nearly capsized the boat. He fell towards the other rowboat, his hands steadying himself on the rail. Tied to the inside of the boat was the body of Clément Duval. Without the note attached to the man's jacket, identifying the faceless man might've taken a long time.

It was late afternoon the next day in a quiet corner of Battery Park when Voltairine introduced Lena Jager to Marie. The three women stood together facing each other as Lena handed Marie the gun, a Remington Model 1875. It was sleek, with a long black barrel and a wooden handle. Marie weighed it in her hand and turned it over, inspecting it.

'Have you ever used a gun before?' Lena asked.

'I've shot my grandfather's rifle.'

'Well, that won't help. But this is easier. Just pull that hammer back all the way.'

Marie's thumb dragged back the hammer. The barrel turned.

'When you pull the trigger, the hammer will drop and hit the cartridge. Bang. The bullet will fly out,' Lena said. 'Pull the trigger. See how it feels.'

'It's empty?' Marie asked.

'Of course,' Lena said.

Marie pointed it at the floor regardless. She pulled the trigger. The hammer dropped with a click.

'It'll obviously make much more noise,' Lena said. She took the gun from Marie and started loading it. 'Don't forget to pull the trigger back every time you want to shoot, though. Just get up close. Put the muzzle to his stomach or his back, and you'll only need one shot.'

'Once you've shot him, Marie,' Voltairine said, 'Don't stand there looking at him in shock. Shoot him and get out of there.'

She handed Marie the loaded gun. 'Don't try and come to us either,' Lena said. 'After we've witnessed you pass the test, we will leave and go our separate ways. Don't try to follow us or catch up with us.'

Marie placed the gun into her satchel. With the added weight, the strap pulled down on her shoulder, and she readjusted it to be comfortable.

'Are you sure you are up to this, Marie?' Voltairine asked.

'The bâtard is responsible for killing my sister,' Marie said.

'This man killed Capucine?' Lena asked, surprised at the accusation.

'He represents those responsible,' Voltairine said, harshly shutting down any further discussion. 'Time is getting on. You should go and wait for him. He'll be happy if you look eager to see him. He won't suspect a thing.'

Marie took a deep breath. 'He won't be expecting this at all.'

Voltairine put a hand on Marie's shoulder and looked into her eyes. 'People have forgotten what it is to live. We only know what it is to be ruled over and the imposed order of others. It is time to reclaim what has been stolen from us, Marie.'

Marie nodded. Defiance burned within her eyes. She turned and walked off across the park.

Beside Voltairine, Lena had her arms crossed. 'Was it this police officer that killed Capucine?'

'Marie has arrived at that conclusion. We must trust her.'

'But do you think it was?'

The two women stared at each other.

'It does not matter what I think,' Voltairine said.

'Of course it does. You're bringing in this random girl who is killing some seemingly random police officer.'

'That random girl is Capucine's sister.'

'You idolise Capucine too much. It blinds you. You don't see even Capucine did not introduce her to our cause.'

'Because then, Marie lacked a motive to join us. Now, Marie has as much motive as any of us. If she passes this test, then she proves her commitment.'

'And if she fails and she talks, they will come for you.'

'Marie will not fail.'

They watched as Marie paced back and forth along the esplanade, waiting for Joe Petrosino. Eventually, a man approached her. They talked for some time as they walked. Voltairine and Lena followed, watching them from a distance.

Lena tapped Voltairine on the arm, drawing her attention. Two police officers patrolled through the park.

'Damn it,' Voltairine said.

'She can't shoot him now,' Lena said. 'They'll go after her. She'll never escape.'

Voltairine immediately started striding over to the police officers. 'Excuse me, officers! Officers, I need your help.'

The two men diverted towards her. 'What's the matter, miss?' One of them asked.

'There's been an accident by the entrance. Please hurry.'

'Please, lead the way.'

Voltairine led the two men away, striding past Lena, who continued to monitor Marie, who was oblivious to what was happening.

'What's happened, Miss?'

'There was a horse and cart. It hit a young girl. She looked to be in a bad way.'

Voltairine reached the gates of the park when the gunshot rang out. Then another. The two police officers stopped. They hesitated. They looked back towards where they'd come from.

'Those were gunshots,' one of the officers said to the other. 'Miss, wait here.'

'But they need help. It's just there on the street,' Voltairine pleaded.

'We'll come back if we can.'

They ran back into the park. Voltairine sighed. She hoped she'd done enough. She waited by the gates as Lena walked swiftly towards her. Panic gripped the other people in the park. Some ran for the exits. Some just stood there bewildered by what had happened. As people communicated what had happened, everyone began to flee.

Voltairine went over to Lena as she approached. 'What happened? Did she get away?'

'She shot him. He fell back off the esplanade into the water.'

'Was he dead?'

They both kept walking, briskly heading out of the park's gate.

'Two shots. Close range. He must be,' Lena said.

'And Marie?'

'She fled immediately. Nobody tried to stop her.'

'Good, good. I'll see you at the meeting point.'

The two women split up and went their separate ways. Voltairine smiled as she walked away. Everything had gone to plan. Just about. She was proud of Marie. And she was sure Capucine would've been proud of her sister, too.

Voltairine felt confident for the first time in several weeks. Clément Duvall, who had proven to be a liability, was dead, and the nature of his death would serve as a warning to others within the Black Veil not to go rogue. And now Marie would take the place of her sister. The Black Veil's aims would soon come to fruition.

CHAPTER 28

The office the Black Veil occupied was more opulent than Marie had imagined it would be. She sat looking at everyone around the table.

'As we all agreed, Voltairine has taken care of Clément Duvall,' Benedict said.

'A little too enthusiastically by all accounts,' Lena, who'd given Marie the gun to kill Joe with, said.

Marie steeled her nerves and her expression. She clenched her jaw to hide her fear and surprise. Had Capucine been like this? She still couldn't believe her sister had really been an anarchist, not to mention being associated with people like this. Hopefully, it was more with people like Lena. But even she had given Marie the gun with which to kill Joe. Marie remembered the gunshots and saw him falling from the esplanade into the water.

Voltairine leaned back into her chair. 'It should serve as a warning not to betray the Black Veil. After all, he killed Elias.'

'We don't doubt your dedication to the cause, Voltairine. Or what Clément did. We question your methods.'

'I use appropriate methods for the job.'

'Cutting off a man's face? Sounds like revenge for what Clément did.' Lena looked at Marie. 'It's too late now, but are you sure you two realise what you've signed up for?' She then looked over to a middle-aged man called Amos. Amos had been introduced and invited to join the Black Veil by Alberta as their new explosives expert to replace James McGarrity. A miner from the Midwest, he was propelled to join the cause after many of his colleagues had died in mining accidents over the years. The mine's owners had never been prosecuted for the accidents.

Marie took a sideways glance at Voltairine and then looked back at Lena.

Lena raised her eyebrows at Amos for a response. He shrugged.

'Though Voltairine's methods are gruesome, they were also effective for our cause. It caused terror and panic. It further reinforced the authorities can't protect the people,' Benedict said.

'Not to mention, the people also believe the authorities did it in reprisal for Clément killing one of their own,' Alberta said.

Lena chewed on the inside of her lip and said no more.

'You're convinced the organisation isn't at risk, Benedict?' a man with an American accent asked.

'Because of Clément's actions? No. He may have used the name of the Black Veil, but there is nothing to suggest he compromised us or revealed our meeting place or our plans. Again, we have Voltairine to thank for getting to him before the police.'

'If we are finally done discussing Clément, maybe we can actually talk about things that will further our cause,' Voltairine said and looked at Alberta's new recruit, Amos.

Amos leaned forward and looked for permission from Benedict. For an apparently egalitarian group, Marie was surprised at how everyone looked to Benedict as their leader. Benedict nodded for the man to speak.

'McGarrity's plans are sound in theory. If you can bring down one of the towers, the main cables will fall, and so will the deck. But you need a lot of explosives to take down one of those towers from the water. Which you haven't got any more.'

'Which we haven't got any more,' Voltairine corrected him. She smiled. 'You are one of us now, after all.'

Amos nodded. 'Even though you have another boat, you don't have enough explosives to bring down one of the Brooklyn Bridge's towers.'

Marie looked to Voltairine.

'Do you have something to add?' Voltairine asked Marie.

'We're going to destroy the Brooklyn Bridge?' She tried to let her surprise filter into her voice as excitement.

'Yes,' Voltairine said. She smiled confidently, pleased Marie was enthusiastic, but her smile faded.

'We need a new plan, though,' Amos said. You can't bring down the bridge from the water.

'Do you have a suggestion on how to then?' Benedict asked.

'The base is bigger, thicker, stronger. So you need more explosives to blast through it. Obviously, higher up, at bridge level you have the arches. So there is less tower to break through. With the explosives we still have at our disposal, that is where we should strike.'

Voltairine placed her hands on the table. 'Granted, it is easy to load a boat full of explosives and detonate it beneath a bridge. But how on earth do you propose to get it all on the bridge without anyone being suspicious?' Voltairine asked.

Amos looked to Alberta. She was smiling. 'Because the bridge has become so popular, they plan to run more carriages on the trains across it. They are currently testing the stress on the system to see if the engines can handle it. These extra carriages aren't carrying people but are being loaded with weight for the testing. We can load one of these carriages with explosives rather than the bales and barrels they are currently using.'

'Once the train reaches one of the arches and the carriage is beneath it, we detonate it,' Amos said.

'And this is done when?'

'At night, after the last train has run.'

'You mean we can't do this during the inauguration?'

'No,' Alberta said. 'There is no way we can do that. It just isn't possible.'

Voltairine shook her head. 'We lose the symbolism. The impact.'

'I don't call a big, gaping collapsed wreck that was once the triumph of engineering in full view of the inauguration any less symbolic. In fact, it only shows the irony of their self-congratulating failure,' Alberta said. A smug smile was etched across her face.

'The only thing that matters now is that we still can proceed,' Benedict said. 'Not that I need to ask, but have you done your due diligence on the feasibility?'

'Of course,' Alberta said.

'It is the only plan you have,' Amos said.

'We have,' Voltairine said. 'We have.'

Charlie had bought a long dark jacket and trousers and changed out of his usual attire. He knew Marie would subliminally look out for his light-coloured clothes and fedora. It was, of course, a long shot that she'd return to her studio, but he had no hope of otherwise finding her. He'd waited on the street and then in a cafe in sight of the entrance to the building her studio was in.

It was early evening when he finally spotted her leaving the building. He was annoyed he hadn't seen her enter but relieved he could now follow her and see if she could lead him somewhere important. Of course, he could have waited for her inside the studio, but he knew she wouldn't talk. She was too stubborn.

Charlie still reeled from Joe's murder. He couldn't believe Marie's descent had taken place at all yet so quickly.

Ever since she'd gone missing a couple of nights ago, claiming to have slept on the beach past Coney Island, she had acted strange.

Maybe she'd had learnt the truth. Perhaps someone in the Black Veil had told her what had happened. But then she might've tricked him all along. It was a possibility. Had she always been an anarchist? Had she played him and tried to derail his investigation? But why kill Joe? It didn't make sense. Why hadn't she wanted to kill him instead? He wondered if he was to blame but then told himself it wasn't worth ruminating on until he had cold, hard facts. He followed her from across the street, at a reasonable distance and always with people between them.

They walked a couple of blocks before he knew Marie had spotted him. She'd clearly retained what he'd taught her. She remained calm. She didn't turn to look at him but stared into a shop window. He didn't try to hide himself. He stood there, crossed his arms and stared straight back. Marie adjusted the satchel strap on her shoulder and walked off down the street.

Charlie followed her. After a while of casually strolling from shop to shop, she went into a haberdashery. The bell rang above the door as she entered. Clever girl, he thought.

He watched through the windows across the street as she talked to the shopkeeper. Then, she casually walked back out onto the street. She stood on the sidewalk and held eye contact with Charlie across the street.

Marie walked off down the street again and stopped at an apothecary. She headed for the door but went past it to a door that led to the apartments above.

Charlie followed after her. He made it to the door before it closed and locked on itself. The hallway was dark, served daylight by a skylight four storeys up.

He heard Marie's footsteps as she bounded up the stairs.

'It's a dead end, Marie. You should know better than to head upwards. There's nowhere to escape to when you go up.'

She didn't reply. He heard her footsteps ascend the stairs and a door slam shut from above.

He scowled. He reached for his gun holstered at his hip beneath his jacket but hesitated. How could he shoot her? You fool. You've fallen for her, he thought. She's played you like her sister played Phillip Moses. His jaw clenched. He withdrew his gun and held it up in front of him. He started up the stairs.

He kicked open the door onto the flat roof. He half expected to see her standing there, but she wasn't. He edged out of the stairwell and went through the doorway. The smell of various stewed meats and boiled vegetables filled the air. There was an iron structure with a water tower sitting atop it. A couple of skylights hugged the rooftop. Iron ladders curled over the edge of the building. He stalked around the perimeter of the square stairwell that had housed the stairs he'd come up. She wasn't hiding there. His guard dropped momentarily, and his gun wavered from its raised position.

'Drop it,' she said.

He glanced over his shoulder.

'Is that the gun you killed Joe with?'

'I said, drop it.'

Charlie threw his gun onto the floor. 'Just get it done.'

'Not before I have answers. Raise your hands.'

He did what she told him to do. 'You're the one who suddenly switched sides, Marie. Or were you just lying all along?'

'You bâtard,' she said. 'All you've done is lie to me since we met. You knew all I wanted was to find out who killed my sister and why. You knew it was the only thing that would give me peace. But of course. You couldn't tell me, could you? Because you killed her. You killed Capucine.'

Marie held the gun and pointed it at Charlie. 'You killed my sister,' she said. 'Admit it.'

Charlie sighed. He said nothing for a while and stood gazing at the floor, then nodded.

He turned around to face her and looked up and held her gaze. 'Yes. I did. I killed Capucine,' Charlie said.

Marie felt dizzy. Her stomach tightened. Her heart rate increased. 'How? Why?' She shook her head. Though she'd suspected it, finally hearing the truth was disorientating.

'Capucine was an anarchist,' Charlie said.

'She was?' What Voltairine had told Marie had turned out to be the truth after all.

'Yes,' Charlie said. 'I should've told you, but I didn't know you weren't one too.'

'I wasn't when we met.'

'But you are now,' Charlie said.

'And I bet you want to kill me too?' Marie asked.

'How could you kill poor Joe? Why not me if you suspected me?'

'Who says I'm not going to kill you.'

Charlie narrowed his eyes art her. 'Justice needs to be served for what you've done, Marie.'

'And what did my sister do that required the kind of justice you deliver?'

Charlie's jaw clenched. 'She was plotting to blow up that theatre and all of its anti-suffragette patrons during that play's opening night.'

Marie's frown grew deeper. 'She couldn't. Capucine wasn't

like that.'

Charlie stepped towards her. She raised the gun at his head.

'Keep your damn hands raised,' she shouted at him.

Charlie stepped back and raised his hands beside his head. 'I know you don't believe me, but it's the truth,' he said. 'Did you even really know your sister?'

'Of course. I...' Marie clearly hadn't known her sister. 'So you killed them both, hung them above the stage, for something they hadn't done?'

'I didn't hang them. I told you. And Phillip wasn't, as far as I can tell, an anarchist. I believe your sister had used him. Faked their relationship for him to become besotted so that she, the anarchists, might gain access to the theatre.'

Marie stepped towards Charlie. She raised the gun and aimed it from his chest to his face. Her hand shook, so she gripped it with both hands to steady her aim.

'That's enough, Marie.' Joe Petrosino stepped from his hiding place behind a chimney tower.

Charlie's mouth dropped open in surprise. 'Joe?' Charlie said, unwilling to believe his eyes.

Joe didn't respond. He kept his attention squarely on Marie. Her finger was curled around the trigger. Tears streamed from her eyes. Her whole body trembled. Joe stepped between the gun and Charlie.

'You don't want a man's murder on your conscience,' Joe said.

She exhaled as if the trance had been lifted. The tension in her arms eased. The gun lowered. Joe reached out and took it from her. Charlie sighed in relief, and Marie collapsed to the floor and sobbed.

Joe glanced back and nodded at Charlie in

acknowledgement, then knelt beside Marie and hugged her.

The sun had lowered towards the horizon and cast the sky in various brilliant shades of pink. Lights illuminated the city one by one; the street lamps, on horse-drawn carriages, and in apartments and shops. It was still busy, and the noise of hooves, cartwheels, and voices drifted up to the rooftop from the street below.

'It's a dangerous game you played, Marie. I would've killed you if I'd needed to. But I understand. I would've done the same myself. You completely outmanoeuvred me, Frenchie. You're one hell of a spy.'

Marie lifted her chin. She hated that a part of her felt proud of his compliment. How could she still feel that way when he'd killed her sister? 'All I want is the truth,' she said.

'Well, I owe you that kid.' He took his pipe from his pocket and started filling it with tobacco. 'Capucine used her status as a suffragette to first meet Phillip Moses as a ruse to confront him. As you're aware, he was a playwright who wrote anti-suffrage plays. He was known to fall for women easily, and she made it look like she fell for him despite their political differences. Naturally, they had to keep their relationship a secret. This played into Capucine's ulterior motive, though.'

Charlie didn't look up as he lit his pipe. He extinguished the match with a wave and continued.

'I learned about their plot a couple of days before the opening show you attended. We found a couple of barrels of black powder and timing devices. One was hidden beneath the stage. One was beneath the audience.'

'We?'

Charlie swallowed. He clenched his jaw. 'Another agent was working the case with me. Gray. He was the one who got the lead on the bombs being planted in the theatre by James McGarrity.'

'So where does my sister end up getting killed and McGarrity escape?'

'While Phillip Moses was occupied with his play, Capucine slipped away. We walked straight in on your sister and who I now suspect was McGarrity, setting the barrels in place.'

'Why didn't you know who McGarrity was then?' Joe asked.

'He wore a bandana and a bowler hat, plus it was dark down there. Anyway, Phillip heard the commotion and came beneath the stage to see what was happening. Capucine grabbed him and held a gun to his head. James took the opportunity to shoot at us. He hit my partner, Gray, and as he went down, he pulled his trigger. The bullet accidentally killed Phillip Moses. I then shot back and got Capucine. McGarrity fled. I went to go after him but hesitated and went to Capucine. She was still alive. I begged her for answers, to reveal who they were, what they were doing. She just said something cryptic that's stuck with me since.'

'What?' Marie asked.

Charlie shook his head and frowned. Then he raised his eyebrows as he looked at Marie. 'Homer has all of the answers.'

'Homer has all of the answers?' she asked.

'Is that it? Her final words were Homer has all of the answers? Does it not mean anything to you?' Joe asked.

'No. Nothing,' Marie said. 'What happened then, Charlie?'

'Well, she wasn't going anywhere, so I went after McGarrity, but I'd left it too late.'

'Did you not think of informing the police?' Joe asked.

'No.'

'Why on earth not?'

'I didn't want anything to slow the case down, and because—'

'Why did you hang them then?'

Charlie pointed his pipe at Marie. 'I told you, kid, I didn't. I came back, and the bodies were gone. Vanished. Capucine and Phillip were nowhere to be seen. Gray was the only one remaining. I don't know who took them and how on earth they got up onto the flytrap above the stage.'

'What happened to Gray's body?' Joe asked.

'I had to take care of him.'

'Was Capucine alive when you left her and went after McGarrity?' Marie asked.

Charlie shook his head. 'She was. But her wound was fatal. There was no way she was getting out of there alive.' His eye twitched on having delivered the news so bluntly to Marie. 'I'm sorry.'

'What do you mean you took care of this Gray fellow?' Joe asked.

'I dragged him out from under the stage. Got him on a barrow, under a tarp, and I wheeled him several blocks away.' Charlie sighed. 'I believe his body was discovered a day or so after we met.'

'That's how you treat your friends?' Joe asked.

'He was a good agent. He knew the risks and the consequences. In our line of work, you don't expect recognition dead or alive.'

'I should arrest you for this, Charlie. Not only this. You blew up that boat. Your fight with McGarrity led to the Mills-Parker Building burning down. You shot up half the

Camorra in Brooklyn.'

'Collateral damage.'

'You've gone rogue,' Joe said.

Charlie didn't say anything. The two men stared at each other.

After all of the lies and deceit, Marie found it hard to trust Charlie. But what he'd said sounded genuine. If Capucine was going to kill all those people she deserved to be stopped. But why had she become so extreme? She wondered if she'd ever stop needing to find answers. She'd found her sister after she'd gone missing. She'd now discovered who'd killed her. One answer was just replaced by another question. She couldn't let it consume her. She had to stay strong. The Black Veil still existed and they still plotted to destroy the Brooklyn Bridge. They needed to stop them, and to do that they would need Charlie's expertise.

'Luckily for you, Charlie,' Marie said. 'Although I don't know why. We're going to need your help.'

After what had happened with Charlie and the Camorra, Marie was surprised the Italian crime syndicate were still involved with the Black Veil. Since Marie had infiltrated the cabal, she had not heard any talk of attacking the Statue of Liberty, which is what she, Charlie and Joe had initially believed the Camorra and the Black Veil were planning to do. The Veil's efforts seemed to have been focused on bringing down the bridge during the inauguration. Marie hadn't dared to question if the statue had ever been considered a target.

A group from the Black Veil comprising Marie, Voltairine, Nils and Leon, along with the explosives expert Amos, had arrived at the Camorra's warehouse on Brooklyn's waterfront that Marie, Charlie and Joe had no idea about throughout their investigation. The kegs of gunpowder, disguised in barrels, were loaded onto the horse and cart. A mob of Camorra foot soldiers armed with rifles and pistols loitered nervous something similar to what had happened at the pier over in Manhattan was going to happen there, too. The pickup occurred without incident, and none of the Italians joined the Black Veil's members when they departed.

Marie and Voltairine had dressed as men with their hair tied up and hidden beneath hats. They wore trousers, waistcoats and shirts. They walked one in front of the other beside the horse and cart. The streets were dark and quiet on the journey to the Brooklyn Terminal. Ahead, the Brooklyn Bridge could be seen between and above the buildings they went past. Marie couldn't imagine something so big and strong collapsing. Though the cart was full, and they crept along, it didn't seem like there would be enough explosives to bring down one of the towers. She had to remind herself it wouldn't actually happen. Becoming a spy and living a double life was incomprehensible at times. Even in the short time, she had been doing it. She wondered how people didn't forget themselves. Living a double life would surely change a person. It had altered Capucine clearly.

She questioned why she was still there. She now knew who had killed her sister, and with it, she had discovered so much more about her sibling that she was still yet to comprehend. Surely, Charlie, Joe and their team could've handled this without her. She should've just left them all and returned to France. She looked at the others who quietly escorted the cart. Nobody wasted their breath. Mostly, they held it. The road wasn't in good condition. Potholes and puddles of unknown depth marred their route. They plodded on slowly, surely. Nobody wanted a barrel to fall off the cart.

She knew they all had personal stories about why they'd turned to anarchism. Whether it was killed family members or great injustices, the rich, the powerful, and those in authority had always benefited from endured misery. She wondered what had ultimately led to Capucine's descent. It must have been the death of their father. Marie had been young, barely seven, when he'd been killed during the Bloody Week. It affected her, but it must've changed something in her sister.

'Vee,' Marie said. Voltairine looked up at Marie, who had fallen into step beside her. 'Did Capucine ever tell you why she found solace in anarchism?'

It starts to rain and the drops pit and patter against the barrels. Nils, who rides the cart with Amos, reaches back and pulls a greasy tarp over the barrels.

'She said she was raised that way. Were you not?'

Marie scrunched up her face. 'I, we. No. I mean, I can't really remember. I spent a lot of time with my grandfather. More than Capucine did. My mère never held any love for authority after Papa died. Or to begin with, I guess.'

'That's it. She said your parents fought in the Paris Commune. That your father was slain.'

'He was. By the Versaillais troops. It seems so long ago, though. I guess ten years is a long time when you're a child.'

'Not when you're older. It blinks by as swiftly as anything.

'But to harbour such hatred? She never told me. She never talked about it.'

The rain fell heavy now. A pool collected in the tarp. Everyone is drenched. Water runs off Voltairine's hat as it does the nearby rooftops.

'You know why we are secretive,' Voltairine says grimacing.

'I don't mean necessarily the Veil. She never...I had no idea what was driving her.'

'Do we ever really know the motivations of others? And even if we did, would we believe them? We only really know the stories we tell ourselves about others.'

'So you're saying I could tell you one thing, and you could believe something else about me, and regardless if I told you the truth, you'd believe only what you thought?'

'People see the corruption and the inequality every day of their lives. Yet they tell themselves that's how it is meant to be or things will eventually improve for themselves. Or they're protected. Or they should go to war to protect their country. People only want to believe what they want to believe. When has working for the man ever delivered a fair share?'

'Okay, Vee. I know. I agree.' The last thing Marie wanted to hear was another sermon from Voltairine. But maybe she proved the woman's point. Marie knew she just wanted to be left alone by all of them.

They soon arrived at the Brooklyn Terminal, where they would load the barrels onto the train. They took the horse and cart up the departing ramp leading to the platform.

The foreman came over. 'Head over there with the others, and we'll instruct you.'

Three other carts on the platform were also loaded with bales of hay and barrels.

'I thought we were the only one?' Voltairine asked.

'Alberta said this would be the case,' Amos said.

Voltairine shook her head. 'She could've thought about telling all of us.'

The ten-minute wait felt longer, but the clock above the platforms struck ten o'clock when the last train across the bridge arrived at the Brooklyn Terminal. The members of the Black Veil stood waiting with the cart full of black powder barrels.

The few passengers disembarked from the carriages and headed off along the platform. Everyone except Voltairine appeared nervous. For once, Marie didn't have to hide her emotions. She scanned the terminal, wondering when Charlie and Joe would choose to arrest them. She knelt down and tied the lace of her boot. She hoped Joe was watching. It was the signal they'd agreed on to inform them that all members carried guns.

She stood. Still nothing. All seemed quiet.

The foreman who'd greeted them on arrival came over waving a cigarette in his hand. 'Once those carriages are coupled to the fourth one, you can start loading the barrels.'

He went to walk away, then stopped, turned, and came back over. He went to take a drag on his cigarette and, realising it had gone out, got a matchbox and out and struck a flame. Marie held her breath.

'Say. What's in them barrels? I don't want them leaking all over the carriage.'

'Oh, just sugar,' Amos said.

'Well. Just make sure you clean up after yourselves if you make a mess.'

Nils and Leon smirked at each other. Voltairine scowled at them both, and their smiles faded.

'Right, boys. You heard the man. Start loading up. Carefully.'

The cart was backed up towards the carriage. The barrels were then lowered onto the platform. Marie worked with Nils to carry the barrels into the carriage. She wished Joe and Charlie would hurry up and start the raid. The thought of being so close to so many explosives terrified her. It had done since they'd left the warehouse.

'Ah good,' the foreman asked. 'All of the barrels are loaded, correct?'

'Yes,' Amos said, 'But—'

'Great,' the foreman said. 'The quicker we get the trains making these runs, the quicker we can go home.'

'What's going on?' Voltairine asked. 'Is everything ready?'

'They're coupling the carriage up to the others. They want to start testing as soon as possible,' Marie said.

'We're not ready,' Amos said. 'The barrels are all loaded, but I still need to connect all of the fuses to the timer.'

'Then you need to be in that carriage.'

Amos nodded and ran to the carriage, carrying his bag of tools. Marie and Voltairine exchanged glances.

'We should stall them somehow until he is done,' Marie said.

Voltairine shook her head. 'No. I'll be happier when that train is moving. I don't like it just sat here. And we would do well to get as far away from the bridge as possible.'

'But we should wait for him.'

'Wait for him? Are you forgetting what's going to happen, Marie?'

'Well, no—'

'If he doesn't want to become a martyr, he will have to find his way off the bridge.'

A whistle blew. High pitched and shriek. Another one. Then another. The whistles kept blowing. There was the thunderous sound of boots running and hooves galloping.

Nils and Leon were the first to react. They ran towards the bridge, but Charlie and several police officers on horseback rode down the walkways, blocking their escape. Scores of policemen filtered onto the platform, accessing it via every exit, doorway and staircase. Marie and Voltairine exchanged glances as the police officers surrounded them, kicked and struck them with batons to the back of their legs. The two women dropped to their knees and were pushed to the floor. They grabbed Voltairine's wrists, pulled her arms behind her back, fastened handcuffs, and started doing the same to Marie.

'Get those cuffs off immediately,' Joe said, running over and pushing one of the police officers off Marie, who sat astride her back.

'What the hell are you doing?' The officer shouted at Joe, who pushed him away.

'She's on our side,' Joe said.

Voltairine struggled and turned her head to glare at Marie.

Joe came over. Voltairine smiled at him. 'You may not be dead. But you're too late,' she said. 'The train has left the platform.'

Joe looked at Marie. 'She's right.'

Charlie rode the horse over to them. Steam rose from the animal's flared nostrils. Charlie leant down from the saddle. 'It's on the train, isn't it?'

Joe nodded.

Charlie sighed. 'I said we'd lose time getting this many men into position.'

'I know, Charlie. I know.'

Charlie pulled on his reins, turning the horse about. He slapped the leather on each side of the horse's neck, and it jolted forward into a gallop.

Charlie rode the horse up the ramp and onto the bridge. He took a route straight down the bridge's centre along the walkway. The horse's hooves thundered against the wooden slats.

The cable trains moved slightly slower than the horse, so Charlie was able to catch up with it. About a quarter of the way along the bridge, the tracks dipped away from the walkway and were surrounded by iron railings. Charlie kicked his heels, and the horse galloped on, breathing fast.

Charlie reached out for the handrail at the rear of the carriage. He missed it. He kicked his heels again, and the horse approached the carriage. It was now or never. Charlie leapt from the saddle and reached for the handrail. He caught it, and his feet landed on the boardwalk at the rear of the carriage. He swayed backwards but caught his balance and pulled himself towards the carriage's rear door.

The carriages entered the covered section of the track. The clatter of the wheels against the rails reverberated.

He pulled open the door and went inside.

A man was crouched among the barrels, and he turned around in the dim light.

Charlie went to draw his gun, then hesitated.

'Yeah, that's right. One rogue shot in here, and we're all blown to kingdom come,' Amos said.

'I thought that's what you wanted?'

Amos reached for the top of one of the barrels and grabbed a flick knife. He clicked it open and held it aloft. Charlie sighed. The carriage wobbled on the tracks.

'I don't shoot rogue shots...I only shoot rogues.' Charlie drew his gun and, in one swift motion, shot Amos in the head. The Black Veil's new explosives expert fell backwards, dead, and clattered onto the floor of the carriage.

CHAPTER 32

October 28, 1886

Two days later, the morning of the unveiling of the statue Liberty Enlightening the World was wet and foggy. One million New Yorkers prepared to line the streets and banks of Manhattan and out towards Bedloe Island, an armada of boats already filled upper New York Bay, jostling for a prime position close to the island.

The copper statue glistened in the rain. The sodden French tricolor clung to Liberty, veiling her face.

Despite the weather, Manhattan was ready to celebrate. Church bells rang, and people lined Broadway in anticipation of the great parade due to depart.

Joe and Charlie stood outside the Tombs prison in Five Points, the last place either of them wanted to be.

Joe raised his hands in surrender. 'I assure you, Charlie. They checked her this morning. There's nothing in there. Nothing in the base. Nothing in the statue itself,' Joe said.

'Why do I still have a bad feeling?'

'After everything that's gone on in this city these past few weeks? I'd be worried if you didn't.'

'I don't know. Stopping them the other night just seemed too easy.'

'We recovered the gunpowder. Hell, the statue wasn't even the target. You know this. The Black Veil's no more. Why don't you just enjoy the day?'

'I'll be glad when the day is done.'

'Charlie. You're a hero. You and Marie. You're both heroes.

Nobody will ever know you are, but you're both heroes.'

'It's bittersweet though, Joe.'

'It sure is. But she'll deal with it all. In time.'

'Do you think?'

'Marie? Yeah. She's the most resilient person I know. But you could help her start by telling her more about the investigation that led you to her sister.'

Charlie laughed the suggestion off.

'Come on, Charlie. You two had something going on, right? Take my advice—'

'Is this professional police advice?'

'Advice from a friend, Charlie. Enjoy the day. Together.'

'You're a good man and a good cop, Joe. Celebrate tonight?'

'If I don't fall asleep. Sure. Let's drink the town dry,' Joe said.

A police officer came out of the doors and spotted them both talking on the steps.

'I'm sorry to interrupt.'

Joe rolled his eyes, and the officer looked taken aback.

'Sorry,' Joe said. 'That wasn't for you. What's up? I'm guessing it's our anarchist friend?'

'She refuses to talk. And those guys in there are gonna beat her to death before she does.'

'She won't talk to us either,' Charlie said.

'She'll only talk to that French woman friend of yours.'

Charlie and Joe looked at each other.

'I know,' Joe said. 'That's what she said to us.'

'It ain't happening,' Charlie said.

'That may be so. But now she's saying time is running out.'

Charlie looked to the sky as he took a deep breath.

'Maybe it's worth trying?' the officer said.

Joe and Charlie both said no in unison. Then they both

sighed.

'I'll go and see if she will,' Charlie said.

Charlie took the elevated railway to Greenwich Village and thought about what Joe had said about Marie. He wondered if they could ever get over him killing her sister despite what she was plotting to do. Charlie shook his head. You fool, he thought. She's going to France anyhow. It was the first time he'd admitted to himself that he had feelings for her. Looking out the window, he saw the Star Spangled Banner and the French tricolor hanging everywhere from balconies and windows. The mood in the city was bully. Regardless of what had happened, it was a time to celebrate, and they had more to celebrate than anyone else after thwarting The Black Veil's final plot to blow up the Brooklyn Bridge. Then he wondered if Marie would think it was a time to celebrate. Sure, they'd busted the cabal, but her sister had been one of them who'd been prepared to kill many. That would still be raw in her mind. He knew she hadn't given herself time to grieve. She had thrown herself headlong into the investigation.

The train slowed as it entered the station, pulling him out of his thoughts.

He saw a flower seller on the street and knew that grieving could wait one more day. This was a time to celebrate a new start. If she wanted to talk with Voltairine, she could. If she didn't, so be it. He bought a bunch of sunflowers from a flower seller. Despite whatever secret Voltairine kept to tell Marie, for the first time in a long time, Charlie felt good about life. He bounded up the steps into the building and climbed the now familiar creaky stairs to Marie's rooftop studio. As he went up, he felt a tinge of sadness, realising there probably wouldn't be many more times he would take this journey.

Enough of the negative thoughts, he told himself. 'It's time to celebrate,' he said like a mantra. He knocked merrily on the door. The door opened at his touch. He frowned. He removed his gun from his holster and went inside. A man turned to face him and froze on seeing Charlie's Colt pointing at him.

'Who are you?' Charlie asked.

'The landlord,' the man said.

Charlie looked around the studio. It was in the process of being emptied. Marie's canvasses and many of her art supplies were stacked up on the floor.

'Where's Marie?' Charlie asked.

'I'd be more willing to converse without a gun pointed at me.'

Charlie placed the flowers on the windowsill and holstered his gun.

'You wouldn't happen to be Joe or Charlie?'

'Yeah,' Charlie said.

'Marie's gone. She's leaving for France today,' the man said, handing Charlie a letter.

Marie arrived at the Compagnie Générale Transatlantique building entrance on West Street and saw the four masts and two funnels of SS La Champagne towering above the ticket offices, waiting rooms, and various other storage buildings.

She showed her ticket and was directed to the waiting rooms. She was early. She took out a sketch pad from her satchel and started as she meant to go on. She was determined to immerse herself in her art more than ever. She looked at the clock. There were four hours until departure. And there was nobody to sketch, just an empty waiting room. She leaned her head against the wall and closed her eyes.

When she woke up, there were people in the waiting room. She'd been asleep an hour. Her neck ached. She sat upright, stretched, and grabbed her sketchbook as it slid off her knee. Her pencil hit the floor and rolled across to a family sitting opposite. A girl around the age of seven got up and took it. She looked at Marie, and her mother encouraged her to return it. The girl came over to Marie and handed her the pencil.

'Merci,' Marie said.

The girl smiled and looked at her sketchbook.

'Can I draw your portrait?' Marie asked the girl in French. It felt good to speak her native language and be understood.

Marie looked to the parents, who didn't protest.

'Sit here,' Marie said, pointing to the bench beside her. She made the girl sit further back and adjusted her to sit at a ninety-degree angle. As Marie sketched the portrait, the girl's younger sister shyly approached.

'Bonjour,' Marie said.

The little girl smiled.

'Is this your sister?'

'Yes, Aimée,' the older girl said.

'And what is your name?' Marie asked.

'Aurélie.'

'I'm Marie,' she said, smiling as she studied the girl's face.

'Do you have a sister?' Aurélie asked.

The ache throbbed in Marie's chest. She didn't stop smiling. 'No. No. It's just me,' she said. She concentrated on the lines as she sketched out the girl's jawline and managed to contain her tears. Looking back up, her gaze drifted past the girl, and she saw Charlie standing in the doorway. Her lips opened. She hadn't expected to see him again. He pushed his hat higher on his brow and closed the door gently behind himself.

He waited, leaning against a post as Marie finished the drawing. Aurélie beamed as she took her portrait. She ran over to show her parents.

'That's incredible,' the father said. 'You are very talented mademoiselle.'

The younger sister stood there expectantly, wanting her own portrait sketching. With about three hours to fill, Marie told the younger girl to sit where her sister had sat. Charlie was more impatient. He came over and sat on the bench behind where Marie sat.

'You'll have to wait until I've done this one now if you want your portrait done,' Marie said.

'That's real sweet, Frenchie. We need to talk.'

'So talk.'

Aimée shuffled uncomfortably in her seat at Charlie's presence.

'It's okay,' Marie said, winking and tapping the girl's knee, encouraging her to sit still.

'Sit still,' Aurélie said to her sister as she came back over clutching her portrait.

Marie started sketching the younger girl's hair.

'I can't let you leave,' Charlie said.

'Why?' Marie asked, and they held each other's gaze.

Charlie swallowed.

'Voltairine. We think something's going to happen today. But she'll only talk to you. She won't tell us.'

Marie smiled ruefully and shook her head. She continued sketching again. 'I'm going to France,' she said.

'It would appear so, kid. But first...'

Marie closed her eyes tightly and bit her lip. She sighed.

'She'll say anything to save herself now. She just wants to spread more anarchy.'

'That's what I said.'

'Then where does it stop, Charlie? When do we all go our separate ways and get on with life?'

'After today.'

Marie shook her head. 'Hence why I'm here.' She gestured at the ship out through the window.

'Marie, people might die if you don't help us.'

'That's blackmail, Charlie.'

'It's the truth.'

'You don't know for sure,' Marie said, swallowing her emotions. She twisted her lips. She said nothing more as she finished Aimée's portrait and held it up to show her. The young girl's mouth dropped open. She grabbed it, slid off the bench, and ran over, calling to her mama and papa to look. The parents thanked Marie again and offered her some money, which she declined.

Charlie touched her forearm as Marie slipped her sketchbook and pencil back into her satchel. 'I know if you get on that ship, there's a big chance I'm gonna regret letting you leave.'

Marie looked up and held his gaze. She knew what she needed to do.

CHAPTER 33

The prison cell was dank and dark. Greasy daylight struggled through the tiny window. Voltairine lifted her head to see Marie open the heavy iron door and walk in. Voltairine was shackled to the wall. Her face was bruised and cut. She'd obviously received a beating. Her hair was lank. She still wore part of her disguise, the trousers and the shirt, but her boots had been taken.

'It's not what I expected an Egyptian temple to look like inside,' Voltairine said. The cell was in the Tombs in the Five Points. From the outside, the prison looked like an Egyptian mausoleum. Marie remembered tailing Charlie, leaving it when she'd first thought he was Capucine's killer. Weeks later, it turns out she'd been right. The circumstances, however, were far from what she'd imagined.

Screams and moans echoed down the corridor. Joe closed the door behind Marie, leaving the two women alone.

'There are no mummies, jewels, or hieroglyphs...' Voltairine said.

'You wanted to see me?' Marie asked.

'Please, take the weight off your feet.'

Marie glanced around the cell. There was no furniture. Not even a bed or a pot to piss in.

'Was it worth it?' Marie asked.

She couldn't believe this was the same woman she had marched alongside on the suffragette rallies or who had consoled her at Capucine's funeral.

'I almost feel sorry for you,' Voltairine said.

'You feel sorry for me?'

'You still don't see it, do you? Even now. This is how they control the population. Fear. To go against them is this. Lost liberty. Well, the illusion of liberty. Lost.'

'Listen to yourself,' Marie said. 'You're in here because you wanted to blow up a bridge. Because you killed how many people?'

'I only killed one.'

'Even if that is true. You still killed him. And you cut off his fucking face,' Marie said.

'He was dead when I did it.'

'You're deranged, Voltairine.'

'Am I? What would the state have done to him had they caught him?'

'They would've served him justice.'

'He would've rotted in here for how long and then been hung for killing a police officer. His throat squeezed until he couldn't breathe. His legs would've kicked for minutes while he struggled. Can you imagine what that is like?'

'You tell me.'

Voltairine smirked. 'He killed Elias. He killed many people. Of course, that's what he did. That's what we did. But he was the one that decided it would be good for the cause to hang your sister and her boyfriend above that stage.'

Marie glared at her.

'It's no less than she deserved,' Marie said. She turned to leave the cell.

Voltairine stood and lurched forwards, her shackles strained. 'Don't you dare say that about your sister?'

Marie turned back to face her. 'At the meeting, Lena alluded to you killing him for reasons beyond his betrayal. For what he did. Was it because he did that to Marie?'

Voltairine lifted her head in defiance. 'How could he kill

her and use her like that?'

'Is that what you think?' Marie let out a surprised exhale and shook her head. 'My God. That's what you were talking about when you said people only believe what they want to believe. Clément, he didn't kill Capucine. I know who killed her. He may have used her body and her lover's—'

'Phillip Moses wasn't her lover,' Voltairine said, her eyes alive and burning with passion in the dirty, beat-up face.

Marie realised Voltairine had been Capucine's lover. 'Oh,' she said. Yet another revelation. She really hadn't known her sister at all. 'Oh. Then, I truly am sorry for you. But you. Clément. McGarrity. Capucine. All of you. You're all murdering bâtard's. You deserve the same fate as the rest of them. You failed. Maybe you should live a little longer to ruminate on that.'

Voltairine began to smile again. She laughed.

'Goodbye Voltairine,' Marie said, and she went to leave.

'You think we failed? As if we wouldn't have plans for today of all days?'

Marie hesitated at the heavy iron door. 'You'd say anything now to try to cause more anarchy or save yourself.'

She was almost gleeful. 'One last hurrah for the Black Veil. What a stage. Oh, you'd better bring your boyfriend in. You know, the one you pretended to kill.'

'Joe,' Marie shouted.

Joe opened the door and entered the cell. 'Are you done?'

'No, she's not done,' Voltairine said. 'I believe we're only just getting started here.'

The interview room was on the same corridor as the cells. It was not much bigger than two cells and just as dour. Charlie,

Joe, and Marie had gathered together to try to escape the wailing coming from the cells and discuss what Voltairine had told them.

'She's playing us, Joe.' Charlie said. 'You must see that?'

'What choice do we have,' Joe said. 'If the Black Veil has planned something and we do nothing...'

'But you can't just release a killer like her back onto the street. Today of all days,' Marie said.

'She'll tell us what they're going to do though,' Joe said.

'Of course, she will,' Charlie said sarcastically. 'She's bending you over a barrel.'

Joe shook his head. 'We're gonna have to trust her.'

'It's a fucking gamble, Joe.'

Joe ignored Charlie and turned to Marie. 'Do you think she'd betray the Veil?'

'Not willingly. At least I didn't think so.'

'So you think she might?'

Marie paced the room.

'What is it, Frenchie?'

Marie shook her head. 'From what I could tell, Voltairine was the most committed to the cause out of all of them. She suspected everyone of lacking the desire needed to achieve their aims.'

'What motivated her?'

'Capucine,' Marie said. But neither Joe nor Charlie understood what she meant. 'Benedict,' she said, a theory forming in her mind. 'Nobody knew who he was, but he was the one who'd assembled them all. Yet he's stayed unknown the whole time.'

Marie suddenly walked out of the room. She headed down the corridor, past the muffled sound of someone thumping on their cell door, past the prison guard and to Voltairine's cell.

She pushed open the door.

'What the Black Veil stood for was your life. Why would you give up one of their attacks?'

'The organisation is rotten from within. I don't abandon anarchism. I condemn the one who set up the Veil in the first place.'

'Benedict?'

'Yes, him. If that even is his name.'

'You could lead us to him?'

'I will do more than lead you to him.'

As the two women glared at each other, Marie knew they'd only discover the Veil's next attack by releasing Voltairine from the cells.

CHAPTER 34

Outside the Tombs, Marie stood with Voltairine, Charlie and Joe in the middle of the busy street. Each person didn't know if they could trust the other. Liberty fever had even penetrated this dank neighbourhood. American flags hung from windows, and there was the feel of a festival. Nearby, a thin man and a stout woman sold shellfish from a cart. People spilled out from the bars and drank on the street. A man with a hook in place of his hand shuffled past, calling out begging.

Charlie bristled with anger. His hand rested on his gun, holstered at his waist. The beggar veered away from Charlie, who didn't take his eyes off Voltairine. Marie glared at the gun and him. He stared back and kept his hand where it was. Joe had warned Charlie that if he tried to shoot Voltairine, he would be arrested for attempted murder or murder if he was successful, which Charlie usually was.

They all turned their attention to Voltairine, waiting for her to keep her part of the bargain. Voltairine was dressed in the male clothes she'd worn as a disguise to load the black powder onto the train cars. Oblivious to them looking at her, she dusted down the jacket she wore. She turned her face to the sky and smiled as she felt the rain beginning to spot. Her bruises looked sore in the daylight, but she didn't wince.

'Ma'am,' Joe said and coughed to get her attention. Voltairine glanced at him as if they'd never met before.

'Oh, well, I suppose time is ticking on,' she said, smiling and looking past him at Charlie. 'There's a bomb.'

'Where?' Charlie asked.

'Bobbing around somewhere close to Liberty, I'd imagine by now. Or at least on its way there.'

'You didn't?' Marie said as she realised what Voltairine had done. 'The suffragettes?'

'Me? When could I have set a bomb on a boat? I was busy trying to demolish the Brooklyn Bridge. And then I was in there,' Voltairine said, her smile fading as she thumbed towards the prison.

'When is it due to detonate?'

Voltairine looked around. She spotted a clock on the side of a building and squinted. 'Their boat is set to explode in an hour. Give or take.'

'Give or take what?' Charlie asked.

'Well, you can never trust a timer, can you? Who knows if the pocket watch of the person who set it was right or not,' Voltairine said and shrugged.

Charlie glowered at her. Marie stood between them.

'Charlie, can you stop it?' Marie asked.

'I don't know,' he said turning from Marie to Voltairine. 'Can I?'

Voltairine shrugged. 'Anything assembled can be disassembled. If you have enough time, that is,' Voltairine said.

'Voltairine? Will he?'

'Just about. Maybe. You've got an hour, but you'll have to find the boat. I'm guessing there'll be a fair few out there today.'

Charlie glared at her one last time, and then he walked away. Joe stepped beside him. 'Charlie, head for the Harbour Department on Pier A. Find Henry. He'll get you a boat out to it.'

Charlie nodded. He looked past Joe to Marie. He frowned.

She'd gone, along with Voltairine. Joe turned to look but couldn't see either of them amongst the public celebrating the day. The pair of them hesitated.

'Charlie, go. There's no time. I'll try and see if I can't find them.'

Charlie nodded. He'd spotted a couple of horses tied to a hitching post across the street. Charlie approached one of them, reached up, and touched the saddle horn. He put his foot in the stirrup. Then he took a deep breath and climbed up onto the horse. Before the policeman could turn around, Charlie had kicked his heels, and the horse galloped off. Charlie took a route straight down Broadway, headed for Battery Park, and soon encountered the parade.

People stood on rooftops as the military and civic procession marched down the middle of the road, the sidewalks full on each side, uncountable bodies deep from curb to building, as ticker tape streamed out of the stock market's windows onto the ranks of soldiers, police officers, firemen, and brass bands belting out triumphant tunes. At the same time, children sold official guidebooks by the thousand featuring some of the artwork that Marie had created.

'Why are you following me, Marie? You can't possibly hope to stop me.'

'Who says I want to?'

Voltairine was distracted by Marie's comment. She glanced at Marie as they strode into the side streets. Then she looked over her shoulder to see if Joe was following them. She couldn't see him.

'I thought you wanted to see me pay for my crimes?' Voltairine asked.

'I don't believe justice is as black and white as Charlie and Joe see it.'

'He is not your relative then?'

'Charlie?' Marie shook her head. 'No.'

Voltairine stopped and grabbed Marie by the lapel of her jacket. 'I should kill you for all of your lies. You destroyed the Black Veil.'

'You'd kill the sister of the woman you loved?'

'Just because you were her sister doesn't mean you are anything like her.' Voltairine let go of Marie's collar and pushed her away.

'It would appear so,' Marie said.

They glared at each other.

'Would you have done the same if Capucine hadn't been killed? Would you have taken on her and the Black Veil?'

'If she'd murdered all of those people in the theatre? Yes. I would've.'

Voltairine shook her head and started walking again. She sighed as Marie doggedly fell into step alongside her.

'So how do you envision me atoning for my apparent sins?' Voltairine said.

'If Benedict had the means to finance the Black Veil, he might do so again.'

'And why would I not want that?'

'Because you don't believe his intentions, do you? And I don't believe my sister did. Did she tell you her suspicions?'

'They were only suspicions. She was beginning to question his motive. I think she was on to finding out about him, but she was trying to make the theatre incident happen at the same time. I hadn't seen her for a few days before...before she was killed.'

Marie thought about how her sister's death had played

out. Her last words played on her mind. 'Does Homer has all of the answers mean anything to you?' Marie could tell by the flash of recognition in her eyes that it did. 'It does, doesn't it?'

'It was just something she used to say.'

'I think she was trying to tell us something.'

Voltairine shook her head. 'I told her she spent too much time in the library.'

'That's it!' Marie said. 'That's where she must've been leading us.'

'To the library? To what end? To read classical literature? I don't think so. If she had something to tell me regarding Benedict, she would've told me outright.'

'No. You said she was suspicious about Benedict. Do you know who he is? Where to find him?'

'I'll find him. In time. In my own way,' Voltairine said.

'She didn't tell you because she didn't trust you. You're too hot-headed.'

'I'm not.'

'You believed in the cause more than any of them. And that's why she didn't trust you.'

'You're not making me want to not kill you.'

'She knew that if there was even a sniff of him not being committed, you'd go after him. Whatever his motivations, he still needs to be brought to justice. That's what I want. Bring him in, and it will help you.'

Voltairine laughed. 'It won't help me. Do you think they want to help people like us?'

'Then if you think that, we must go to the library. You don't have time to search for Benedict, but we do have a lead that could lead us right to him. If you help me find Benedict and help me discover the truth that Capucine was looking for, I'll vouch for you. When the time comes.'

Her shoulders slumped, but only momentarily. She threw her shoulders back and walked taller. 'I don't need your help. They won't catch me. But alright, let's go and find out if Capucine has left us a message.'

Marie had never expected to return to her sister's former place of work, the Astor Library on Lafayette Street. Marie and Voltairine were surprised to find the library open. They strode through the doors and across the reception hall to the desk where Amelia sat. She looked upset until she recognised them both. 'Marie! Vee!'

'Amelia,' Marie said. 'We need your help.'

'We need to find a book. Urgently,' Voltairine said.

Amelia stood from her chair. 'Are you okay?' Amelia asked, concerned about Voltairine's bruised and cut face.

'It's nothing,' Voltairine said, waving the concern away.

'Nothing? Was there a march?' Amelia's asked, rushing around the desk.

'Homer,' Voltairine said, changing the subject. 'What books do you have by Homer?'

'The Greek poet? Well, they're poems, and you'll want either The Iliad or Odyssey,' Amelia said.

'You know where they are,' Marie asked.

Amelia nodded. 'Of course.'

'Take us to them,' Voltairine said.

Amelia looked eager to please the two women. She led them across the reception, up the wide staircase and into the library's main hall. It was deserted compared to when Marie had last seen it when she'd first arrived seeking her sister. The desks were empty, with chairs neatly tucked beneath them.

'Why aren't you on the suffragette boat?' Marie asked Amelia while glancing at Voltairine as they walked.

'Mr Everett won't allow us time off.'

'Today?' Voltairine asked. 'As if anyone is going to come looking for a book today.'

'Umm, you two are. In fact, I'm surprised you're not on the boat yourselves. It was your idea, after all.'

'We were heading there when the police stopped us,' Voltairine said, and she tapped at her face.

'Oh, that's awful,' Amelia said, pointing to one of the bookcases. 'It'll be over here.'

They came to a bookcase twelve feet tall in one of the alcoves. Amelia went and got a set of ladders and wheeled them over to where she'd located the books. She scuttled up the rungs, piled a few books in her arms, and climbed back down.

Marie took a couple off her pile, and they went over to a table.

'Why are you so desperate to read Homer?' Amelia asked.

'It's something Capucine once said. I just want to see if it has any meaning,' Marie explained.

'Amelia, we have done a lot of walking today, and we're really thirsty,' Voltairine said, changing the subject.

'Oh, but we're not allowed to bring drinks into the library.'

'There's no one here,' Voltairine said.

Amelia nodded, easily persuaded by the older woman she looked up to. 'Okay, I'll be right back.'

Amelia left, and Marie and Voltairine started looking through the books, expecting to find a note or passage Capucine might have underlined.

'You should be careful what you tell her,' Voltairine said.

'Just look for whatever Cap might've left for us,' Marie said.

As they leafed methodically through the books and scoured

the inside of the covers, Marie didn't notice Voltairine slide the glass vial along the inside lining of her jacket. She pulled at the exposed thread, loosening the stitching, where she pushed the vial out and slipped it into her pocket. All the time, she turned the pages of the book, and Marie remained unaware.

'There's nothing here,' Marie said, shaking her head. Marie couldn't find any marking or even a note that Capucine had left. After all, it had only been a theory. A long shot at best. Why wouldn't Capucine have just told Voltairine?

'Do you mind me asking what your relationship was like?'

Voltairine looked up from the book, surprised by the question. She shook her head as she looked to her memories.

'I don't know, it feels like a dream.'

'I just mean, if you were close, why didn't she share her worries about Benedict.'

'It...it doesn't matter. Capucine was suspicious of him. She was looking into who he was, but that's all I know. Look again,' Voltairine said. 'There must be something in the books.'

'What are you looking for exactly?' Amelia asked as she returned carrying a tray of three glasses of cordial.

'We don't know,' Voltairine said.

'It might pertain to who killed her,' Marie said.

Amelia raised her eyebrows, then put the drinks on the table.

'Did he write anything about murder?' Voltairine asked.

Amelia smiled, then felt conscious that her reaction was patronising, so she shook her head. 'What doesn't he cover? Murder, love, betrayal—'

'Betrayal?' Marie asked.

'Well, yes. Of course,' Amelia said. As they flicked through each book, she explained the themes of Homer's work. As the two women were distracted, Voltairine moved around the table. She picked up one of the glasses and sipped the drink. She looked up at the bookcase.

'Are you sure you haven't got all the books down?'

'I'm pretty sure I did,' Amelia said.

'Please, check again. Marie, help her.'

Amelia and Marie raised their eyebrows at Voltairine's impatience but went and did as she suggested. While Marie's back was turned and Amelia climbed back up the ladder, Voltairine dripped a couple of drops from the vial into each of their drinks. Then she went back to the books.

'There's no more books up here by Homer,' Amelia said.

Voltairine sighed as they came back to the table. She finished her drink and pushed the tray over to their side of the table.

Marie took a glass and thirstily gulped down the drink. Amelia didn't even pick her drink up.

Voltairine held up one of the books to them. 'We haven't time to read all of these,' she said. She dropped the book onto the table, and the noise echoed through the cathedral-like space.

Marie turned around and sighed as she looked around the library hall. Countless books lined the shelves. Busts sat on plinths. The whole building reminded Marie of a place of worship for literature. Though Capucine loved stories, Marie couldn't imagine her sister bending the knee to any of these gods of literature. Her eyes narrowed. A realisation formed. She walked around the table as Voltairine and Amelia watched on.

'What is it?' Voltairine asked.

Marie arrived at the nearest bust. Shakespeare. She spun

around and looked at the others dotted around the hall, trying to find the one she wanted. 'Where's Homer?' Marie asked.

Amelia's face lit up. 'Over here,' she said and started off in the opposite direction to Marie. Marie quickstepped over to her, and Voltairine did, too.

Homer's marble bust stared blankly past them. Their eyes darted all over the head and the plinth it sat on.

'There's only one place we haven't looked,' Marie asked.

Voltairine pushed forward and grabbed the head. Marie and Amelia, sensing she was about to pull it off, grabbed the head, stopping her. Marie felt lightheaded from lurching forward so quickly.

'Hey, you're gonna get me into trouble,' Amelia said.

'Just look underneath, Vee,' Marie said as they tilted the head off the base.

Voltairine crouched. She gasped.

'What is it?' Marie asked, trying to peer over the head.

'A piece of paper,' Voltairine said, pulling it out from beneath the bust. They lowered the marble head and looked on as Voltairine unfolded it. Marie instantly recognised her sister's handwriting.

'What does it say?' Marie asked as Voltairine paced off away from them. Marie went over to her but again felt lightheaded. She rubbed her forehead, but the drowsy feeling washing over her didn't subside.

'It's an address,' Voltairine said, facing Marie. 'Are you okay, Marie?' she asked. 'You look pale.'

Marie stumbled to a table. Amelia rushed over to her.

'Get her the drink,' Voltairine said, pointing to the glass on the table across the hall. Amelia hurried off to get it as Voltairine put her arm around Marie. Marie shrugged the embrace away.

'You look ill, Marie.'

'What have you done?' Marie asked. She tried to shake the weariness from her eyes. Her vision couldn't focus. Her eyelids were heavy. She struggled to stand and leant on the table. 'You, Vee, can't change...world. Ideal...stic. No...body. Wants. Cares.'

Marie dropped to her knees. She could barely keep her eyes open to see Voltairine standing over her. Amelia returned with the glass of cordial. Marie batted it away, spilling its contents, and the glass shattered across the floor.

'Goodbye, Marie,' Voltairine whispered as she cradled Marie's head and lowered her gently onto the floor.

CHAPTER 36

The horse was flagging when Charlie arrived at the NYPD's harbour department headquarters, Pier A.

As he rode down the boardwalk towards the harbour, people moved out of Charlie's way, where everyone was gathered. Charlie sat in the saddle on the horse above everyone and looked for the rookie officer who'd help him and Joe early in the investigation.

'Henry!' Charlie shouted. 'Henry Selwyn!'

The rookie officer turned from the glassing the harbour with a pair of binoculars and saw Charlie. He pushed through the crowd to get to him.

'Mr Blaine.'

'Kid. I need your help,' Charlie said, climbing off the horse.

'Sure, what do you need?'

'I need a boat. Have you got one?'

Henry laughed and then it faded as he saw Charlie meant what he said. 'You'll be hard-pressed to get a boat now. Every vessel is out there,' Henry said, pointing at the armada of boats out by the statue.

'Have you seen the women? The boat full of suffragettes out there?'

'Sure. They're not allowed on the island, but no rule says they can't be on the water.'

'Well, they're not the only thing on that boat. There's a whole load of gunpowder and a bomb that's...' Charlie checked his watch. 'Gonna go off in thirty minutes. And the whole boat is going to blow to smithereens. So I need to get over there and get it defused. Do you understand?'

Henry nodded. 'I think I have an idea.'

Charlie followed Henry into the harbour department building and onto the balcony facing the water. Henry scanned the harbour with the binoculars.

'What are you hoping to do, kid?'

'I'm hoping there's a trawler coming in. If they've got a boatful of catch, they're gonna want to get in as soon as possible. They'll be the only boats not wanting to head that way. There we go, look.'

Henry handed Charlie the binoculars, and he pointed them in the direction of a flock of seagulls above a fishing trawler. Henry went over to the signal lamp. 'Let's hope they know Morse.'

Henry opened and closed the shutter on the front of the signal lamp.

'What did you say?'

'I told it to dock. Pass me the glasses,' Henry said.

Charlie handed him the binoculars. He put them on the boat and didn't see a response. He sent the message via Morse again and held up the binoculars again.

'He's lifting a flag. It's Charlie.'

'What?' Charlie asked.

Henry glanced at him and grinned. 'The letter C. Phonetically Charlie. It means affirmative.'

'Oh,' Charlie said. Then he checked his watch. Time was running out.

While the trawler made its way over to Pier A, Henry got one of his colleagues to signal the vessels out in the harbour to get the suffragette's boat to move away from all of the others. Charlie and Henry headed back down to the waterside.

'Nothing as yet, Henry. I'll keep trying, but everyone

has lost their minds as they try to get as close as possible,' Henry's colleague shouted down from the balcony. Charlie and Henry waited until the steam trawler, Pioneer, arrived and pulled alongside the pier.

Henry stepped across the gap onto the vessel and climbed up to the Skipper, who leant out of the bridge door.

'We need passage on your vessel,' Henry said.

'Where to?' the Skipper asked.

'Out to the statue.'

'I can't go back out that way. I got a boat full of fish. Can't you smell it?'

'Apologies, sir, get us out there and then you can be on your way.'

Charlie had climbed onto the boat. 'Henry, get us moving. We don't have time for this.'

'You can pilot the vessel, sir, or I will commandeer it,' Henry said.

'Goddamn it. What's your heading?'

'Like he said. Out there!' Charlie said, heading to the bow and pointing towards the Statue of Liberty.

The trawler struggled back out into the bay. Charlie paced back and forth. He looked up to the bridge where Henry stood with the Skipper.

'Can't this thing go faster?' Charlie shouted. The rain slapped against him, and the waves hit against the hull. The fishing boat's Captain shrugged and kept on a heading for the statue.

Charlie glassed the armada surrounding the island with a pair of binoculars. He lost count of the vessels of all shapes and sizes, with no standing room left on the decks and the sailors of the tall ships clinging to every foothold and handhold of the mainmasts. None of them appeared to be full of protesting suffragettes, though.

Bells rang out everywhere there was one, from the steeples of churches to the decks of the ships.

Charlie went from the deck and climbed the ladders up to the bridge. A couple of the fishermen stood amongst the hanging nets and their baskets of catch, smoking and scowling at their delay.

'Goddamn it. It would be quicker to swim,' Charlie said.

'That can be arranged,' the Captain said.

'Don't tempt me.'

'Have you spotted them yet, Charlie,' Henry asked.

As they edged closer, even more boats came into view further around the island.

As the fishing boat bobbed up and down on the water, the vessels came in and out of view in the binoculars. He sharpened the focus. People on the boat held placards aloft. 'That one!' Charlie pointed. 'Set course or whatever it is you guys say.'

The Skipper raised his eyebrow. 'Aye,' he said sarcastically.

Henry took the binoculars and saw the suffragette's boat.

The Skipper turned the wheel a few degrees to the left. The boat responded and veered steadily to the right before the Skipper set it straight. The suffragette's chartered boat lay directly ahead. But the fishing boat continued to chug slowly across the bay towards it.

Charlie retook the binoculars off Henry and kept them on it as they approached, occasionally lowering them to check his watch. There was just over ten minutes to go until the bomb detonated. That was presuming, like Voltairine had said, they had used a decent timer or had had their watch wound correctly when it was set.

'You're gonna have to get right on close to it so we can

jump across,' Henry said.

'The wind's picking up. The water's getting choppier. We can't risk the two boats colliding,' the Skipper said.

'Well, just get me as close as you can, and I'll see if I can learn how to fly,' Charlie said, handing the binoculars over to Henry. 'You don't need to board.'

'Are you serious? You'll need help.'

'I need all these boats moved away, but that ain't gonna happen.'

The fishing boat slowed as it navigated between the other vessels and weaved through to the suffragettes. Charlie climbed over the coiled ropes and crates to the bow of the fishing boat. Finally, the Skipper steers the fishing boat alongside the suffragette's boat, and several women start shouting at Charlie. One leaned over and tried to hit him with a placard as he reached for the taffrail. Fearing they would collide, the Skipper steered the fishing boat away from the Suffragette's boat.

'Get me closer,' Charlie shouted.

The Skipper steered the boat as close as he dared to. Charlie didn't allow the women to swipe at him with the placards as he jumped from one boat across to the other.

His foot landed on a rail but slipped off. He fell, but he grabbed the taffrail. The fishing boat bobbed up towards Charlie, and the bow threatened to crush him against the other boat. The Skipper increased the speed and steered it away. Charlie held on and dangled off the side of the boat. A couple of the women continued to hit him with the placard.

'What the hell are you doing?' Charlie said.

'You can't stop us,' one of the women yelled.

'I'm not here to stop you. I'm here to save you.'

'We don't need no saviour.'

'There's a bomb on the boat.'

Her eyes grew wide.

Charlie angled his head to look at his watch on his outstretched arm.

'This whole boat's gonna blow in less than five minutes.'

The placard fell from her hand and hit the water. A couple of women helped Charlie climb over the taffrail and onto the deck.

'I need to find the engine room,' he said, clambering up off his hands and knees and standing.

Murmurings of what Charlie had said about their being a bomb started to spread. Charlie ignored the questions as he pushed through the crowd that began to panic. He had a bad feeling. The bomb could go off at any time. All he could think about was how inaccurate the timer might be.

Matilda Joslyn Gage pushed through the crowd of women to reach him. 'What's happening? Who are you?'

'Ma'am. I have reason to believe there's a bomb on this boat.'

Explosions suddenly sounded. Everyone froze and looked on in horror. They awaited the flames and the boat they were standing on to erupt, but it didn't happen. The twenty-one gun salute from the canons placed on Bedloe Island had begun. Charlie looked over to the statue. The French Tricolor fluttered from Liberty's face and into the canon smoke that lingered, obscuring the statue's base. It looked like Liberty floated in the sky. Brass band instruments mingled with the further pounding of the canons as they set off, one by one, and the sound of all the ships blowing their whistles and fog horns.

Charlie didn't say anything else. He pushed his way through the crowd of women. And found a hatch that led below the deck. He climbed down the ladder and looked about in the dim light. He swore under his breath as the boat swayed on the pitch and roll of the water. He ventured deeper and lit his lighter, aware of the naked flame and the prospect of several barrels of gunpowder waiting to blow. He found the barrels surrounded by bales of hay. He saw the device on the lid of the barrel and immediately recognised its design. A few years ago, Charlie had worked a case that led him to England to work alongside the Special Irish Branch during the Fenian Dynamite Campaign. The bomb itself was simple, an outside case of sheet iron, about ten inches square; the miner compartment contained the clockwork movement that, at the time fixed, liberated a knife which cut a string and let fall a spring onto the percussion cap causing the machine to explode. The bomb and where it was positioned next to the hull was powerful enough to cause a rupture that would no doubt sink the boat. But it was the added barrels of powder the bomb sat on that would cause the symbolistic event the anarchists wanted.

Charlie had defused one of these infernal machines before, but he knew that they had modified their devices so that opening the case lid might instead cut the string inside and spring the detonator.

He couldn't risk it. Not with all of these people on board the boat. He picked up the device and weighed it in his hand. It would likely sink, but he couldn't be sure. What if it floated and caused damage to more vessels beyond the one he stood in.

'Fuck,' he said. He would have to weigh it with something heavy enough to pull it down to the Upper New York Bay depths. He rubbed his stubbled chin as he thought. 'Come on, man,' he said to himself, knowing the bomb could go off in his hand.

Charlie ran back to the ladder. He climbed it, careful not to drop the device as the boat swayed.

The women, who had stopped protesting, parted as he climbed back onto the deck. He started towards starboard but decided against it as that side faced Liberty.

He sighed and went to the port side, cradling the device and feeling sick at the impending explosion.

Matilda Joslyn-Gage followed him with a couple of other women in tow.

'Is that it? Is that the bomb?'

'Yeah, but just stay back,' he said, even though staying back wouldn't save them. 'Actually, no, come here. Give me your hat.'

Matilda hesitated.

'Please, quickly,' he said.

Matilda took the pin out of her hat and removed it as she approached.

'I need the ribbon. Take it off.'

Matilda untied the purple, white and gold ribbons and handed them to him. He placed the small iron box on the deck and tied the white and purple ribbons around it like a parcel. He then tied the other ribbon to them. Sweat poured from his brow. His shirt was soaked from his sweat as much as the rain. He removed his revolver from his holster and sighed, regretful that he had to use it as a weight. Still, it had saved his life before, and its final use would hopefully provide the same outcome.

He tied the end of the gold ribbon to the trigger guard and pulled the knot tight.

'Hey,' he shouted to Matilda, 'Grab my belt so I don't go over. Everyone else get back.'

Matilda followed him and took hold of the back of his belt as Charlie leant over the side of the boat. With his arms outstretched, pivoting on his stomach, and his feet coming off the deck, he lowered the device onto the water. It initially floated until he dropped the gun. The revolver immediately sank, pulled on the ribbon, and dragged the bomb down with it. Charlie watched it descend, and he could see it for much longer than he'd hoped. Matilda pulled him back onto the deck. 'Hey, move the boat towards the island,' Charlie shouted to the Captain, who watched what was happening at the cabin door.

'The anchor is down. We need to raise it up before we can move her.'

Charlie rolled his eyes.

'Was it really a bomb?' Matilda asked, peering over the edge into the water.

'A Fenian special,' Charlie said and looked into the water.

'Why would Fenian's want to attack us?'

'It wasn't for their cause—'

A white cloud erupted under the water and quickly rose up toward them. As it reached the surface, the boat rocked on the shockwave like a wave had hit it.

Charlie looked towards Matilda and raised his eyebrows. 'I hope this makes me an honorary member of your association, ma'am?'

'I'd say it does. For life.'

The next day Voltairine sailed into Port Washington harbour on the ferry. She headed a short distance north to Sands Point and walked down the meandering lane. Leaves from the copious Red Maple and Eastern Red Cedar fluttered down from the high branches and drifted into heaps. Various grand Dutch Colonial houses were spaced far apart with large grounds and gardens surrounding them.

Voltairine was almost at the end of the lane nearing the beach when she arrived at the address Capucine had written on the piece of paper and hidden beneath the bust of Homer. She walked up the gravel path, shaking her head at the grandeur. The closer she got the less she thought she'd find Benedict residing there. How could a man that lived somewhere like this believe in anarchism.

She walked between the pillars on the porch and pulled on the doorbell and waited on the gravel until a maid answered the door. 'Yes, can I help you, ma'am?'

'I'm here to see the master of the house,' Voltairine said.

The woman looked at her suspiciously. 'Is Mr Richards expecting you? He didn't tell me he was expecting anyone today, least of all a lady,' she said, studying the cuts and bruises on her face.

'Then he must be getting forgetful in his old age. I presume he is here?'

'Yes.'

'Well, will you make me wait on the doorstep like a common peddler?'

'No, ma'am, she said and opened the door.'

Voltairine walked up the couple of steps into the hall. A staircase led upstairs directly ahead. Four doors, two on each side of the reception hall, were closed. Several portraits were hung. One was of Benedict, but the caption plate displayed his real name, Marcus Richards.

'If you'd like to sit while you wait, ma'am, I'll go fetch him from the potting shed.'

'Potting shed?' Voltairine laughed and shook her head.

The maid shuffled off across the polished mahogany floor.

'Tell me, is he a keen gardener?'

'Indeed, ma'am. He prides himself on his petunias. They're the best I ever did see.'

Voltairine was astonished. So the man who sought a bloody, anarchist revolution and who oversaw murders in the name of the Black Veil grew petunias. And was proud of them.

The maid waddled off, exited via the furthest door, and closed it behind her. She wouldn't be back in a hurry. Voltairine went over to the nearest door and tried it. It was locked. She knelt and looked through the keyhole. It appeared to be his study. She withdrew a lock pick from her pocket and set to work. It was an easy lock to pick, and she had it open within a minute and went in. Two tall windows flooded the room with light. Towards the rear wall was a desk and chair facing the door. Bookshelves lined the walls. She went over to the desk and tried the drawer. It was surprisingly unlocked. She carefully lifted some papers and found his gun. She took the bullets out one by one, dropping them into her pocket, and then she placed the gun back under the documents and went to close the drawer. She hesitated. She pulled the papers out and unfolded one of them. It was a plan for a bridge. It was then she realised it was a replacement for the Brooklyn Bridge.

'The bastard used us. He set us up to use us,' she whispered to herself. From the selection of plans and correspondence, it appeared that Marcus Richards planned to benefit significantly from being one of the men who would rebuild the Brooklyn Bridge had it been destroyed.

She quickly folded the plans, gathered the papers and placed them back in the drawer.

She went over to the rear window, where there was a cabinet with a crystal decanter and glasses on a tray on top of it. The maid had only just made it to the potting shed. Voltairine kept watching out of the window as she poured herself a drink from the decanter. Marcus Richards came out of the potting shed looking all flustered. He immediately spotted her standing in the window of his office. She placed the stop back into the decanter and sat in a high-backed chair in the corner of the room facing the desk.

Marcus Richards's footsteps hurried across the reception hall, and then the door swung open, and he came rushing into his study. Voltairine sat relaxed in the chair. She sipped on the glass of whisky she poured for herself and placed it back onto the side table.

'What do you think you're doing showing up at my house like this?'

'Having a drink.'

'And letting yourself into my office. If you were followed—'

'I'd be dead. Or arrested. But I'm not. I'm here.'

'What do you want?'

'To see if you're still committed to the cause.'

He walked around to his desk and stood behind it. 'I'm afraid it's time we must accept defeat, Voltairine.'

'Why? It was just a minor setback. The bridge is still there.

They can't guard it.'

'It's not worth the risk.'

'Not to someone with all of this to lose.'

Marcus Richards shook his head. 'It is a folly. The project is dead. The Black Veil only has a handful of murders to its name. We have accomplished nothing that will instigate any kind of change. Yet, we still have the chance to return to a normal life.'

Voltairine laughed. 'No. You do. They know who I am and what I've done.'

'You can flee the country and return to Europe. I'll pay for you to go. It's not safe here for you anymore.'

'Leaving you free to continue your life as if nothing ever happened. Here. In this.' She looked around his fine office, and then she looked at him askance. 'It didn't escape me how you managed to stay clean throughout all this. And now everyone who might implement you in this plot is gone.'

'Everyone but you,' he said, opening a drawer in his desk. He removed a gun and aimed it at her. 'I am sorry, Voltairine, but your emotions have always ruled you. It seems they still do. And I can't have loose ends.'

Voltairine took a sip from the glass and defiantly glared at him as she placed it back on the table.

He pulled the trigger. The hammer fell on an empty chamber. He tried again. Then, it dawned on him that the gun had no bullets.

'It was never about anarchism for you, was it?' she asked, revealing her own gun that she had tucked between her leg and the side of the chair.

He looked down at his gun and saw the barrel devoid of bullets. He placed it on the desk.

'Our guns share the same bullets.'

His shoulders slumped. He sat down in his chair in defeat. 'Anarchism was a means to an end.'

'What end?' she asked.

'Power. Wealth—' Bang.

Voltairine had heard enough. Haze drifted from the barrel of her gun.

She went over to his desk and stood over his dead body. 'Now I am the Black Veil,' she said.

Marie Cadieux climbed the last few rungs of the ladder and pushed open the hatch above her head. Breeze and light flooded into the claustrophobic passage.

She hooked her arm around a rung of the ladder and pushed down the lever on the paraffin lamp, raising the glass globe, and she blew out the flame. Then she climbed out onto the narrow platform of Liberty's torch.

The static copper flame licked towards the sky, glistening in the sunshine.

Charlie followed, climbing through the hatch after her.

'There you go,' he said as he stood, and they both took in the view of the Upper Bay where she had first arrived in America. Staten Island, Jersey City, Manhattan, and Brooklyn surrounded the water, with buildings rising in height and number by the day. A steady stream of boats and ships brought more people to the New World, but Marie had set her sights on leaving it and returning to the old.

Marie and Charlie walked around the flame and looked towards the Narrows and the Atlantic beyond.

'You must have friends in very high places, Charlie Blaine.'

Charlie smiled. 'Sure do, Frenchie. Sure do.'

'Friends that get away with it,' she said, crossing her arms.

'They're not all like that senator. And I did it all by the book and handed it to Joe. It was his investigation that got shut down immediately by his superiors.'

Marie sighed. After Voltairine had drugged her and brought her own particular brand of revenge fuelled justice on Benedict, also known as Marcus Richards, she had exposed a wider conspiracy. It turns out Marcus Richards had established the cabal of anarchists to bring down the Brooklyn Bridge. He and seemingly several other men with power and influence stood to benefit significantly from being the ones to rebuild it. Their identities were kept a secret, except for the senator for New York. Voltairine had sent evidence to Marie exposing the conspiracy. But the senator and the other perpetrators above Marcus Richards were too powerful and connected to bring down. Joe Petrosino's superiors had taken the evidence and seemingly closed the case.

None of them would face justice. At least not in the judicial way, Marie pondered. 'I don't think the senator will survive for long with Voltairine still at large,' Marie said.

'She is a danger that should've been dealt with,' Charlie replied.

'Like my sister?'

'Why do you think she did it, Marie?' Charlie asked. 'Why do you think she became an anarchist?'

Marie shook her head. 'Injustice, I suppose.' It was only speculation. She didn't really know what had motivated Capucine. She suspected it was because their father was killed by the Versailles troops while he sought revolution in Paris when she was a child. Perhaps the apple didn't fall far from the tree. But she couldn't be sure. The truth is she didn't really know her sister. Not after she'd left France and came to America.

Charlie sighed. 'I'm sorry for killing her, Marie.'

Marie shook her head. 'It's no more than she deserved. And prison would've been a fate worse than death for her.'

'The strange thing is Frenchie, and it worries me more than you'll know. I don't disagree with some of their beliefs.'

'That's because you're a good person when it comes down to it, Charlie. I feel the same, but their methods...killing innocent people?'

Charlie wrapped his knuckles against Liberty's flame. 'That's why we must stand for what is right and go about it correctly.'

'One person's right way is not necessarily another's.'

'Liberty is to faction what air is to fire, an ailment without which it instantly expires.'

Marie raised her eyebrows and slowly turned to face Charlie. 'Is that poetry?'

'I guess you could say so, a political kind.'

She smiled.

'So,' Charlie said, stretching his arms and leaning against the rail. 'My bosses are extremely pleased with what you've done. They want to offer you more work.'

'Spying?' Marie laughed. 'I'm done with spying. I'm going to Paris.'

'That's a shame because one of the jobs is there.'

'Really?'

'Really,' Charlie said.

'Purely, out of interest, what jobs?'

'Matters of national interest. Ones that your French heritage can be of use towards.'

Marie shook her head in disbelief. 'Spy against France? I'm not even American yet. I'm still a French citizen.'

'The U.S. government wants control of the Panama Canal. If they control the canal, they not only control world shipping but the speed at which our navy can sail between the Pacific and the Atlantic.'

'From what I've read, the French will willingly give it over to the Americans at the rate that Panama dig is becoming a scandal and a disaster.'

'That is precisely what they're banking on happening. Your mission will be to ensure that happens and accelerate it where possible. You will, however, just be a cog. There are many operations taking place to ensure this event happens. Panama or France? The city in the jungle or the city of lights? The choice is yours, Frenchie.'

She smiled, 'Well, tell them I choose Paris, Charlie. But I'm not going there to spy. I'm going there to be an artist.'

Marie Cadieux returns in

Marie Cadieux and the Fever Coast

HISTORICAL NOTE

Historical research is a funny thing. You often stumble across amazing people who seem too heroic or incidents too far-fetched for a novel.

As always, I like to skirt in and around recorded facts and imagine what might not have been recorded alongside such events.

During this period, anarchism began to flourish across the globe. A few months earlier, a bomb had been thrown at the police by suspected anarchists in the Haymarket Affair. Bombings and assassinations were a regular occurrence.

In 1916, an anarchist did, in fact, attempt to poison some 100 guests by putting arsenic in their soup. Earlier in 1882, the World Building, home of the New York World newspaper, caught fire and was notorious for burning to the ground as quickly as it did.

A few of the characters in the story are based on real people, notably Joseph Petrosino and Matilda Joslyn-Gage. Joe was indeed an NYPD officer and a pioneer in the fight against organised crime. Beginning his career in 1883, there was no better cop (real or fictional) than Joe, who could take on the Black Veil alongside Marie and Charlie. His career is legendary, and he has been featured in numerous films, dime novels, and TV productions.

Marie could not interact with the suffrage movement during this period without encountering Matilda Joslyn Gage. Gage worked tirelessly, contributing to women's suffrage in the United States, among other causes.

Indeed, Gage did join the New York City Woman Suffrage

Association to protest the unveiling of the Statue of Liberty from a cattle barge in the bay. I'd like to imagine a certain detective enabled this.

Though Voltairine in the story shares the same name and a few characteristics of real-life anarchist Voltairine de Cleyre, they are not the same person. It would have been interesting to have featured de Cleyre as herself, but ultimately, my story dictated the need for a character far darker. Her name is amazing, though, so I kept that!

ACKNOWLEDGMENTS

Firstly, I want to say a big thanks to all of the readers of my debut novel, Marie Cadieux and the Fever Coast. Your support and love for Marie made me determined to write another adventure featuring our heroic French spy. Special thanks go to Simon Crossley, Lisa Bentley, and Margaret Elston. I hope you enjoy reading about how Marie first fell into spying in this prequel.

Thanks to my writing group, Jan, Paul, and Phil. In January 2024, Paul suggested we do the 100-day writing challenge, and their encouragement during that period led to me writing this story at a pace I've never encountered before. Massive thanks also go to Jan, who helped me edit this one in a suitably record-breaking time. I'm looking forward to returning the favour.

Thanks to Caroline Cauchi. Our chats about writing and your encouragement to just get on with it and believe in being a writer helped fuel the creation of this novel.

As always, my biggest thanks go to my family: Liz, Lauren, Evie, and Mum. Your encouragement and support are a source of endless motivation. I hope I didn't reveal too many of the plot twists that happened while I was writing, and it's all still a surprise.

REVIEWS

Thank you for taking the journey with Marie and reaching the end of Marie Cadieux and the Liberty Conspiracy. I hope you enjoyed this story.

As an independent author, without the backing of a big publisher, your review would really help me to reach a wider audience. If you have a spare couple of minutes, I would really appreciate it if you could post a review from where you purchased this book.

Each positive review I receive makes a huge difference meaning more people discover my writing.

Not only that, I love hearing how you felt while taking the journey with Marie.

Thank you once more.

David

ABOUT THE AUTHOR

David Gennard graduated from The University of Manchester with an MA Creative Writing studying under M.J. Hyland, Jeanette Winterson, and Ian McGuire.

When not writing, David can be found on set shooting promotional photographs on films such as The Unlikely Pilgrimage of Harold Fry and TV shows like Billions. He's also often found out in the countryside, on a beach or paddling across a lake. David lives on the Wirral with his partner, two children and his border collie, Buddy.

Find out more about David's writing and sign up for his reading crew at: www.davidgennardauthor.com

www.ingramcontent.com/pod-product-compliance
Lightning Source LLC
Chambersburg PA
CBHW011554190726
48287CB00010B/2891

9 781739 502317